W9-ALN-177

The
Art Fair

Also by David Lipsky

DAVID LIPSKY

The
Art Fair

DOUBLEDAY

NEW YORK   LONDON   TORONTO

SYDNEY   AUCKLAND

PUBLISHED BY DOUBLEDAY
a division of Bantam Doubleday Dell Publishing Group, Inc.
1540 Broadway, New York, New York 10036

DOUBLEDAY and the portrayal of an anchor with a dolphin
are trademarks of Doubleday, a division of
Bantam Doubleday Dell Publishing Group, Inc.

Library of Congress Cataloging-in-Publication Data

Lipsky, David, 1965–
The art fair / David Lipsky. — 1st ed.   p.   cm.
1. Mothers and sons—United States—Fiction.
2. Artist colonies—United States—Fiction.
3. Women artists—United States—Fiction.
I. Title.   PS3562.I627A89   1996
813′.54—dc20   95-43685   CIP

ISBN: 0-385-42610-0

May 1996

First Edition

1   3   5   7   9   10   8   6   4   2

Book design by Claire Naylon Vaccaro

For Evelyn, and for JHL

The author would like to express his appreciation to Deb Futter and Virginia Barber, without whom this novel could not have been written. I would also like to thank Lee Boudreaux, Wendy Hubbert, Jennifer Rudolph-Walsh, Alison Becker, and Alison Cherwin for their often invaluable assistance. Without dropping into the Academy Award pitfalls of this genre, I should also mention the many friends who offered their assistance and readership to the drafts of this book: David Samuels, Pat Sutton, John Barth, Katie Roiphe, Mike O'Donnell, Joel Lipsky, Elizabeth Wurtzel, Clement Greenberg, Jeff Giles, Stephen Sherrill, and (with love and regret) Amanda Filipacchi. A book, like a writer, has friends before it has readers. This novel was fortunate to find such good ones.

The
Art Fair

Sell while you can: you are not for all markets

—ROSALIND,
As You Like It

I learned how to fly first-class when I was ten. My brother and I were saying goodbye to our father at the airport. I hugged him and started to cry—and I could tell this cry perked Dad up. He tried not to show it—it wasn't dignified, this pleasure he took in thinking he was the parent we loved best—but there was a little smile, and then his hand thumping me on the back, and then a little exploded laugh at the fact that I was still crying. "Just two weeks, Rich," he said. In fact, what made me cry was the prospect of seeing our mother in New York for the first time in a year. There would be the finicking week of getting used to each other again— her anger that we had left, our introduction to the life she'd built without us, then gradually getting warm to us again—and finally two good days. She would take us to all the kid-sights in New York, the art museums, Natural History, the zoo, FAO Schwarz, as if we were no longer kids whose exact tastes she knew but simply generic children whose tastes the city could agree upon and for whose distraction it had erected a number of amusements. Then the two days of getting ready for the airport again. Then the horrible departure—and the watching our mom return to where she'd been before we arrived. She would watch from the big picture windows at Kennedy, tapping the glass and waving, although she couldn't tell precisely where our seats were—waving at the big dumb white animal of the airplane that had swallowed her children. That's what I was crying about. It seemed an awful amount of preventable heartache, for a slim reward—the two good days. I didn't want to get on the plane. We waited till everyone else had boarded, the stewardesses urging us to get moving, my brother trying to cheer me up. We trudged finally to the counter, one reluctant group, the last people at our gate. Our dad gave me a hug and said, "Be nice to your ma," as though he had to encourage this. "These visits aren't easy for any of us." I burst into tears again. Jon put his hand on my shoulder. We checked in our boarding passes. The time-anxious stewardess walked us down the tunnel briskly. I was still crying. She turned around at the door of the plane and said, "Let me see your passes." My brother surrendered them—maybe we'd broken some no-crying-in-the-airport law, and they weren't going to let us fly. The stewardess knelt down. "You know what we're going to do?" she asked, with one of those bright stewardess voices that seem to have makeup on the breath. "We're going to bump you up to first class."

What I had never anticipated was how much *nicer* it was. The larger seats. The footrests. Those ads that bragged about legroom—they weren't kidding. I had shuffled through first class to coach maybe ten times in my life, and had never looked around. They were bringing the adults there champagne and orange juice. They brought us two glasses of orange juice each. Jon and I became very quiet—as if we might jar our good fortune by making too loud a peep. We looked at each other silently, in sparkly first class. I walked back to peek behind the curtain into coach—where we would have been sitting. It suddenly looked awful and cramped and shabby—and it made sense to me. This was *second* class. It wasn't meant to be as nice. It was meant to be workmanlike and shuffling; you weren't *supposed* to enjoy it. It seemed an important distinction; you could travel through life with the minimum, just get through, or you could enjoy it. I tried to find the seats Jon and I were supposed to have occupied. I looked at our fellow passengers and thought, *Those boobies.*

They brought us big porcelain bowls of mixed nuts where the salt was like a fine soft coat the almonds were wearing. They gave us free headsets for the movie and the plane's audio program, with its light seventies hits and TV comics like Bob Newhart and Bill Cosby, whose original comedy programs we'd never heard. We had only seen the fame that had come *after,* but never the thin, youthful, uncertain way in which it had begun.

The meal came with a real linen napkin, beautiful silver, and a box that said GODIVA. I didn't know what Godiva was—only that it was wonderful, for it came in a gold box we had to unwrap. Jon and I ate slowly and carefully, not wanting to miss anything. "Did you try the bread?" Jon whispered. *"Sesame seeds."* He pointed at the crumbly white disk on the edge of my plate. "That's chèvre—goat cheese. *Delicious.* That's focaccia." When we unwrapped the gold box—a gift the airline seemed to be giving us, just for being ourselves—we looked at each other with delight. Our faces lit up. It was wonderful chocolate. During the movie, the stewardesses kept coming back and bringing us huge Toll House cookies. Every time we finished one, they would bring us another. When the plane landed, the stewardess brought us our carry-ons from a special closet, and we got off the plane first. Stewardess goodbyes are pretty worn out by the time they get to coach. But we got fresh goodbyes. You could tell the difference.

After that, I always made sure to make a scene in the airport. Returning from New York to California. Going from Los Angeles back. The only times I couldn't were when we visited our grandparents for one gray week each February. I was so wretchedly bored—all those old people at the condominium, with their old smells and their days by the poolside, as if they really were dinosaurs killing time around the tar pit—and so eager to get home that I would walk right on the plane.

This was OK. Flying coach sharpened my appreciation for first class. I would get us seats near the check-in counter. I would catch a stewardess's eye early on, and give her a red-faced sniffle. Sometimes, if the stewardess was a hard case, I would run back through the tunnel to give our dad one last hug. He learned to wait for this last hug, and the whole thing proved to him what a good parent he had become. I'd put my arm around Jon as we walked down the tunnel, and, at the last minute—the airline offering what resources it could to these devastated boys—the stewardess would stop. And turn around. And say, "You know what we're going to do? We're going to bump you boys up to *first class.*" After a certain point, the hardest thing was producing the gratified surprise. When I was a grown man, I understood the meaning of *foreplay* immediately. It was what it took to get you on the airplane. After a certain point, I wanted to walk up to the check-in people and say this: "Look, we're both going to cry. Our dad's going to look stunned. I'm going to hug him. It's going to tear your heart out. And then you're going to bump up our tickets. Why not just skip all this and bump us up right now?"

It was in this way that I developed my reputation for being the more emotional of us two. The more delicate. The son being more damaged by the divorce. I think at a certain point my brother figured out what I was doing—but he never said anything. He preferred first class too, but not so ardently as me. Sometimes, when it was a male steward taking tickets, or when the airport was really crowded, it looked as if we might not make the switch. Then I really *would* cry—and we'd get our adjustment. Jon enjoyed it, but he never started the crying himself. He would wait for me. People think first children have it easier. That they are more confident, more loved, more sure of deserving attention. That's wrong. First children have always struck me as more cautious—it's second children who get the easier ride. First children are right up there ahead in the cavalry charge on life. They're the first wave. They're the ones who take the first bullets, who dash ahead not knowing what they'll find. Second children are safe behind them, in the clear.

I never had to fake emotion with our mother. There was something so brave about her, in her dealing solely with our fractured family. After all, Jon and Dad and our stepmother and me—we were all together. We had each other, for better or worse. Mom was alone in New York, a city not known for its conduciveness to that state. When I hugged her, she would hug back, fiercely, and say, "This stinks. It *stinks*. But I guess we all have to rise to the occasion. We all have to be stronger." She didn't laugh with delight, the way our father did. Her big hand on my back had *force*—as if she were trying to press its imprint into her hand, so she'd remember how it felt, that she'd held her children, once we were gone.

And then she'd voice her private hope, in a small and careful voice, as careful as Jon and I when we first unwrapped our Godiva chocolates: "You don't have to go, you know. You could always move back." When I was fourteen—and we had been flying for four years—I saw that it might have been nicer of me not to have done this. That if I had been manly and stoical—the way my brother always was—these scenes might not have taken on the horror they did. I was fourteen, and I had begun the crying thing, which felt a little young to me. The stewardesses were watching, the gate was emptying out. I was tall and woolly, with glasses. My blond-haired brother, who adored taking care of me, was checking the weights of our various carry-on bags, trying to select the heaviest for himself. Mom said, in her careful voice, "You know, you don't have to go back if you don't want to." And suddenly—and the whole gate seemed to whirl with color and flash at my choice—I didn't. I whispered into her ear, "I'm not. I'm going to stay." My mother's hands jolted on my back—I don't mean she pressed me harder. I mean there was a rhythm to her hugs, and this was interrupted. Then she acted fast. When you made a decision with my mother, she liked to act quickly on the consequences, so that you could not escape from them. "What are you doing?" Jon asked—startled and sixteen, and his face turning . . . well, what, really? His eyebrows and mouth and expression lines did different, muscular things at once as various thoughts were shot out by his brain over his features. He was going to be making that cavalry charge alone. He asked, "You're not coming back with me?" in a quiet voice. We separated my bag from his. Mine was the heavier one. I actually had to take the strap from his shoulder, until he realized—"Yeah, this is yours"—and slipped it off. I had never put someone on an airplane before. We walked Jon to the gate. "You don't want to do this," he whispered to me. "What will Dad say? School starts in a week. Are you sure? Are you sure?" I felt Mom's apprehension that I would change my mind—as we tried to rush my brother onto the plane—and I hoped she would not try to defend her new territory. I felt this possibility flash through her body, and then I felt her reject it. She was always surprising me. She said, "Stay, Jon. You stay too. No one has to go back." My brother shook his head. "Richard—" And then he said, for our mother was right, and we were all rising to the occasion, "You guys take care of each other." He walked onto the plane. I don't know whether he got to fly first class or not.

There were amends to make. And arrangements to work out. My mom gave me her apartment's one bedroom, so my development into adulthood would be normal, so I would have this egg for my adult personality to hatch in. She slept in the living room, on a fold-out couch that was cramped and whose mattress was spiny with metal rods. This was how I ended up able to love only one person in the world.

We *started out* first-class. My mother was a painter—everything else came out of that. My mother painted pictures for a living—it was all she'd ever wanted to do, and it was what she did. My father was in advertising. He sold pictures of the good life for a living. They were both illustrators in their various ways. And they never cared about money, not the way I did. But of course, they never cared about it because they always had it. I don't remember my first five years, really—and anybody who tells you they do is lying, because nobody can; it's like someone telling you they tape-recorded an opera on an answering machine—but I have isolated memories of where we lived, and of myself, incapacitated by my youth but happy. Little messages from that life in the past. Rooms with lots of windows. Beautiful furniture. A maid.

Everything changed the summer my mother became a painter. This was the last year of the sixties. They were driving their old Thunderbird to Connecticut. My mother would have been wearing sunglasses—she was very beautiful, and deep into the Jackie Kennedy fantasy then gripping most of her friends. My dad was ignoring her cigarettes. Quitting cost him something. Even two decades later, when I took up smoking, his face would brighten at the sound of a match, at the crinkling of plastic on a pack, as if something *good* were on its way. They would be in their late twenties. They had already bid goodbye to our doormen for the summer. They had already left the city behind—all those contacts my mother had spent years collecting, she wasn't going to able to tap them for three months. (Would those powerful people forget her?) My brother and I were parked at our grandparents' for the day. The city's influence thinned out as they left the Bronx. It was as if the city had gotten tired, had given up throwing tentacles out from its heart to rope in the countryside. They passed the old rusty industrial scaffold of the railroad, and they were into pure green.

My mother said, with a wicked smile, "Let's not go."

My father was tricky. When he didn't like what you said, he would ask "What?" tilt his ear in your direction, and give you the chance to reconsider. The night ten years later, when I called from the airport to tell him I was moving to the city, his voice turned querulous, as if I were saying something very stupid. "You're staying in New York to go to *which* movie?" He would develop emotional spot deafness. That afternoon, he switched off the radio. "Let's not *what?*"

My mother repeated herself. She didn't want to go to Connecticut, where nothing was happening. My father pulled to the shoulder and turned off the car. He made his listening expression, and my mother confessed. There were dealers in East Hampton. East Hampton was where painters went for summers. She knew of no painters in Connecticut. If she went to Connecticut—it logically followed—she wouldn't become a painter herself. She knew they'd already paid for part of the Connecticut house. But who said that had to matter? (Do you see what I mean about first class? It was like getting the two glasses of orange juice.)

My father restarted the car and drove to an Esso station. My mother, of course, did not talk. She blew cigarette smoke out the window. What a *good* couple they made, with their complementary deafnesses! My father left the car. He crossed the baked parking lot and stepped into a phone booth. He called the family who were renting us their Westport house, and canceled. Just like that. My mother sat in the car worrying that he would have second thoughts, but she shouldn't have. My father loved the gesture too. His own father had been deeply concerned with money—my grandfather's bed had green pillows on it, and I thought this was because what he always wanted to do with money was wrap his arms around it and snuggle in close—but *my* father wanted to be the kind of person to whom money didn't matter, in the kind of marriage where choices weren't limited by cash. Fantasies, too, get passed down in the genes. He had married my mother at college

because she was a painter. This was the sort of thing he
had put himself in for. My father hung up the phone
happy. He walked back to the car, feeling like the sort
of man he wanted to be: the sort of man who could
stroll cheerily away from a one-thousand-dollar loss.

He got back into the car and swung the Thunderbird around. They were at the beach by three. My father—who had his own instincts for ceremony—drove
them up Bluff Road, to Indian Wells beach. My mother
kicked off her shoes and walked with her arms spread
wide, the salt wind flapping her white shirt behind her.
"It's beautiful, beautiful!" My father said, "The boys
will love it."

My mother became a painter that summer. My
father worked in the city, visiting on weekends.
He played out the role of breadwinner, of upper-mid-
dle-class New York parent. He played it with a little
hangdog look of imposture—it was my father's weak-
ness to believe that a man's personality was too complex
for any one thing, to want you always to see the complex soul staring out from the single, reductive part. My
mother converted one bedroom into her studio. She
bought a roll of clear plastic and stapled it over the
floorboards. She put up curtains to get less light. She
painted on the floor. We'd gone to Celia Kapplestein's
retrospective at the Guggenheim that winter. Celia was

a painter ten years older than my mother—a painter who was where my mother wanted to get. Celia was painting on the floor. So my mother painted on the floor. She was twenty-eight. She had an adaptive mind, and a punch-clock mind. It was time to be a success. It was time to have a show. She had been at Hunter College. She *knew* what to paint: stain paintings, like Celia's but a little flashier, a little *younger*. The first week, we played in her studio. We chatted with her and stamped our feet until she watched us roll Tonka toys on the plastic, making little rips that at the end of the summer would be filled in with paint. My mother knew this wasn't going to work. She placed an ad and hired us a mother's helper. This girl showed up every morning at ten—a short, clean-faced girl with three blue towels folded in her beach bag, along with two sodas and a novel by Hermann Hesse. She took Jon and me to the ocean. She took us to the marina, where we fished for crabs. We turned red. In the afternoons, my mother would kick off for the day. She would change into a swimsuit sans shower, drive out, and meet us at the beach. Jon and I would be paddling in the water. We would see her walk powerfully across the sand. There were lots of other mothers on the beach, but we knew that walk. We knew that figure. She would wave to the mother's helper. Halfway to the ocean, she would whoop and begin to run. She would dive in, and bubble up in front of us. She'd tickle our feet. She'd grab our ankles and dunk us. My brother was seven to my five. He copied our father's helpmeet style: "How'd it go?" "I painted *great* today," she'd say. She'd take us by our wrists and kick us in a circle, the three of us in the water. She painted with reds and greens and yellows, and as we circled, the tints would release from her skin, so that we were floating in the sunset colors of her paintings.

They had my brother one year after college. They had me two years after that. My brother was blond. I was brown. I think if we'd both come out brown, or both blond, they would have had another kid. But my mother did everything in series. She had the two colors she wanted, and she closed up shop, as far as childbearing was concerned. She swam with us, chattered about her day, fed us, and got us into bed.

On Fridays, our dad arrived by train. The platform was a reunion station, all us semi-families awaiting completion. When the miracle of fathers arrived, we all turned quiet and solemn and curious, after the festival hugs. These were the dark-suited men who allowed us to live free by the water. There was all this excitement on the platform, and lots of perfume, and lots of children running around. You got to recognize the mothers from the platform every week. During the days, their hair got salt-stiff, they wore T-shirts with white smears of suntan lotion over their arms. On the platform they dressed up like starlets. Our mother would chat with

them—enjoying *her* imposture as a young wife. Jon and
I ran around with a group of young boys. We caught
fireflies in jars—sometimes, we crunched them between
our fingers and smeared the yellow dye on our foreheads like war paint. We stepped down to the tracks—
our mothers nodding *be careful*—and placed pennies
there, and waited for the train to smash them. Every
week, it was a wonderful surprise, to see how powerful
and heavy the train actually was. That train pulled
up—and there were the dads, late arrivals to our party.
My father liked to watch my mom step toward the stairs
as the engine slowed. He liked Jon and me walking to
him, our foreheads glowing with firefly juice, carefully
presenting our bent pennies. "Thank *you*," he'd say, as
he pocketed them. He always did one thing, the same
thing, whenever he arrived. He would take our mother's
hands, palms up. He'd stroke the palms with his thumbs
and turn them over. Paint got stuck in her fingernails,
in the knuckles, and not even the most patient scrubbing could work it out of the skin, as if the paint were
veins of gold in the earth she was rummaging among.
"Painting hard, I see," he'd say. The crowd would break
down to its component cars, all the engines starting, all
the headlights wheeling around on neighboring walls,
on bushes, on trees.

At home, in our beach-smelling house, our parents
would eat chicken. After we were in bed, we could hear
our father pacing in her studio room, his city shoes

sticking to the plastic. Our mother turned quiet whenever anyone looked at her paintings. We could hear our
father expressing enthusiasm ("Gorgeous! Joan, I have
to say, you are one of the five best painters *alive.*" It was
his way, this breathless ad-speak, of saying he loved her.
It was innocent, and it inspired our mother, but she
couldn't quite forgive herself for being so easily inspired. At the supermarket, Jon and I would stroll
alongside her, and when we pointed out things we
wanted, she would say, "I have to say, Chef Boyardee is
one of the five best cooks *alive.*" It was our first experience of family treachery). Then we could hear our
mother using her stapling gun to pin yet another canvas
on the wall. We would fall asleep to that steady chunking sound. What they did after they finished looking
was anyone's guess—but there were other bumpings,
other steady sounds as well, and in the morning our
plates would still be on the table, the frayed meat going
a little gray on the chicken bones. Our mom would pick
up a plate of broccoli and admire the deep watery green
it had turned overnight. "What an *interesting* color,"
she'd say, as she slurped it into the trash.

By the end of August, it was rainy and cool in the
mornings. Leaves were firing, and closing up, and turning into red fists. My mother was running out of time.
But she had enough paintings for her show.

She even knew the dealer. Gregor Krumlich had a
house in East Hampton. *He* was the reason she had

brought us here, instead of to Connecticut. East Hampton advertised that she was in the same world as him, with the same values as his. Gregor was Celia's dealer—he was a tall Austrian man, with square glasses and very little hair. He was *extremely* professional. That was all he was. He had disappeared into his role as art dealer, until the role was all that was left, and there was no man, no personal man there, at all. Just an art dealer. My mother loved the grandness of that gesture. He had already visited her studio twice in the city. Our mother painted in the cellar of our high-rise—among the tenants' trunks and spare furniture, and the lockers of the doormen. When Gregor visited the second time, I snuck downstairs in the elevator. I brought some finger paintings from nursery school. I ran into her studio, shouting, "Gregor, Gregor! Will you be my dealer, too?" My mother looked at me in horror. Later, when Gregor was gone, she took me aside and explained that I hadn't even brought my best work. "You only get one chance with these people, Rich," she said. My stuff was pictures of Dr. Seuss characters—I guess she thought it was derivative. My parents' couple friends, and even my mother's art world friends, would have been charmed by my behavior. But Gregor didn't even kneel down. He looked at my mother and said, "Joan." Then he turned away, bringing his fingers to his chest, as if tapping his tie would remind both of them who he was, and why he was there.

She didn't call him first. It had been two years, and
she couldn't get Gregor to commit to anything. She was
twenty-eight, and had a young person's lucky feel for
strategy. She called Karl Olken, who ran a gallery in
SoHo. SoHo was not as posh as Fifty-seventh Street,
where Gregor's gallery was. This was fine. She had a
plan. She invited Olken for a Tuesday dinner. He
brought his wife. Our mother had made them a wonderful fish supper—a big salmon had been caught and
was willing to be cooked for our amusement. She mari-
nated it in dill and wine, with bulby mushrooms and
horseshoe slices of celery ringing the dish. This was set
up on the patio.

First, she showed the Olkens her paintings. This
was for real. Showing them to Jon and me, to the
mother's helper, even to our father, had been good practice, but our opinions didn't count. We weren't *profes-
sionals,* and a lot of her freedom of movement, mentally,
was gone. Olken was an older man—a Polish immi-
grant—who was lofted to great vistas of greed by my
mother's work. She watched him closely until she could
guess his reaction. Once she'd guessed it—Olken kept
bustling up to the wall, then pacing an exact number of
steps back, so that she knew he was imagining them
from various sight lines of his gallery—she ceased to
pay strict attention. She turned her attention to Mrs.
Olken. Mrs. Olken walked timidly beside her husband.
She was careful not to say anything that would commit

Karl to any course of action. When Karl liked a painting, Mrs. Olken murmured something in support. When he nodded, she did. When he became silent, she ceased to exist. Finally, she stood in a corner. Mrs. Olken showed what twenty years of life in the art world could do to a person. After the last canvas—my mother put down the staple gun and wiped her hands on her jeans, the same way she did after finishing a meal—Olken turned to my mother with a grin. "These are *truly wonderful*, Joan," he said. "They truly are," his wife faintly repeated, and sank down in the room's sole chair, as though an ordeal for her had ended.

My mother served us dinner in a state of giddy triumph. I had never seen her like this. She floated back and forth from the kitchen, carrying out wine, iced tea, bread, lemon for the fish. Usually when she served a dinner, she had various anxieties—Was the conversation flowing? Was the food all right? Now there were no anxieties, and she could concentrate on sensations—as if this highly sophisticated and human brand of satisfaction had paradoxically freed her up to become wholly animal. She watched us. Jon, with his big appetite, chewing salmon and pushing the mushrooms aside to form a toadstool meadow at the edge of his plate. Olken waving a hand in front of his nose—to push aside a diligent mosquito—as if someone were whispering urgent advice he intended to disregard. Mrs. Olken, loyal but famished Mrs. Olken, finishing up the last bit of fish and looking softly at her husband, to see tonight's policy on second helpings. There we all were. The evidence that my mother had painted the right pictures, that she'd made the right choices, that she was about to move ahead, was working on her like a drug.

I pushed my plate away and tapped Olken on the back of his smooth hand. The time had come, I saw, to bargain. "Would you care to buy some of my work too?" I asked.

My mother froze. She was the doomed, talentless mother of an imbecile. This is one of my first memories—the entirely adult look she gave me. The look an adult gives an ally when you have let them down. But Olken smiled, lifted his wineglass, and said, "Richard, I did not come to *buy*, but to help your mother *sell.*" Mrs. Olken laughed. In this world, my mother saw, spouses served as interpreters for their husbands, to help get their point across to the rest of the room. Karl was using me backward, to slip messages to my mom. "In fact, Richard"—he had a foreigner's gusto for words, relishing them not for their sense, but in pleasure for having the right ones at his disposal—"I was just now about to offer your mother a *show*, when you raised this important *question.*" He turned away from me. "Joan?" he asked.

My mother was hiding her reactions in the salad. She said, "Give me one day to think about it."

The Olkens seemed crestfallen—Karl looked to his

wife for advice, she looked back to him with none—and finished the dessert in silence. We all followed them out on the lawn, to see the Olkens off, to watch the complex human spectacle of car doors being locked and elderly bodies belting themselves in. The night was full of crickets, and salt winds, and a cicada sound that was like the telephone wires singing. Olken rolled down his window and reminded her, sternly, "Tomorrow, Joan." He started his car and drove away.

Jon and I went to sleep. My mother picked up the phone and started a number, and hung it up, and restarted, several times. We could hear her, and smell the peppery smell of her cigarette—the smell that meant a decision was coming. After a moment, she started dialing again. Frederic Beaumont was Gregor Krumlich's second in command. He was a playful man, who dressed in silly sixties clothing and loved gossip. At the gallery, he would telegraph Gregor's actual intentions when Gregor himself was especially impenetrable—he was Krumlich's art-world wife. She said, "Hi, Fred. It's Joan Freeley," when he answered.

Frederic's voice turned from dull to playful—he had a tic, of wanting to inject more wit into a conversation than it could comfortably hold. The jokes were fine. But they tended to prolong discussion, and made the same point—that Frederic was a witty man—again and again. When what my mother really wanted was to exchange information, hear simple yeses and nos. "Ah," he said. "Joan Freeley—honeymoon summer at the beach. And what is the weather in East Hampton?"

My mother enjoyed the surprising card she found in her hand—her ability, for the first time, to end Freddy's words with some of her own. "Nice. Karl Olken and his wife just dropped by. He offered me a show. I have to let him know by tomorrow."

Frederic said, "Don't say anything until you hear from me or Gregor."

An hour later our phone rang. On the other end was Gregor, with his personal, peculiar combination of anticipation and annoyance. Like most powerful people, what he wanted most was not to be surprised. He said, "I will come *Thurs*day afternoon."

On Wednesday she packed. Jon and I went to the beach for the last time with the mother's helper, who still had not finished *Steppenwolf.* My mother put her studio into boxes. She pulled up the plastic. She took down the curtains. She scrubbed paint from the floorboards. On Thursday, when Gregor arrived, she'd taken that house back in time—it was, effectively, the untouched house we'd first rented. My mother showed the pictures to Gregor. She'd been waiting for this moment for two years, yet the experience was quite different from her experience with the Olkens. Her whole future depended on Gregor's response. His was the only gallery she wanted to show in. His collectors were the buyers she wanted. His artists were the artists she wanted to be listed among. She could hardly bear to look at Gregor, there was so much condensed *want* shimmering around his body. Gregor didn't nod, didn't move. When he had finished looking at a picture, he would click his tongue against the roof of his mouth until my mother put up another. She felt he could tell how much this meant to her, that he knew this was all a formality, and what it came down to was that Gregor could change her life with one word. It was horrible. Her desire shifted; what she wanted most from Gregor now was for him to leave. She sat down. Gregor sighed, tucked his tie deeper into his sport jacket. He patted her on the shoulder, said a few words, and invited us outside. Then he kissed my mother on the cheek, nodded formally to Jon and me, and squeezed himself behind the wheel of his tiny and surprising convertible. The gravel in our drive chattered for a few seconds after his tires had gone.

We drove back to New York the next evening. The farm stands were closing down—there were a few farm families standing beside them, offering hairy brown ears of corn and wilting, drooping sunflowers. For a while, we were beside the train—and this appealed to me, for we had so often driven to meet this train, which carried my father. Now we were driving alongside the train to New York, to be with our father all the time. "Pass it, pass it," we cried. And our mother sped up, so that when we looked out of the back window we could see the thin, bottle-nosed face of the engine, and none of the cars behind. Our mother was relieved. She thought about how close she had come, sitting in the front seat of this car, to going to Connecticut. Her life would be very different now if she had said nothing, if she hadn't been in this environment, she would not have painted the same pictures. Life was as chancy, as rickety an affair as that. She lit a cigarette. My brother picked up her pack and said, "Don't smoke these, Mom. We want you to live a long time." "I stop today," she said, and blew some smoke through her nose, and threw the pack out the window. The train was long gone. For a while, the sun wanted to race us. A big orange ball, skimming close to the surface of the potato fields. Every time I thought we had ditched it, it would pick its way through trees and electrical towers to reappear by our side. I knew then we were never going to pass it, that it was riveted to our car, because we were the people it loved best on the road. I didn't know if I should let Mom and Jon in on the secret. When we joined the expressway at Westhampton, the sky had turned watery gray and the other cars had their headlights on. Our mother repeated Gregor's words, in a good approximation of his voice. It was a strange thrill to watch her become someone else. "*Some*body is going to make a *great deal* of money from these pictures, Joan. It might as well be me." We laughed, and badgered her to repeat the words—the words that we knew meant something special, that she'd gotten what she wanted. We didn't know that from now on this was going to be our family, the three of us. My mother cackled—she had the loudest laugh of anybody I knew. This was the most beautiful summer of our lives.

And then we hit real first class for two years. And then it was over—and after that, we were in coach. After that, it was economy all the way. All the way into the present. Other people were still flying first-class— that was the horrible thing. We knew how terrific it was up there, but my mother and I, we had been bumped back to coach. And then my father, because he was so interested in making sure my mother and I weren't having any fun—he kept waltzing back in to check up—he got knocked back into coach too.

My mother had her first show. She sold seventy-five paintings that year—an unheard-of number, in the sedate art world of the seventies. Celia Kapplestein demanded Freddy fly out to her compound in Litchfield. She toured him through her studio, showed her new work—"Lovely, lovely," he murmured. Then she spun around and cried, "Why is Joan Freeley selling more pictures than I am?" My mother was written about in *New York* magazine. She was interviewed by *Art in America.* I remember our father going downstairs, the night of her first show. (All of us attended, Jon and me and our father all wearing matching blazers and khakis, so that everyone could tell who we belonged to. We were a six-legged cloud of tan and blue shuffling behind her in there.) He went down to Lexington Avenue for the early edition of the Friday papers. My mother kept Jon and me awake—we were buzzed-up on wine and adult talk anyway, sitting around the big white table. Dad came back with a stack of newspapers, exuberant. Our mother tried to get the papers from him, but he insisted. "I want to read it," he said. It was his way of showing he was part of things. My mother huffed. "Shall I read the headline?" he asked. She didn't say anything. He turned to us. "Shall I read you *boys* the headline?" He lifted the paper. "An Interesting Talent Makes Its Debut," wrote Hilton Kramer. The review got better and better, our mother hugged our father, and then we were rich.

You know what it felt like? It felt like all those invisible rich people were holding a vote. The article under consideration was: Should Joan Freeley be a painter? Should we give her enough of our money to let her *continue* being a painter? They had voted yes.

Dad always had mixed feelings about New York. Once we had the money, he began to torture our mother with those mixed feelings. He didn't like that we had to be chaperoned to school. He didn't like the dirtiness of the city. "All the *dog crap,*" he would say—as if the country, with its large community of unhousebroken animals, promised complete freedom from rogue excrement. After five weeks my mother caved in. She had wanted to buy, with the extra money, a house in East Hampton (which we would have still. I could have taken women there during college, I could have invited friends, Mom and I could have used it, instead of having to arrange and beg weeks and Sundays from wealthy friends. In high school, when we were entirely out of money, she would become morose in the spring. Gloom would set in. Getting away never meant that much to me. I'd been summer-camped so often when I was young that the idea of June and July in the city had a kind of reverse glamour. But Joan would become despondent. She didn't like having no place to go. She didn't like other people *knowing* she had no place to go). Dad lobbied—with all his skills as advertiser—for a farm in Vermont. He headed the Pepsi account. He wrote a Pepsi ad of all of us entirely happy in Vermont, one glowing family. He got Jon and me to approve first, then used the pressure to get Mom in.

He wanted to teach writing in the country. He wanted to write novels himself. That was the bargain he wished to make. He had supported Mom as a painter. Now she was set—an Interesting Talent had made its Debut—and it was Mom's turn to give him *his* chance.

When she has described this logic to me, she has always sounded surprised. She lifts her eyebrows and asks, "What do you think of a man like that?" But this was the deal she must have known she was striking with Dad. She had married a man interested in the arts—a man who would pay for her paint supplies, for a studio, for baby-sitters to keep us distracted. Only a man who was interested in such work himself would have made such sacrifices. This was the second part of the bargain. So we moved.

What I learned from my father was different. He was good at advertising. He really was. He could compose sentences made solely of images. He could make your heart ping with emptiness, and in the instant of that emptiness convince you that only his cars or sodas could fill it. Dad didn't realize the tragedy of man is that, alone among animals on this planet, he has no natural prey group, no natural food source. A whale is born, or a rooster, and right away all they want to do is sift plankton or peck corn. Immediately they know how to schedule their days. A person is born—and what does it do? Hold on to what you start doing. Once this becomes a question, you're sunk, because you can never answer it. This is what I learned from watching my father.

It was two years in the country. They fought all the time. We were near Bennington College. Our mother

made what contacts she could among the fine-arts
faculty. My father managed to find three or four eager,
not terribly bright kids—two from the campus, two
from the community—who wanted to study writing
with him. You'd come into the room and see them
there. Our dad earnestly reading Kafka aloud, looking
up forcefully after a pungent paragraph. When no one
responded, he would slowly read it again. "What do you
think?" he'd ask. "It's *good*," someone would say. Another would hand-raise. "I think it's liberating, the way,
when Kafka wants Samsa to become a bug, man, he's
just a *bug*." Our father would lean his ear forlornly
out—drop it down, waiting for something smarter.
Then he'd read the passage a third time.

Our second year, he gave up teaching. He started a
film society in town—the classics, as far as my father
was concerned. *Citizen Kane. Shane. The African Queen.*
A movie called *The Sundowners*, with Robert Mitchum
and Deborah Kerr arguing, until I fell asleep, about
whether or not it was ever going to rain. There were
always silver cans of film in the house, and on movie
night Dad would slap his hands together with great
gusto, and run the projector himself. He tried to start
discussion groups afterward. But by *The Magnificent
Ambersons*, most of the campus community had stopped
attending, and after *The Sundowners* (my dad's Water-
loo), no one came at all. Just the four of us. It was

pointless to have a discussion group. My father drove us home smarting, and my mother cleared her throat and said, "I liked the scenery. I've never been to Australia"—which only highlighted how little there was to say.

Then Dad had nothing particular to do at all. He'd given up his book. Our mom painted in the barn, walking home across our big lawn at evening to sit in the living room. Dad no longer looked at her hands (which were as paint-covered as ever) to see the colors she'd been rummaging among. He had a new hobby—wholly private and self-contained. A beard. It came in furry, and made him look old. "I could never have grown this in the city," he explained, marveling—as if this were yet another unanticipated Vermont bonus. When he kissed Jon and me, he would jut his chin out a little and wiggle it back and forth, to give us more of that whisker feel.

Jon and I grew more raucous as things got worse. If Mom and Dad were trying to get away from themselves, he and I tried to eliminate each other. He would invite me to ridiculous dares—bike rides down our hill with eyes closed, jumps from the bridge in town, into the fast-moving river, to catch a crayfish or retrieve a lost ball. The morning of my birthday we played one-on-one, and he elbowed me in the eye, giving me a big shiner. Our grandparents drove up that day—to find my father in his beard, my mother in her painting clothes, and me bruised and holding a bloody towel to my nostrils. I was near the kitchen when my grandmother and grandfather came in for water. "This is turning to shit, huh?" my grandfather asked. "It's not going to last much longer," my grandmother sighed. "The crime," my grandfather said wistfully, "is what they're getting these days for a divorce."

There'd been confusion, all that year, with another couple, the Boydens. Jacob taught sculpture at the college. He had a beard—and this may have been what gave Dad the idea. A facial competition, with the best beard winning Mom, and the less hairy suitor slinking off in defeat. Jacob was South African and very fat. He always laughed and boomed and bellowed expansively, as if his responsibility, as a guest here, was to occupy more space than a normal American would have. He was the only person from my mother's art world in Vermont, and our mother got the two families very closely connected. (I found out how closely only later.) Jon and I would play Parcheesi with the Boyden daughters—an ethereal gang, all blond and always seeming to flutter away, somehow. They were none too pretty, and pale, but I tried to have crushes anyway. I didn't know what was happening on the main floor, where our parents played their own sorrowful games—but the drives home in our Thunderbird were murder, our parents' heads as big and immobile in front of us as backstops. It didn't surprise us when one morning Dad simply left. When the distance between the front seat and backseat of the Thunderbird finally elongated to Dad driving off alone.

That was the end of their marriage. He had gotten our mother into the world she longed to join. Then, gripped by second thoughts, he had tried to get her *out* of that world. In the resulting confusion he had been the one to leave. Jon and I were tangling with each other on the first floor when the Thunderbird drove away. We charged upstairs. Mom was sitting on the bed, staring at her palms. "Dad left," she said. "Good," Jon said. And it was good. There'd been a heaviness to the house that was gone, and though it now felt scary-empty, the emptiness had possibilities. Jon bounced his basketball on the dining room table, shattering plates and upending glasses, which were reluctant to break. He bounced the ball against them two and three times, until they crashed to the floor. I built a Hot Wheels track that went down the stairs, and when this didn't work too well I began chucking the cars at the front door, where the intricately molded hubcaps (someone at Mattel had really *cared*; one of the most heartening things about the world are these pockets of unforeseen craftsmanship) made a silver pile of clippings. Anything goes. Mom got her paints and, humming to herself in the sun, made a brightly colored FOR SALE sign for the lawn. A master of the fast departure, she had us in SoHo within a week.

We were spoiled children, and we hated it. I didn't understand SoHo—the warehouses, the old buildings, the cobbled streets. It wasn't the Upper East Side, and it was dirty. I felt marooned—our mother had taken us off the track of the nice life we'd been on. She'd moored us in a creepy cul-de-sac, with her art-world friends. None of the kids in my school had parents in the art world—it made me feel different, like there was something I had to cover up. There is no more eager conformist in the world than a little kid. You're just trying to get your first foothold in the normal culture at that age. You grip on and start your climb. All of the sudden, we were on a different mountain, and I wasn't a good sport about it. In a way, my being a bad sport guaranteed that I would be climbing that wrong mountain forever.

Jon became my parent. School was a two-mile walk from the loft. Mom was in the art world for the first time; she let Jon take care of me. He dressed me up in the mornings. He walked me to the subway, with its sleeping men and its smells of dust and iron and urine. We would stand there together, at the edge of the platform, waiting for the breeze to start, and for a train to light its threads of gold on the tracks. The wind and lights and rumble—there was a whole different planet down here, with its own turbulent weather systems.

Mom celebrated that whole year. Jacob visited sometimes—sometimes sleeping over, sometimes not. She went out, to art-world bars in the neighborhood where her friends convened, and would come back with her clothes smelling of cigarettes and white wine. "You'll be OK for the night?" she asked. "Just until ten?" Jon nodded. It was strange being left alone, in the loft with its ticking sounds, with its windows turning black as the sun went down. Our loft had once been a factory. Our bedroom had a huge heating unit, with metal coils and pipes, and at night, when we were alone—when she had gone out to a party, or to Broome Street Bar for a drink with the other painters—it felt like we were inside a large snake, whose coils were slowly constricting shut. In the absence of our father, Jon seemed to decide he would become our dad. He picked up our father's mannerisms—the dropped head, the tendency to say "What?" a great deal, the way of ignoring what you said and walking on until you said something he liked better. When we came home from school, we weren't to talk to our mother—she was painting. We would watch cartoons. Sometimes, we would make a net out of blankets and chairs, and play tennis in the huge living room.

At seven, she would open her door. We would hear the clicks, and see her poke her head out of the studio.

"Whew!" she'd say. This meant we could talk to her. We'd bound in. She'd be doing stretches on the floor of the studio—bouncing her head into the bow of her knees. "How was your day?" she'd ask, her voice roughened by stretching. The room smelled of paint—a bright, plastic smell—and was spotlit by ten lights. We were walking on a stage. "What do you think?" she would ask. And she'd ask very seriously, pointing out a canvas grid of a hundred colors and asking if one square of blue was too blue, or if another section was too monochrome. There was the idea—now that Dad was off in his own pastures—that any criticism had the potential to be helpful, and valid. I don't know what Jon's feelings were. But I could usually not tell one from another. If she was in the middle of a painting, she would say, "Don't say anything. I haven't decided how I feel about this one yet." Her paintings to me were simply our anonymous livelihood. They were something the world wanted from her. Every three months, Gregor would come to the house. On these mornings, our mother would be up early, makeup already on. She would draw her face away from the stove as she cooked, to keep the cosmetics from melting, and when she kissed us she would hold her face only in proximity to ours and invite us to touch our lips to her sweet-smelling ear. This was my first experience of a social kiss.

In the afternoon, when we came back from school—with Devil Dogs, with Yoo-Hoos, ready to lower our heads back into the stream of television from which school had obligated us to remove it for eight hours—she'd be back in her painting clothes. "Don't talk!" she'd call, and when we entered her painting room a number of the canvases would be gone, and she would be moving with the quick steps and pursed expression that meant she was serious. She still smoked— which meant she was especially serious. She could never quite remember where she'd left a cigarette. So there would be four or five going at once, their smoke snaking into the air, and as she moved around the room she would pick up one or another, drag on it, and put it back down. She kept the pack in her jeans pocket. It killed her to part with paintings—and yet, on the days they went out, she was giddy. She would wrap them lovingly in plastic, as if outfitting them in mufflers for the winter. She would plant a kiss on the frames and say, "Don't come back." They only came back if they didn't sell.

I'd met Gregor once myself—so I could understand why she smoked the way she did. A year after we moved to SoHo, our mother threw herself a huge birthday party, and I met him again. Our loft had been a wreck when we moved in. Now it was finished, and lovely. That was worth celebrating. My mother's paintings were selling extremely well. Four years as an artist, and she was friends with all the people she'd admired while a student. That was also worth celebrating. She was about to get her divorce. She had many lovers. This was something I didn't want to celebrate. The lovers were a parade. They came by to audition for the role of stepfather every few months—not just Jacob, but other sculptors, and a lawyer, and a handsome cameraman from PBS. They went with us to the beach for weekends—my mother found she could trade paintings for months by the sea—and they would mount imitations of our own father that somehow *missed*. They couldn't sit still. They would be fatherly for one moment; then they would act like older cousins the next. Then, when they felt they had lost us, they would retreat to a wounded distance, whispering with our mother and answering our questions with *mm-hm*s and *no*s. Our mother became irritated with us for vetoing their performance—"You didn't give Albie a chance"; "I thought you were both *very* hostile to Ken"—but our response was as important to her as it was to these men. If we didn't like them, she couldn't. They would give a few more auditions, each more constrained than the last, and finally they would mouse off the stage, and our mother would find a new man. But the party, it is clear to me now, was her coming-out party. She had made a decision, that morning driving to Connecticut, about the life, in her best fantasy version of life, that she wanted to lead. Now, through an outrageous combination of circumstance, she actually *did* have that life. This was what we were celebrating, on her birthday, at the age of thirty-two.

It was catered. The caterers came in the morning, a busty Irish woman and her sullen teenage daughter, and set up camp in the kitchen while Jon and I stalked hungrily around. These caterers were clear on the fact that they weren't there to cook *our* breakfast—"We didn't come to be maids-for-a-day, Mrs. Freeley," the mother told our mother—and so Mom grudgingly put together our Cream of Wheat and orange juice. These were the ways people defined themselves—that they would make so much sacrifice for money but no more. Jon and I ate, Jon verified that I had some kind of subway pass for the morning, told me to zip up my coat, and walked me to the subway. All of this was with a vague sense of grumbling. Our normal routine was being disrupted. Now, as a twenty-two-year-old, the idea that my mother had caterers in her house, that she was dressing herself and our loft for a party for three hundred, seems impossibly glamorous. I love the idea of it—of the power she could command. But then it just seemed another oppression of her life as an artist. We both had friends in school, Jon and I, and it seemed their parents' work intruded in their own lives far less often than our mother's did. I felt bad for the Irish girl—because her mother was a caterer, she had to be in this humiliating position of going to other people's houses, as a servant. Her mother's work was barging into *her* life, too.

In the afternoon, Mom's work intruded on us again. She met us after school. She took us to one of the barbershops in Little Italy. Jon's haircut came out fine—he had straight hair, and there wasn't much you could do with it. They sat me down in the chair and put that long robe over me, so that I couldn't use my hands to protect myself. They kept cutting until my hair met some vision of theirs as to how young boys, perhaps in the old country, looked. There was one moment at which it looked good—but I didn't speak up, and they kept cutting more. I was all forehead and mouth—and the extra skin felt as exposed as an overtrimmed toenail. Mom took Jon by both arms, ran her eyes over his face, nodded. "Perfect," she said. She turned to me, my difficult woolly head. Her eyes scrunched up around my unfortunate length of brow. "Is there anything you can do?" "You wanted short," the barber said, trying to deny responsibility, sweeping up the hair from the floor. We went with her to Saks, and she bought us new blazers and new Qiana shirts, and I understood that we were part of her display, too. Part of what she wanted to show was that she was managing everything—being a painter, being a woman, being a mother. She had an ideal for how we should look, and in the mirror, while I was trying on my shirt, she played with what hair I had left, curling it over my brow with one finger. "You look nice," she said, dubiously.

We took coats, as the guests arrived. That was our job. For the first hour, our mother stood by the door, greeting people as they came in. The caterer's daughter was only a few years older than Jon—but somehow, she was wearing a skirt uniform, and carrying a tray, and handing out food to strangers. She wouldn't look at us. I liked taking the coats. Each one had a different scent. The heavy leather jackets smelled very much like the cows that had worn them first. Windbreakers smelled of rain and breeze. Wool overcoats were gardens of trapped cigarette smoke. I liked thumping them onto my mother's bed, in her room—the allowed vandalism of chucking the coats down there. I avoided the sight of myself in the mirror. The room filled up. My mother had bought new records. David Bowie, Mick Jagger, Bob Dylan. The music thumped around.

Everyone showed up. Hiroshi came—a Japanese artist I liked, because he was around Jon's size, and because his vocabulary was about as large as ours. He liked to talk to us. His English was unsure—when he said something, he would wait to see if you understood, and then, when you did, he would smile. It was so human. He had done some contracting work on the loft, and he grinned at our mother and said, "Joan—place looks great." Lars Stevensen showed up: he was a fat

sculptor, always high-spirited, and I learned later that
that high-spiritedness had to do with being drunk. He
had lived with us for one month at the beach. He had
meaty, sculptor's hands. "Want to have a pinecone
fight?" he asked me. We had once chucked pinecones at
each other for an hour. My mother's boyfriend arrived—this year, the little sculptor from Maine, who
had decided to win over Jon and me by being naughty
with us. His version of adulthood was that it was all a
ruse, and he was still a kid using age as an excuse to
break rules. He led us to the bar and got us drunk on
wine. I didn't want to drink—but Jon was hungry for a
father downtown as well as uptown, and he said to me,
"Drink." So I drank. "What do you guys think?" Ken
asked. "I would like," my brother said, "to try a beer."
"Oh—a beer man. Any particular label? Domestic? Im-
port?" My brother lifted his chin, considered like a man
in a beer ad. "You decide," he said. Jon tried a Bud. No
matter how good this man's impersonation of a stepfather was, every time I looked at him, all I could remember was the morning I had walked into my mother's
bedroom, ready for breakfast, and seen his pale back
laboring, and an odd, preoccupied expression on my
mother's face. She had seemed to be trying to remember
something. Whenever I was around Ken, this was all I
could think of—this very odd moment—and I was
afraid, when he saw me, that he could *tell* I was thinking of it. I tried to be with him as little as possible.

We took more coats. The famous artists came later. There was a division. My mother had made it into the first group, like Lars and Hiroshi, people who sold paintings and were reviewed. There was another group—immortals, like Celia, and Jack Atski, and Leonard Chichikov. That was her next step. You could hear marching outside, coming up the steps, endlessly, more people arriving, a machine of coats for us to carry into the other room. The party was spreading onto the stairs, and you could hear hellos out there too. When the famous artists arrived, they would glance around with a look of comic dissatisfaction—they had come against their better judgment, and things were a little worse here than they had feared. They gave Jon and me their coats with preoccupied faces. They weren't as polite as the younger artists were. When Neil Hollander came in, he gave me his wonderful trench coat, and his gloves— then on second thought he put those deerskin gloves in the pocket, said, "Don't lose these, OK?" and slinked away to where Jack was drinking with another man, and he made smiling remarks that made all of them laugh. I took Neil's coat to the bedroom, took the gloves out of the pocket, and slipped them on. They were still warm from his fingers. I wore Neil's gloves the rest of the night, until another boy I ran into—the son of a divorced mixed-media artist—demanded one, and then I lost track. I think I eventually left mine by the kitchen sink. I kept thinking, as I stood by the door, that Dad was going to show up. It seemed implausible, that in this party of three hundred invitations, one had not been mailed to him. I kept thinking I would take his coat, take his gloves, and he would ruffle my hair.

Everyone smoked. Some people danced. Some people smoked marijuana—that very sweet smell, from pockets of the living room. Many people brought kids, and eventually we had a gang going. We ran around, eating peanuts out of bowls, playing tag, watching sweatily the TV in our bedroom while an Alfred Hitchcock movie made its broadcast premiere on the *ABC Friday Night Movie*. The party began to feel like any other SoHo party—it was hard to remember it was our loft anymore. This seemed to relax my mother. In her dress, and her careful makeup, she hadn't wanted to have her *own* party. She had wanted to have the *standard* party. This party looked pretty standard to her. She laughed, in her tight dress. She kissed many people. She loved to dance—I watched her dance with Ken. At a certain hour, I walked into our bedroom to watch TV, and the lights were off. Jon said, grouchily, "Turn that *down*." He had gone to sleep. "Why don't you go to bed, Richard?" I walked outside the door to find our mother. I found her in her studio. The lights were off. She was searching through all her ashtrays.

"Have you seen my cigarettes?"

"You shouldn't smoke," I said automatically.

"I know, I know." She put her arm around my shoulder. "You haven't seen Gregor, have you?"

"Jon is asleep," I said—meaning Jon might have seen him.

"Here they are"—she had felt in the pocket of her painting shirt, and brought out a pack. She lit a cigarette. She put her arm back around me. "It's late for you, isn't it? Go to sleep if you want to. You don't have to stay up for me." It was strange—the studio felt like our home, and the noise outside did not. She kissed me on the cheek, nuzzled warm next to my ear. "I think you boys did an excellent job with the coats. But you don't have to worry about the party anymore. Anyone coming this late doesn't have the right to expect as charming a staff as you two. If you're tired, go to bed." And I stumbled back to our room.

I awoke twice. The first time because the music had all at once stopped, and a blue light was flashing under the door, and my mother was speaking in a very careful voice to someone. The police had come, because of the noise. This meant the party was a complete success— you wanted to be having so much fun that the neighbors complained. After the front door closed, and I could hear the policeman going downstairs, a cheer went up. The party resumed, louder than before.

I awoke the second time many hours later. The moon was slicing through our window, making shadows

on the floor. I needed to pee. I'd been dreaming myself
walking through a large, sunny house, looking for a
bathroom. I had found one, and was undoing my pants.
This I knew to be a bad move. Jon had warned me once,
"Whenever you think you're peeing in a dream, stop,
because it means you actually *are* peeing." I had learned
this the hard way—the soggy and humiliating way—
myself, a number of times. Sometimes—to be perfectly
frank—the loft scared me. I hated to cross that dark,
empty space the hundred yards to our bathroom. So I
would pee into the wastebasket. This seemed quite sensible. Jon never woke up, and there were lots of wrap-
pers and wadded papers in there to absorb the stuff. No
one seemed to notice. But about six months after we
moved in, Maria (who cleaned the place once a week)
said something to our mother. It did not occur to them
that it was me. Their belief was that Wilbur, Jon's cat,
was urinating into the basket. Somehow, this absurd
theory went over. I can't imagine how they pictured
it—Wilbur climbing up the basket, straddling with four
cat legs, it seemed awkward and impossible—but Wilbur took the rap. He was shipped off to a friend of
Jacob's in the country, and then I was too embarrassed
to confess. I was afraid to pee in there now, because
then everyone would know, and Jon would blame me
for having lost his pet. So the basket wasn't an option. I
lay there. The feeling was urgent. It had to be the
wine—my body wasn't used to it, and the wine really

wanted out. It was in a hurry to resume its journey, to get wherever it was going. It had lurked in a grape. It had bided its time in a bottle. Now it really wanted to see the Hudson River. I thought about staying in bed, and trying to sleep. But I knew that eventually I would have another peeing dream, and I wasn't sure I would be able to stop myself a second time. I stood up. Jon was asleep. I had pajamas with little socks built into the feet. Mom was casual about doing the wash, and the sock part had gotten crinkly with dirt and foot-sweat. My feet made soft, cardboard sounds as I stepped to the door, opened it, and walked into the party.

It was dark, but the party was still in full swing. There were the people dancing. There were the people smoking. There were the people who weren't dancing or smoking, but who were drinking. The party was like one big many-legged animal, sprawling in our loft, coughing out smoke and noise. I pushed among people's legs toward the bathroom. I had hoped, of course, not to be noticed—but everyone was drunk, and they saw me as more entertainment. "Look—here comes the new curator of the Whitney!" someone shouted. I walked past the bar, and Ken—playing up to some other young artists—stopped me. He held my arms as if he didn't know me, as if I were a strange boy outside a 7-Eleven trying to buy beer. "All right," he said. "I think I'll need to see some ID." I hated him for selling me out for a laugh. A woman, all at once, grasped my hands and whirled me away in a ballroom step. But I made myself totally stiff in her arms, and she let go of me and flitted back to her friends, to her cigarettes and drink.

There were many people. They were in three groups. The younger artists huddled in a big loose clump near the door. They made a smaller group than the non-artists. The non-artists (the ones who weren't girlfriends or boyfriends) circled them enviously, and sometimes talked to them. Sometimes the younger artists would seek out the non-artists, and they all laughed together. Then the famous artists were in their own, much smaller, group. Jack and Len Chichikov and Neil and Darryl Bayer. They talked only to each other. Occasionally, one of the younger artists would break away from his group, and walk over and try to join them. Jack would lower his head, and regally listen, and then laugh, and repeat what had been said to Len and Neil, who also laughed. This gave the younger artist the excuse to stand by them for a quiet moment and sip his drink—to get their view of the party, their perspective, a little taste of what it would be like when he could officially join them on their mountaintop. After a few minutes, he would return to his own group. The non-artists didn't speak to the famous artists at all. The object seemed to be not to have to talk to *anyone*—to keep breaking away from larger groups to smaller and more select circles, until finally there was no one who would dare speak freely to you at all. This was the objective in that room. I tried to picture my mom this way—as cool and distracted as Jack Atski. It was a frightening image. I would have to think of something witty to gain the attention of my mother.

I made it to the kitchen—the older caterer was washing dishes, her daughter was back in jeans, sitting slumped and asleep at our kitchen table. Guests were here too, in a long line before the bathroom. I joined the line, until I realized they weren't waiting. They were just hanging around—they had gravitated to the bathroom as a fun place to stand. I walked into the bathroom. A woman was at the sink. A woman I didn't recognize, performing a bit of last-minute emergency touch-up work, dabbing on mascara in the mirror. She waved a hand by her face and then held it out to the toilet. "Don't mind me," she said. The woman was not leaving her post—she was waiting for me to begin. Because I was eight, I was obviously not supposed to know what a penis was. I lifted up the seat. I couldn't do it. I had never been naked before in front of a woman who wasn't my mother. I stood there, and then I spit in the bowl, flushed. "That's better," I told the woman, and walked out of the bathroom.

The sight of the toilet had only made my bladder more urgent—it was as if I had shown a castaway, for one cruel second, a glimpse of land. I walked back through the party. My mother's room was to my left— and she kept a big mug on her night table. That was

what I would use. I could use it, and then empty it into
the toilet the next morning. (I could also make sure
never to drink from that cup again.) My bladder, sensing relief in sight, began chugging itself back up. I
opened her door, which Hiroshi had helped us hang. I
stepped in, closed the door behind me, and there was
Gregor Krumlich.

He was reading. He was reading a yellow book
called *Sensibility*, which my mother often read. She
would read at the table while Jon and I were doing our
schoolwork, and sometimes she would dip into it with a
pen, as if she were trying to correct a mistake, or to add
her own small float to that black stream of words.
Sometimes, she would read a passage to us—like Dad,
as if Dad's spirit had slipped a few genes into her code.
The book was about art. The passages she read us were
ways of looking. I thought this was stupid. You looked
at something and then decided whether you liked it.
"That's Ernest Steinman's whole *point,*" Mom would
say. "You've grasped it instinctively. That shows I'm
bringing you up right." It seemed that Gregor, with a
slim smile and a glass beside his hand, wasn't truly
reading. He was flipping through pages, searching only
for those very sentences where my mother had tossed
her own inked words into the calm printed stream.

He was wearing clothes that frightened me: a blue
shirt, and a wonderful double-breasted suit. These were
clothes that said "You can't talk to me," as clearly as if

Gregor was saying it himself. His shoes were shining dark brown with lots of scrollwork, and they repeated the same message. The shoes said, "We are unapproachable—and if you don't want to take our word, take a gander at the suit." I knew that, in Gregor, I had found the calm center of the party—that here was the person so powerful he didn't need to talk to anyone. He had gone as far as you could in the world of parties.

"Gregor," I said. He had grown a beard since I had last seen him. I had met him on the lawn in East Hampton, and since then he had become a rumor in our house, the man who decided when our mother was ready for the world. "Are you looking for your coat?"

He looked up lazily. Then he laid the book lightly aside and turned in my direction—as if this was his office, and I had barged in. "Pardon?" he asked.

"Are you looking for your coat?"

"Its whereabouts are not a *mystery* to me. And you are . . . ?"

"Richard Freeley. I'm Joan Freeley's son."

"Yes . . . the finger-painting *artist.*" And he blinked comfortably—and then the comfort was gone. Just like that. You could feel it suddenly end. I felt he was really *looking* at me, as opposed to just seeing me as an anonymous interruption. He was using me as a way of getting a fix on my mom—to spy on the private life of one of his painters, the type of mother she was, what her personal tastes were, to see if they were up to snuff.

There I was with my bad haircut, in my dirty pajamas—when probably, when my mother had sized me up in the barbershop, she had been imagining me through eyes very much like Gregor's.

"She bought us new clothes today," I said.

"A *practical* and *attentive* mother," he said. "Bearing up well under the *pressures* of a single-parent household." It was as if he were quoting from reading matter that was amusingly beneath his interest. He picked up his drink and took a small sip as the ice cubes tinkled. "Your mother," Gregor said, "is ever the industrious woman."

He looked at me another second, his eyes receding back into comfort. They had taken what they wanted from me, and now I had dropped back to being an interruption. He was waiting for me to leave. But I had given my bladder its I'll-release-you-soon message, and I knew I couldn't make it back to my room, back through all those people. Gregor reopened the book.

After a few seconds he turned to me. "Are *you* looking for a coat, Richard?" His attention wavered in and out like a kind of wind, a dangerous breeze, and it seemed my responsibility to try to hold it. I wondered how my mother could bear up to facing him, four times a year.

"My mother is trying to find you. This is where I'm supposed to sleep."

His eyes took me in a second time—people didn't

often tell Gregor what to do. He looked at the coat-covered bed with mild surprise. Then he looked back at me with lifted eyebrows. "Well. I should try to find *Joan* then. Give her a hand with the *hostessing*." He stood up. Yawned; covered the yawn with a fist. "Tell your mother, I have enjoyed her *underlinings*." The way he said it, it sounded like a euphemism for something dirty and best kept to yourself, like "panty shields." I said, "Good night, Gregor."

He made a small bow. Then he left. I took his glass from the desk. I emptied the drink into the palm plant in the corner—perhaps the palm would become drunk, and mistake its genus, and in the morning produce a rose. Who knew the secret ambitions of plants? Then I pulled down my pajama bottoms, held my little pink penis in my fingers, and peed into Gregor's glass. What a relief! Yet this was how I'd always feel in front of Gregor, for the rest of my life. Frozen with need, things to say clotting me up. As if I had to pee, and he *knew* I had to pee, and I couldn't fully express myself until he was gone. I put the glass back down on her desk.

I couldn't walk back to my room, because then Gregor would know I'd been lying about sleeping here. This seemed like a risk for my mother. I would have to stay. I shut off the lights. I crawled beneath the coats until I was under my mother's blanket and sheets. The sheets had a warm smell that was like her, and there were rough streaks of paint, and they were also like her.

I pulled my head under the blankets and under the mound of coats. I could smell them all again too—the different sweats, the cigarette smokes, the furs, the pungent dirts, all those coats gossiping to each other about where they'd gone and what their owners were like. I was lying under the whole weight of my mother's world. I went to sleep.

In my dreams, I kept on becoming lighter. Every few minutes, I was aware of the door opening and somebody's throaty laugh, or someone shouting through the doorway, or a man gruffly telling a woman, "No, we'll take a *cab."* Every time I heard one of these things, the burden above my shoulders diminished. Finally, many hours later, the lights were blindingly on, and I was blinking. My mother, in her long pink dress, with the fabric that concealed her shoulders. Behind her, Ken, looking blurry and impatient and nervous; the helpless look, I learned when I was a teenager and wore that face myself, of men in the grip of sexual hunger. "What are you doing here?" she laughed. All the coats were gone—just a short leather windbreaker, Ken's, and my mother's purse. "You wanted to sleep in your mother's bed? I'm touched."

"Did you see Gregor?" I asked.

"I never found him," she said. No, Gregor did not take instruction very well—I knew I wouldn't tell her I had given him some. Ken lifted me up and carried me through the living room, where a record was winding itself down, where David Bowie was innocently singing as if people were dancing, singing to an empty room, and then I was in my own bed.

I put a stop to this period myself: Me and Dad, and Jon. We all collaborated on Mom's fall from the art world. I think Dad didn't want to be brushed off so easily. I don't think what he did had a *direct* effect on what happened to her. Only, the things people do are done in *circumstance*. They are a product of mood, of how people feel about themselves—and Mom was about to lose her children, and would feel pretty low, and so whatever she did would be a product of that. Of feeling low about herself. And that became her social persona, and all the decisions other people made about her were about a woman who was feeling low about herself. And soon she was feeling low about the art world, too—and new decisions started being based on that.

Dad got an apartment. He made this apartment very attractive to boys—Dad the boy-catcher, Dad the life-advertiser. It was in our old Upper East Side neighborhood, a few blocks from the park. The divorce went through. Mom wanted a good settlement, and she did kind of a cruel thing. She used the novels Dad had written in Vermont. The first was about a man who loved his painter-wife too much. He helped get her

work commercial, introduced her to painters and critics—and then she became famous, and, well . . . the
novel ended there, with the painter famous, and the
good-hearted husband following her to a party. The
second novel—*Double Life, Double Wife*—was about a
man who quits his job as an advertiser and makes his
wife support him through prostitution. Mom's lawyer
read aloud from this novel in the courtroom—with Dad
at the other table—and the judge, hearing it, immediately doubled her child support. Then Dad made his
second move. He called on the phone. "OK, whisper,"
he said. We whispered. "What's your allowance?" We
answered. "And what is she feeding you?" We told him.
"Do you know," he said, "that I am giving her one
thousand dollars a month, and it's all supposed to go to
you? Why don't you ask what she's spending it on? You
have your father's permission."

We'd get up for school very early, in the icy still-
dark. We'd watch the shabby old Hanna-Barbera cartoons, then *The Little Rascals*, then *Magilla Gorilla*—as
if the programming on TV were warming up with the
morning. By the time Bugs Bunny came on, we had to
leave—we'd stay, and risk lateness, only if the first cartoon was one we liked. But at Dad's apartment we had
permission to watch the whole thing. He would watch
with us, and afterward, he would stand up and laugh.
"Kill the Wabbit! Kill the *Wab*-bit!" he'd sing, and it
was lovable to watch Elmer Fudd's voice channeling out

of his handsome smooth face. He'd give us money for a cab—it wasn't any faster, but it was fun to watch the driver whip around garbage trucks and sneak into the bus lanes. Jon would calculate the tip in front of our school, while our classmates dropped off the steps of the bus.

Our mother didn't understand why we were becoming judgmental. Choosy, like shoppers. There had never been a reason before; we hadn't known there was an option. Now, our father was constantly offering a standard to compare her to.

We were sitting in the kitchen one night. Mom was doing a watercolor. Jon was leaning over the paper, advising her on colors, and I was bringing her water to clean off her brush. We were both half listening for the phone. Whenever the phone did ring, Jon and I would freeze guiltily, like adulterous husbands—the phone now issued a constant source of plots that embroiled us and implied demands for us to meet. But the phone wasn't ringing, and we were sitting with our mother. "Here, give me a hand," Mom said, handing both of us brushes, and we began to paint in our own squares. (The finished painting, *32 Wooster Street*, hangs in a museum in Toledo.) We heard shouts from outside. My mother opened the window. Darryl Bayer was downstairs, in a hansom cab. With him were Lars and Hiroshi. "Joan! Joan Freeley!" he cried. "Let down your hair!" We walked downstairs. "Where're you guys off to?" Mom asked. "Get in, Joan," Lars said, burpily. They were going for drinks at the Carlyle. My mother squeezed in between these three men. Her eyes narrowing happily, she leaned over and smiled something to Darryl. We waved, and blew warm air into our hands, and watched the horse clop down Wooster Street for a block or two. The hooves sounded perfect on the cobblestone—this was what the streets had been made for, not loading trucks and schoolchildren. It felt magical, to have our mother *summoned* this way. This must have impressed me, for when our father asked what she was up to, I bragged, "She goes for rides in a carriage every night." "Really?" he asked, grinning. "She went *once,*" Jon said. "Well, that's got to cost an arm and a leg," Dad said, cheerfully. "How does that sound for a thousand dollars a month?"

We went with her to openings. After the party, I watched, and I had the impression her career wasn't going as fast as before. I had shown Gregor some *messiness* in her life—that her kids didn't have good manners, that she made them sleep in inhuman conditions, on beds crowded with coats. Her openings took place on Thursdays, from six until nine. There was food; but never enough food. They served only white wine and Brie on crackers—as if some art-world specialists had gotten together and decided the best way to sell paintings was to keep the collectors slightly tipsy and light-headed with hunger. No one looked at the paintings.

They came together and turned their backs to the work and chattered. The openings were so *strange*. She would paint for six months. Then, one day, we would go up to Fifty-seventh Street. A rug shampooer would come at five and shampoo the rug. Assistants would speed around the white walls, straightening canvases and checking lighting. Gregor would clap his hands together and touch his tie a great deal. "Now *Joan*. When the guests *arrive*, I want you to . . ." And there was our mother in the center of the room—she had made all this happen, all this energy, just by what she had done on her own. Power. She was a different woman here than the woman who'd taken us to the beach. Or she was the same woman, the woman who had walked up the sand from her car, breathless and sure.

Jon and I had to stand next to each other. If we didn't—if we were alone for even a second—Freddy Beaumont would swoop down and unnerve us. "Rich-ard," he'd say, suddenly bending down behind me. "How about it? Give me your honest take. Is your mother staying commercial? This gallery has a very high overhead. Is she going to sell out the show, earn back our rent, pay our salaries for the month? Rich-ard—you guys have lived with the paintings. You know her last show wasn't *quite* up to expectations. So tell me. *Can we afford to tip the rug shampooer?*" This was his way of joking—Freddy had the kind of humor that depended on making somebody else feel bad. Afterward,

Jon and I would seek each other out. Freddy had a freakishly large behind—it was his liability, and as long as he was facing you, he seemed stylish and perfectly cool. Then, when he turned away, there was his bottom, peeking out from his jacket flaps, confiding, "I am human after all." We called him "the Butt." Jon would say, "I just had a visit from Freddy Buttmont. He brought his behind." I would say, "Freddy-the-Butt just asked if Mom's paintings were going to sell."

Then the collectors would arrive, and everyone would jolly up. I have one very clear memory of a collecting couple—a perfect collecting couple, in their fifties, who had made their money in some ordinary and efficient fashion, and had come to this place where money guaranteed something a little *extra*ordinary, a little tribute to what they had achieved in worlds outside this one. The husband slipped off a brown trench coat and hung it carefully on the coat rack, then brushed down his lapels. His wife burst out of a lovely fur. Looking down at the floor—looking at no one—she grasped her slip through her dress and gave herself a little wriggle, bringing her inner and outer selves into alignment.

Jon and I wandered through the rooms—the roar and chatter of a party, the smell of people. The other artists weren't rooting for her. They weren't rooting for each other, either. But on a night when it was someone else's opening, they were all temporarily united by not wanting any pictures to sell. Any collector who bought one of Mom's canvases this week was less likely to want to buy one of *their* canvases the following week. When Jon and I slipped into a room, there would be Lars and Herb Tingley and Tom Dancer, the art lawyer, laughing about something and careening their eyes to the pictures. They would say, ". . . I guess she decided not to pay attention to *ARTnews* last year." Then they would all Ho Ho Ho. Tom would spy Jon and me—and grasp Herb's forearm, and conversation would halt.

When we were bored, we read the guest book. Everyone signed in. Art critics wrote the names of their magazines in bigger letters than their own names— they knew the magazine name was the one that counted, the one whose sun gave them shine. Our mother's friends wrote little messages in the address box—compact sentiments that exploded with encouragement, like "Great show, Joan," and "Keep up the lovely work!" I would get bored and sign in a hundred different people. I'd sign "R. Redford," very humble and casual. I'd sign "Woody Allen," and include a note promising "I will use your lovely work in my upcoming film!" One Thursday night, I signed in President Ford's entire cabinet, having just that afternoon learned them in school. (The only change I made was in Rogers C.B. Morton's title, from "Secretary of the Interior" to "Secretary of Interior Decorating.") At home, weeks later, Mom would sigh, "Richard. *I* get the joke, but I don't think Gregor appreciates this. He turns these books into mailing lists." I couldn't stop myself; it was for Gregor that I was doing this. I wanted him to believe my mother was exceptionally popular among the Hollywood elite. I thought I was doing her a favor—showing she drew a slightly better crowd than Jack, a more powerful group than Celia. I practiced different signatures, and phoned film studios and memorized their addresses. Once, at the table, reading the guest book, Mom looked up and sighed. "Your *father* came to the show." Jon looked at me—I shook my head. This was one I hadn't signed. Mom looked into the middle distance of the loft for a second. "Well, if you remember, ask him what he thought."

Then the lineup, at eight o'clock. Gregor and my mother in the center of the room. It was an informal line—the people just stood in little clumps, not wanting to acknowledge that they were waiting together at all. Even the artists got on the line, though. Gregor and my mother operated very well together. My mother would shake a hand, then pass the hand over to Gregor. Gregor would smile and nod and suggest to them the picture they might like best—they worked smoothly, like a department store Santa and her floor manager. Mom in fact called it, with a smile, her "Santa routine." The artists—whether they were rooting for her or not—liked to show they knew my mom better than the collectors. They would do more than shake hands. They would kiss, or give her a little hug. She was the star of the evening, and they wanted to shine with her, show they were part of the same constellation. After the evening was over and everyone had gone, our mother's face would be covered with strange lipsticks around the cheeks and mouth, as if she had been beaten by a flurry of friendly people. She would walk to the ladies' room to wash off, and click back up the hall, that walk we knew so well, its exact speed, its exact approach. She'd return flinging water from her fingertips, and Freddy and Gregor would be conferring behind her. The staff would be putting dots on the paintings that were going to sell. Red dots meant a sale. Black dots meant a possible sale. When an evening was a success, the other artists would walk out chagrined—a nightmare field of red dots, a huge blooming diminishment in the available collector funds of the New York City art world. But Gregor and Freddy would be chuckling together, and our mom would toss a paper towel into the wastebasket and say to us, "Boys! Time to hit the road."

Our father found a girlfriend, whose impersonation of a mother was perfect. Emily had two daughters herself. She lived in the penthouse of my father's building. I liked to go up there after school and drop water balloons off the roof, or climb to the water tower. No structures were more enchanting to New York City children than water towers. They were a whole different city—a village of wooden huts, of thatched dwellings like the ones we studied in the Kenya block of our social studies class. The world beneath the streets was another planet, with winds and earthquakes and slivers of light. The world above the rooftops was a primitive nation. And in between were the streets, where everyone walked and made believe things were normal, and up-to-date, and harmless. I felt at home in our father's apartment, with Emily and her daughters—the nicest version of the city of all, the Upper East Side world. Dad would look around and thump the sofa cushions with satisfaction— the advertiser in him trying to find the moment. "This is like a *family* up here." He knew that word had a real, hideous tug for us—that we had watched enough television to know that families had a mother and a father, with office jobs and carpets.

We watched TV there all the time—Dad would join us for *Star Trek,* or sit through the tortuous un-folding of the bare-bones plot of *McCloud.* "I think," he would say, pretending his plot-knowledge was something we shared, "that that guy's old Texas horse sense is going to solve the crime a lot faster than their New York City street smarts." We'd laugh with him—and sure enough, he was right. "Spock! Spock!" he'd cry, on a Saturday when we were just sitting around—and he'd press his hands to my face in a Vulcan mind-meld. It was embarrassing and thrilling at once. As an adult, I understand what he was doing. He was *courting* us— doing things in the present so that we would imagine an

unbroken future of that much attention, that much
charm. Of course, no one could maintain that much
flirting energy for a lifetime. Particularly not in a family, where everything is so backstage and grouchy. But
we had never been courted before, at ages nine and
eleven. "I'm getting a reading," Dad would say, his
hands searching like tentacles over my face. "I'm getting *cold.* I'm getting *sweet."* Jon would laugh. He would
drop my head and race to Jon. Hands on Jon's face. "I'm
getting a clearer reading. The same thing. *Baskin-Robbins.* They want Baskin-Robbins. Captain, beam us to
Baskin-Robbins for ice cream at once." And we'd walk
down to Third Avenue and buy cones.

Our second year in SoHo, Freddy quit Krumlich
Gallery. He was getting married. Gregor casually asked
if his wife's family had money—a fair question.
Gregor's own wife had had money, and that was how
Gregor had opened his gallery. Freddy said no. Gregor
said, "Well, why marry her?" It was a common-sense
question, and Freddy could find no witty response to it
except to quit. But without Freddy there, my mother
had no source of gossip on Gregor's moods, on the life of
the gallery. Gregor made the classic rebounder's mistake
after Freddy. The man who had once run his gallery—
Freddy—had been his opposite, and that hadn't worked.
So the man he got to run the gallery now was the same
as himself. A small duplicate of Gregor, without as
much personal power. A reticent and careful man. Now

there were two kinds of the same strength at Krumlich Gallery—not two different kinds of strengths—and my mother had no further insight into what Gregor was thinking. This made Mom nervous, and added a funk to the loft. But everything at Dad's apartment was cheerful. Work ended at six, and after that work never entered the house again. Work stayed politely outdoors, and if it ever did come in, it carefully wiped its feet and hung its coat and meekly sought out Dad and didn't bother the rest of us. The art world was different. When Mom wasn't working, she talked about work or read books that might help her work, and when we went to parties, they were with painters she worked among.

He doubled our allowance and got all the foods we liked. He gave us dialogue to derail Mom: whenever she asked us to do our chores—we had no chores at his home—we were to say, "Mom, we aren't your *maids*." This drove her wild. She became dangerous with threats. But she believed I was still loyal, that I still loved her enough so that the major threat would stop me. I was waiting for her to make that threat, and one morning she did. It was a Sunday, and we had not gone shopping—one of our weekend chores. Mom had been at a party having fun all night, and now we were supposed to work. Certainly, I had learned from TV, and from watching the parents of my friends, it was the parents' job to work, so that the *kids* could have fun. I convinced Jon that we should stay in. We watched

Wonderama on television, suffering the platitudes of the
host ("Kids are people too," and a hysterical song about
fitness that repeated the single word "Exercise") so that
we could get at the cartoons. Mom came in at eleven
and was disturbed to find us there. Further, it wounded
her to find us watching TV—an insult to her, as if she
had raised us so poorly that we didn't find each other
more interesting than a small glass-covered box, or that
we couldn't generate interest inside ourselves. "You
didn't go to the Grand Union?" she asked. I said, "We
aren't your maids." She sat down on Jon's bed, and she
deployed that threat, that threat we'd all been waiting
for. It had been my job, somehow, to get her to make
that threat; it had been her job to make it. We had
drawn to this irresistible moment together. "Look,
Rich," she said. "Why don't you go stay with your father?"

And I had my opening. I went into the other room
and called Dad. He sounded happy and shaken—he'd
gotten what he wanted, the world had proved suscepti-
ble to his designs. I went downstairs with my knapsack
and sat on the curb waiting for his taxi. A little while
later, Jon and Mom bumped the grocery cart down the
steps behind me, off to Grand Union. They blinked.
Mom was wearing sunglasses. She walked to the curb
where I was sitting. She looked at me. She took off her
sunglasses. She put her hand on my shoulder—and this
was my first taste of power, my first experience of deny-

ing someone something they wanted, and seeing the
pain it could cause. I thought of Gregor. Power wasn't
about capacity to say yes. That was kindness. Real
power was about the capacity to say no. Mom said,
"Richard, I'm apologizing." This surprised me. My
mother was proud, and when she made a mistake her
impulse was to run further along, down the path she'd
created, rather than retrace her steps. "And I'm asking
you nicely to stay with me and your brother in our
home. Your father has been waiting for us to make a
mistake like this for a long time. If you go ahead, I
don't know how, but I know he will find a way to make
all of us pay." I didn't say anything. She squinted. She
dropped her arm and replaced her sunglasses. "Well,
if you are going to go, please come back soon. I'll
miss you."

So I went to live with my father. He turned his
apartment into a clubhouse—bought an air hockey set,
and a Ping-Pong table, and a box where you piloted a
stainless-steel ball bearing along a labyrinth of holes. In
the spring, one weekend when Jon visited, Dad nudged
my back. "Richard has something to say to you." "I
think you should move in too," I said, as Dad and I had
practiced. "It's fun up here—" "Of course it's fun," Dad
said. "I'm a father to two boys. It tears me apart to think
of one of you downtown. I feel like half a father. And I
worry about your mother. She's a painter. What hap-
pens if her paintings stop selling? You belong here, with

your father and brother." Jon asked me carefully, with that first-son caution, "Is it really more fun?" "No whispering," Dad said. "Of course it is. It rips me up inside." "It is," I promised. Jon trusted me. He moved too. Dad's child-support payments ceased; Mom was alone in the loft. We waited, that spring, for Dad's next move. We waited for him to marry. The implicit promise had been that Dad's life was more like TV; a married father would bring us into that TV world entirely. Spring ended. We went to summer camp. When we returned, he was married all right. But he wasn't married to Emily. He was married to Jane.

I learned what happened years later. Mom was at a party—this was during the years I lived in Los Angeles, in that strange town that really was like TV. We had seen years of television with houses and cars and friendly neighbors. We had seen hundreds of movies that implied lawns. Lawns were America. The whole Jeffersonian formula about a nation of farmers—it had boiled down to a nation of men obsessed with their yards. Every Saturday and Sunday they came out, mowing, watering, fertilizing, weed-whacking, growing and chopping, like dogs scratching themselves over and over in the exact same spot. We had never had a lawn before. In New York, we had seen ads for lawnmowers and fertilizers, and been fascinated. In Los Angeles, we had those too. We had stepped into the tranced TV world, and mowing the lawn became one of my jobs. I did it with pre-teenage sweat sticking my T-shirt to my back, and panicked green clippings leaping from the mower to attach themselves to my knee. I spent four years in that strange bright all-over sunshine of Los Angeles, which never changed, but was like the light of a refrigerator door that was left open all year round. Mom went to a party, in the days when Jon and I were visiting her three times a year. She ran into Emily. Emily told Mom that Dad had come up to her apartment in August, after a business trip. He seemed cocky and short with her. He said they would have to marry right then. Emily said it sounded nice—but she wanted to wait. Dad didn't want to wait—he said he didn't have to. Emily said she thought it was best. Two weeks later, Dad had married Jane.

Mom told me this years later, after I had returned to her and we were sitting in her living room and I was revealing—as I never had before—what had become of Dad. I asked, "Why didn't you tell us this at the time, right when you knew it?" She squinted, staring into the mind of the woman she'd been then. "You were living with them," Mom said. "I thought it would scare you. I didn't want things to be any harder for you than they already were."

We came back from camp that summer, and there was Jane. We couldn't believe it. They had moved to the West Side in our absence. The Ping-Pong table and air hockey set they had gotten rid of, for they didn't go with Jane's decor, her Art Deco knickknacks and champion rugs. The rugs *were* her in a sense; you had to walk lightly around Jane, and there were surprising, repeating patterns running beneath your feet, which you couldn't follow but would suddenly swell to be all around you. As if to ensure a successful marriage, she had none of our mother's traits at all. She was blond, where Mom was brunette. She was gentile, where we were all Jewish. And she was mean to us. Or rather, not kind. She had been a child, but never a parent, and so had never made the transition from a child's acquisitiveness to a parent's generosity. It was strange to know that in her fantasy version, we would not have existed. She would walk out of their bedroom, on particularly happy mornings, and find Jon and me there, and be surprised. As if, in her happiness, she had forgotten her husband had two children. She was twenty-eight, incidentally—the age of our mother before she started painting. Our father was trying to replay that part of his history. To get it right.

From Jane I learned table manners and that not everyone loved me—two interesting lessons for a boy. My mom had not been that interested in our manners. She must have figured that if we were ever in a position where bad manners held us back, we would solve the problem accordingly. And she had certainly loved me. I learned from Jane how to act in rooms with people who wished I was absent from those rooms entirely.

Mom moved uptown. She took an apartment in a building six blocks from where Jane and Dad and Jon and I were living in four concentric circles. The weekend she moved, she took us on a tour of the building. Doormen and elevator men. "Just the things you like, Richard," she said. The apartment was a nice, small one-bedroom. She looked at us tenderly, uncertainly. She was trying to guess our tastes, but it was too late. We had already acted on those tastes; it was past the point where she could try to court us back. I didn't know, touring the place, that this was going to be the apartment I would live in for years and years after. That when I would say the word *home*——or in a movie, when the screenwriter and director appealed to that potent concept, so that all the throats in the audience would choke up at once——I would be remembering this modest little place. I don't think she did either. She ditched the loft; it was too lonely without us. She painted in the small living room of the apartment. She wanted to live near her children, for she had no idea who Jane was, and thought we might be in trouble.

After three months, Dad and Jane took a business trip to Los Angeles. Our grandparents arrived to take care of us. "Nice place," Grandpa said, eyeing the rugs, for he could tell they were expensive. Money in a form you could stand on interested him——as long as you were standing on it, no one could pull it out from under you. "A little *fagelah*, for my tastes," Grandma told him. The newlyweds came back, and Dad took his final revenge. He told us, at the table, "Boys. You know how hard it's been these last few months. Your mother hasn't made it easier, living six blocks away. I've arranged to be transferred to California. We're going to leave next month. Remember, you *must not tell your mother.*"

He arranged our flight for a Wednesday. One of Mom's days. We met Dad at his office that afternoon. His desk was cleared off, the posters were down. He called Mom, chatted with her for a second, told her he would have us uptown in an hour. He gave the phone to me, and whispered in my ear, "Tell her you're going to be there in an hour." I took the phone. Dad had already said it, and it seemed too complex to contradict him. I told the phone, "I'll be up in an hour." "That's good," Mom's voice said. "I've got this chicken-in-wine on the stove. Your favorite, right?" I thought of that meal I wasn't going to eat; I wondered what she would do with it. Would she throw it out? Would she eat it, slowly, night after night? Or would that be too painful? "Are you OK?" she asked. "Your voice doesn't sound right." I gave the phone to Jon. He looked at me. Dad had already said it. I had already said it. He said it, too. We got into a cab to the airport. We got our boarding passes—one of my first plane rides, in coach. I didn't then know how much I would soon long for first class.

Mom must have sat there for hours. She must have sat for hours and hours, first watching the clock a little, then getting nervous, then calling our home and getting no answer. By the morning, of course, she would find that the phone had been disconnected. In all the time I have known her, she has never described that night to me.

We began flying back and forth between California and New York. Gregor asked Mom to leave the gallery; she couldn't paint anymore. She was an abstract painter, and the problem with abstraction is that your moods too clearly come through. No one wanted to hang pictures in their home that so clearly told—in the vocabulary of colors—that here was a woman who was depressed because she'd lost both her sons. There was no way she could hide this, paint a picture without this central awful depressing fact being stated. When we told Dad about this, the year I was twelve, he waited a moment to compose his reaction. Then he said, "I told you it was a difficult profession. I told her, too." He had found a new ending to his novel. The art-world husband gets his wife out of the art world.

When letters didn't give us enough of her presence, and Jane complained of the price of our long-distance calls, Jon and I begged for recordings of her voice. She sent us them once a week—Dad, with a little frown, would throw these packages with his ex-wife's hand-writing onto our beds. We played them dreamily, on the mornings when he and Jane slept late. At the end, she would always say, after clearing her throat and encouraging us to be happy, "I *like* taping. It's fun." As if our moving had had the benefit of revealing to her a whole new hobby.

And then I moved back to New York. We had no money. Mom was out of a gallery. Jon was living in California, away from us both.

She didn't have the loft—we were in the small one-bedroom, because of what I had decided to do at age nine. She slept in the living room, and gave me the bedroom. This was the situation I had plunged us into, at age nine, and this was the situation that I promised myself I would recoup.

W e had no money and neither of us had any friends. We went to museums. We dashed around the city, the two of us, with our un-social lives, looking for places where we could invest ourselves guilt-lessly among large crowds. We stole a social hit from these unwitting providers, these innocent groups. We slow-walked past Jackson Pollock, and Morris Louis, and William Merritt Chase, and Vermeer. We crunched over dead Central Park leaves into museums, tracking their shredded remains on our sneakers. We passed grand fountains and cool marble pillars, with their sense of life as a beautiful breakfast party. I got dizzy on the

elegance, the well-dressed tourists making their flattering assumptions about us. Mom would look at a Cézanne and try to show me the way the background
integrated with the foreground. She would hold her
hand over the canvases (index and thumb together to
indicate an imaginary brush) and sketch very rapidly
back and forth, showing how the paint was applied—
until a guard, attracted by the activity, wandered over
and asked us to step a little back. Mom said, "You can
always tell how good a painter is by the transition between the way they do what's behind and the way they
do what's in front. Cézanne was a *master.*" I didn't have
any idea what she was talking about. But I noticed other
people often attentively listening as she spoke, and this
made me happy. We doused our loneliness in these afternoons and galleries, and returned to our apartment
with better manners, with lighter speech. As if we'd
held a little last sip of those museums in our mouths.

She got money for us—how? Life turned out to be
expensive. This was something I had never considered.
Rent, food, phone bills, clothing. Every month, you had
to get these problems licked. Then, just when you
thought you had—you backhanded them off your side
of the court—four weeks later they bounced back at
you, speedier and more dangerously aimed than before.

She sold paintings. She called collectors who had
bought her work in the past, and asked them to visit. I
would hide in my room, doing homework. I would hear

the doorbell ring. I would hear Mom's stiff, pleasant greeting. I would hear the closet open and the hangers tinkle as a coat was stowed. Then rumbles of chairs, feet crossing the living room. Voices that became simply the deeper thrumming of a man and the lighter patter of a woman. After an hour, I would hear them at the door again, Mom's pleased goodbye. Then she would march straight to my room, throw open the door, and collapse on my bed. The vein in her forehead—a kind of branched Y—showed whenever she lay down. "Whew!" she'd say. "I sold one."

She borrowed from rich friends, from older collectors who had become her intimates. We visited beautiful apartments on Park Avenue. Mom dressed me carefully in my best clothes. The nicest sweaters. The plushest corduroys. My great statements, which I tried to separate for days at school, so that I might have a not-great pair of shoes but a terrific shirt, she put together. My clothes were like a speech composed entirely of bons mots. She combed my hair. We sat together on a sofa in front of a low coffee table, while a wealthy woman (secretly applauding the safer choices she herself had made) poured us tea and "caught up." I learned the trick of this after a few times. After ninety minutes, I would go stare at family photographs, which sometimes contained their children and Jon and me, at beaches and piney lakesides. I would find that smiling brown-haired boy who'd been me; the boy who'd been enjoying a first-class life. Mom would walk up to me in these corridors of preserved moments and say, "Richard. We're ready to go now. Unless you want to stay?" As if it were me who had brought us here. On the street, she would tap her shirt pocket and say, "We're good until November."

She cooked. Another rich friend wanted to write a low-calorie gourmet cookbook. In the spring of my first year, they signed a contract together. Every Friday, he would give her a list of recipes, and money for the service, and expenses to buy groceries, and a questionnaire for the two of us to complete. I was instructed never to snack—I broke this law every day at school—and to faithfully record my weight on a scale. This carried us two months. My mother (who had been a wonderful cook) served up great london broils, and rare filet mignons, and ducks surrounded by whatever it was that made duck taste especially good. Our bathroom—what with the asparagus and rich cheeses—became a rather sweet-smelling place, a kind of flowery swamp. "I've never eaten this well," she mused; she had taken to putting out candles with dinner, to honor the quality of the fare. The rich friend eventually moved on to other interests (the rich: they don't get things finished; they assemble the basic *ingredients* to get things finished and this seems to satisfy them—the knowledge that they *could* have done something, that it was within their grasp, and it was not incompetence but their own choice that prevented them from going further), but the food was wonderful, though I know it would have made whoever bought the cookbook gain (if our question-naires were reliable) about twenty pounds a year.

She got me a cat—I named him Claudius, after the devious hero of a novel I was reading. The novel was about political maneuvering in Rome, about game-play-ing—I kept thinking how like the art world it was. Claudius had seemed a very friendly kitty when we visited the man who'd placed the ad in the *Village Voice*. He seemed a furry machine for the production of purrs. But when we got him home, for the first few weeks, he would wake up every night and wriggle out of my arms. I had tried to sleep with him on my chest, as I used to sleep with our old cat Wilbur. But Claudius would slip away and tack around the apartment, crying. He'd peep into closets, scrape his claws against closed doors, let out a little strangled *meow*. "He must miss his brothers," I said. He had been from a large litter. My mother looked at me with a very level expression. "That must be very hard for him," she said. Now, of course, I see what I was saying to her—just as my mother must have seen it. I *did* miss Jon, more than I could have said. When I visited, I felt horribly guilty, having lured him to Los Angeles and then left him there. I could not think about it. When I first visited California for Christmas, there were only four days of crossover before Jon had to fly east. In our new republic, the Christmas skies were alive not only with sleighs and reindeer but with the floating children of divorced families, migrating from one set of chimneys to another. Jon put his hands to my shoulders and turned me around. He went back-to-back with me, to see if I'd grown. His buttocks pressed against mine; I had known that feeling for all my growing up. At our old house, he took me into the bathroom. "Bear with me a sec," he said. "I don't know when I'm going to see you again—Easter I guess. And who knows when this is going to happen? But I just started shaving, and in case *you* have to start shaving in the next three months, I want you to know how to do it right." And he showed me. Hot water on the face, to soften the whiskers. Work up with the razor on the neck and jaw, down on the cheeks. If you're careful, you'll keep the sideburns level. We did it together, the two of us in our bathroom mirror. "A lot of people will tell you to shave *before* the shower, so you can rinse off in the tub. I say *after*. So your face is soft." It's the way I still shave now.

One day in the February of my sophomore high school year, Mom received the announcement for Celia Kapplestein's show at Krumlich. She still went to openings, of course, as well as carting her work and slides around the city, trying to interest dealers in her work. Celia's catalog was beautiful, longer than it was wide, and shiny, like a fish newly tugged from the water. Some real expense and care had gone into it; someone clearly believed they were about to make a *great deal* of money off Celia's show. I came home from school, and Mom flapped the catalog by her cheek. "Do you want to go to this, Richard?" "It looks *awful*," I said, turning some pages. To say Celia's paintings looked fine would be to compound the envy she must be feeling. Mom surprised me by taking the catalog back and spreading open the pages. "You think so? A lot of the pictures look good to me. What do you think of this, for example?" *"Awful,"* I said again. Sheepishly, gingerly— and I didn't understand why she was walking so carefully around this topic, "So you don't want to come along?" I thought of all the openings I had gone to with her, from the first, with Dad and Jon. "I'll go," I said. This was where I saw what had happened.

By Thursday night I had more or less forgotten. I came home from school and shed my backpack and plopped down on the sofa—the sofa that at night folded into her bed, and which during the day had a musty sleep smell that made me embarrassed and guilty at once. The smell said, Your apartment only has one bedroom, and you have it, and your mother sleeps on the couch. I didn't know why Mom wasn't there. I sat around for half an hour, walked into the bathroom and found her hair dryer on the sink, which was also puzzling. Had she gone out? Then I realized and put on my coat and ran outside, into the starry February cold which shocked my cheeks.

A few heads turned when I entered Krumlich's gallery. But seeing I was no one important—just a teenage boy in an orange down jacket—they went back to their conversations. Just like that—they saw me, they didn't need to look at me. This wasn't something I was prepared for, this clear perception: you are not important here. I took off my coat, and their lack of interest must have infected my movements, for everything I did felt clumsy and unworthy. My coat slipped off the hanger. I picked it up, looking to see if those people were watching.

I found my mother in the fourth room I searched. "Richard!" she called. She was talking with Hiroshi—and I saw that at openings she needed people to speak with, in order to be invisible. Hiroshi was a safe bet, because of his difficult English. Even at his own openings, people rarely spoke to Hiroshi.

"How are you, Richard?" Hiroshi asked. He was wearing black Buddy Holly glasses, which he pushed up on his nose. "God. Long time, long time."

"Fine, Hiroshi. What about you?" I turned to apologize to Mom, but she—changing position so as to be standing beside me—tapped my forearm, meaning I was being rude and should listen to Hiroshi.

Hiroshi dropped his head, an abbreviated version of

the bow he'd never unlearned from the Royal Academy of Fine Arts in Tokyo. "Fine. Thank you." He tilted his head at Celia's work. "What do you think of the show?" I asked what *he* thought, and he nodded rapidly. "I think it's great, great. Such wonderful *color.*"

Mom's hand was still on my forearm. "I was just telling Hiroshi," she said, "that I haven't seen Celia's work for two years. These new ones are quite a change."

"True," Hiroshi said. "This work is a *departure.*"

As if this word signaled the end of his own conversation, Hiroshi made another stifled bow, held up a farewell index finger, and stepped away from us. I would learn, in the years to come, that there were two kinds of goodbyes at openings. There was the friendly kind, like Hiroshi's—which promised that the departing person would return later, to get your summing-up views on the event. And then there was another kind, the unfriendly kind, which meant that the departing person was surprised you'd come forward to speak with them, unhappy you were in the same social circle, and was resigned to seeing you either at the next such gathering or—preferably—never.

When he'd gone we circled back to the guest book. Those same dismissive heads took us in, looked away. As if they were *feeding* on something they didn't want us to share. "Sorry I was late," I said. "I forgot." "It's fine. As long as you're here now," she said. And I could see how much this was true—that she was as relieved to see me as she used to be at airports, when Jon and I would stroll glutted with cookies out of first class. "Hey!" she would say, after first examining the faces ahead of ours, with a little disappointment that she couldn't visually shape their features into ours. Then she added, "You must really have been blocking." We walked into the first room. Krumlich was arranged like a large plus sign, with a series of side galleries forming the crossbar off the main viewing area. Gregor and Celia were in this main space—meeting and greeting—so we walked into the side rooms. I saw Mom a second after she saw Gregor. The look that had come over her face—proud and envious, resentful and hopeful—was difficult for me to categorize, and impossible to witness. We passed Celia's work, pale stain paintings she still did on the floor. As we walked, I became aware of an overwhelming burden of *risk*—which I couldn't quite make sense of. All we were doing was going to an opening.

In the first room, we ran into Lars Stevensen, a friend. Lars kissed Mom's cheek, and held out a hand to me. That hand, curling around mine, had the special extra graininess sculptors' hands get, as if they have somehow acquired extra lines in their palms. "How's it going?" Lars asked, stowing those hands into his pockets.

It was obvious he just meant this as a pleasantry— and actually, at home, my mother rarely summed up her professional situation. So it was a surprise—a painful surprise—when she gave her self-estimation as "so-so."

"I know what you mean," Lars said quickly, putting a lid on this. "It's been a shit winter." He looked over our shoulders—Lars, the man we'd lived with two summers at the beach—and said, "Excuse me, I haven't said hello to Celia yet. It's a great show, no? I'll talk to you later." Then he kissed Mom on the cheek again, and looked at her with a little wariness as she prepared to speak. They had been friends for years, and now this friendship he seemed to regard as a manipulative trick she'd once played on him—as if he feared she was going to remind him of this friendship now in order to unfairly get something out of it.

"It *is* a nice show," was what she said, and Lars left. To conceal both our disappointments, she pointed out, "You haven't said what you think of Celia's pictures."

I looked. The paintings did not turn away—they stared back, blues and pinks and yellows, very smooth, very like the paintings I'd been seeing of Celia's all my life. "She's really breaking new ground. These look like star charts. She should have been an astronomer," I said. Mom laughed, and it was the first moment when she had seemed at ease since I'd found her. It seemed that was what I was here for—to keep her relaxed, to make her laugh.

"Try to really *look*, though," she said.

"I *am* looking," I said. But what I was searching for,

in the smooth surfaces of the pictures, was the foothold
of a joke, the crevice of a comic idea I could latch on to.
The titles seemed to have nothing to do with the
work—and I felt something brighten and quicken in
my head. "Plus, these titles. *The Swan's Knowledge* and
Transfigured Gaiety. What's the point? She should just
call them by their prices: *Sixteen Thousand Five Hundred* or *Twenty Thousand Dollars.*"

"They're quotes from Yeats," Mom said, sobering.

I was about to say something else, but I saw she
wasn't listening. She'd altered her face into an intelligent, attentive expression. I didn't understand why—
and then I looked up and recognized the woman coming
toward us. Lara Kilmer, the art critic. She had a long,
tubular nose and squinted eyes, as if she was trying
to physically edit the crowd down to just those people
she wanted to see. "Hi, Lara," Mom said, as they
passed. Lara said, "Joan," flatly. It was a neutral
fact—my mother's name—and not a greeting. Mom's
face relaxed.

"That was Lara Kilmer," she whispered.

"I thought it was," I said.

"That bitch," my mother said.

In the next room were a number of people I knew,
standing in small clumps, drinking and socializing. People I'd met at my mother's old openings, or at their own
openings years before. Their heads rustled up—artists'
eyes were in constant motion at openings, seeing who

was coming in or leaving, who they might make a connection with, who they should avoid—and then those heads dipped back into the underbrush of conversation. I understood it a little more. My mother wasn't showing, and that was a sin. It made her invisible. What was worse, when it didn't make her invisible, it was like a clumsy sandwich board she was wearing, a sandwich board that hampered all her movements. A sandwich board that said I AM NOT SHOWING. Herbert Tingley was standing in the corner, talking with his wife and another couple I couldn't place. Herbert had always liked to gesture while he spoke; he was revolving his cigarette-holding hand so vigorously he seemed to be trying to make a lariat from the smoke. The Tingleys—Herb and Bea—had baby-sat Jon and me, they had come to the loft for dinner, there was a long backlog of life between us. Now they saw us, and quickly pretended they *hadn't* seen us. Their drifting heads found ours and stopped short, but their bodies—those less subtle bodies of theirs—told that they had seen us. They shifted position. They shuffled, those bodies, until their bottoms were facing us, so that a stiff Tingley wall of human backsides prevented us from trying to join their conversation. What I couldn't understand was *why*—my mother wasn't showing. But didn't this mean they should have been *nicer* to her, not less nice? They should have rallied around us.

In the room past the Tingleys was thin Ken Worthy, a museum curator. He was in conversation with two painters and a doughy couple, collectors. Collectors, at least, had not changed since my childhood. They had the look I remembered—of staring blandly at the world from a moving vehicle, through a windshield tinted by money. I followed my mother over to them; we stood beside Ken while he wrapped up what he was saying.

"Hey, Joan," Ken said, angling his head toward her. The doughy couple, seeing this was someone Ken knew, smiled in neutral unison.

"Hi," my mother said. "What've you been up to?"

"Visiting different studios, poking around. What about you?"

"I've been painting," my mother said. And Ken's face underwent a quick change, and I saw that by mentioning her own work she had violated what seemed to be a silent agreement between them.

"That's great," Ken said, making ready to return to his conversation.

"You should come by and see the work while you're in the city," Mom said.

"That would be great," Ken agreed. He took her hand. "Listen, why don't I give you a call in the middle of next week. All right?" They kissed.

My mother nodded. "So I'll talk to you Wednesday?" Ken nodded, and we moved off.

"Sometimes," she said, "after I say certain things, I get the impression they weren't the most terrific things to say."

"Was it wrong to bring me?" I asked, because I thought then that perhaps I was the problem, that bringing a child was a faux pas.

"No, no, Richard," she said. "I don't necessarily think I could have gotten through this without you."

At the end of that night, Mom and I got on the Santa line, the hand-shaking line. I stood with her. Once, at her own openings, she had been a lucky stone they all wanted to touch; now, it was as if that same stone had turned radioactive, and everyone feared contamination. Mom had slipped down into the first circle of people; the non-artists. I could see Gregor was counting heads, to check how many people were left. Gregor saw us on the line and nodded to my mom. It was a grim nod. I looked at Celia—powerful, happy, adored, aging. She was aging—she must have been in her late forties—but she was aging well, because money allowed you to give time a little tip, to pay time to go a little easy on you. "Good to *see* you," she'd say as she shook hands. "Thanks *so much* for coming." When she liked someone, she would fold her hands against her waist and invite them to converse for an extra second or two. This sharp face was waiting for us at the end of the line like a buzz saw. My hand started to sweat—my hand had this one line to deliver and it was rehearsing itself, remembering handshakes that had gone over well in the past, trying to forget others that had been crap-outs. We reached the head of the line. My mom was right in front of Gregor—and whatever her face was doing, I was glad I didn't have to see it. She shook his hand. My mom said to him, "I'm doing some interesting pictures." Gregor said, "That's *wonderful news,* Joan." And that was that. Celia looked at us complexly; we weren't collectors, and weren't really colleagues. "Joan," Celia said. "Good to *see* you. Thanks *so much* for coming." And that was that. We were at the end of the line, and Celia and Gregor were chatting with two different people.

Hiroshi came to our sides, holding his plastic wineglass with both hands, like a rugby player with a football. "Did you say hi to Celia?" he asked. He had come back, just as he said he would. We told him we had. My mother walked to the guest book and signed in her name. Beside her signature, in the address box, she added, "CK: Excellent show." We didn't talk in the elevator. On the street, on Madison Avenue, with the steam coming up from the grates as if the city were releasing one long sigh, we were the only people waiting for the bus. Behind us was a Gap T-shirt ad, of a man we knew, a bearded heavy man with a soft, merry expression. "Jack Atski, Artist," the caption said. It made sense for the ad to be here—this was the art district. But it showed the difference so clearly between him and us. The poster said, I am posing for a Gap ad, and you are stuck waiting for public transportation. "Richard, I just wanted to say, I very much appreciated your coming tonight," my mother said formally. I said quickly, "Yes, it's good to *see* you," and she laughed. Then she looked at me. She pushed a hair back over my forehead. "I really am very glad you came." I knew that this was what had happened to her after Jon and I left. And afterward, of course, I went with her to every opening she went to.

I had known how to sneak into first class on airplanes; there was a code to it, a code I could learn. Now I wanted to sneak us back into first class in the art world, where we belonged. And I assumed—because I was young, and one starts out with utter faith in one's own abilities, before the world gradually furnishes you with conflicting evidence—that I could learn this code too. I grew up at openings. Mom and I attended two a month. I would come home from high school and drop my bag (all that drab preparation for real life: this *was* real life) and we would eat silently at the table. Then the ordeal of the dresser. I would walk out in a sweater and slacks, and ask, my voice croaking a little, "OK?" "Nice," my mother would nod. Then she would disappear into the bathroom, and I would hear the faucet spurt, and her blow-dryer howl, and she would emerge from that noisy preparatory cave in a blouse and skirt. And we would model for each other, unconsciously, the invulnerable faces we intended to wear at the gallery.

Openings began—openings were won and lost—before they started. The whole thing was so *social.* Everyone got a fix on your position by how others treated you. Then, when the evening was over, they would remember. They would remember if Jack Atski had smiled at you like rain during a drought or like rain on a sunny day. They would keep in mind that Chuck O'Donnell had not given you the time from his watch. And they would make decisions about you accordingly. Well, this was a lot to base on a single night. People were itchy for any shorthand they could get. One bit of shorthand, I quickly learned, was clothes. Clothes sent a message: good clothes said, Maybe you weren't aware of this, but outside of your attention, in my own life, I am doing just fine. Otherwise, how could I afford *this?* If you walked in there looking bad—sending the opposite message, This is the best I could do—you saved them a few seconds of mental time. They scratched you right off. (When you dressed badly, they should have sent *thank you cards.* "You spared me a great deal of effort at a number of openings. Signed, Mrs. Leonard Chichikov.") My mother thought she had left all that clenched middle-class competitiveness behind when she joined the art world—a bedrock misconception. This world was more about status than any other. Except here the flower beds and new cars were shows and reviews and sales. She was *still* on the platform waiting for the train in East Hampton, trying to make herself look good for the men who were rolling up in the cars, the dark-suited moneymen who allowed us to get on with our lives.

She didn't understand this as clearly as I. "Richard," she'd say, locking the door and putting the keys in her purse. "I think it's touching the way you pay so much attention to me." It wasn't only her I was thinking of. There was, in my mind, the ideal girl, the girl I would meet and eventually bring home. I wanted a mother in elegant clothes, a success. If this girl thought my mother was a failure, what would that mean for our romance? How would she look on me? I was being loyal to my mother and this future girl at once. "But I don't think what I'm wearing tonight is going to be at the top of anyone else's list." Life *wasn't* like a movie; what it was like was a movie theater, where the film showing was your own life. She had a seat smack up in the front, where the action was overwhelming and harder to follow, and all she could do was crane her head and feel a stunned identification with her character. I had found a seat farther back, where I could watch the other heads watching me, and experience the action at some remove.

We rode the bus in our evening clothes to Fifty-seventh Street, among the last-chance commuters and the elderly women who were on every bus, who seemed to ride buses just for the pleasure of the trip. And then it was upstairs, in the familiar elevator, to Gregor's gallery. After every opening, I learned to mock the other artists, to parody what they thought were their smart styles of rejection, to attack their work. Mom would laugh. But my insults didn't last. At the start of each opening, they were back, the disparagements scrubbed fresh from their faces, and their bodies shiny and sharp with the capacity to humiliate, to reject.

We stowed our coats and took deep breaths, looking around at the handfuls of art people who had been scattered within each room like tiny pieces of glass, over which we were treading barefoot. We stepped gingerly, testing the surface with our soles.

I learned the grammar, the ritual behavior, the slow walk of openings. It was a Serengeti ballet in here. The slow, sedate head-turnings, the studied calm, as art people lumbered from one room to another, drinks in hand. The lordly thump of elephants. The smaller animals jumped around, nipping at things, trying to find grass and dead stuff to tear at. Phoebe Eagleton, who had quit her critic's post at *Newsweek*, and wandered stunned that her jolly art-world friends no longer wanted to talk with her. Julian Rosenbloom, a sculptor at Krumlich, who was rumored to be always on the verge of being tossed out. He tried to stay settled down—but his eyes went everywhere, there were so many people to *talk* to. He had gotten the call once, the story went, from

Freddy Beaumont. He was out. He had taken a cab to Fifty-seventh Street and zipped up the elevator and confronted Gregor in his office. "Is it true, is it true?" He had counted on Gregor's pained sense of decorum, his desire for control. And it was a good gamble. Gregor— in person—couldn't say it was true. So he gave Julian a two-week show every fourth year.

My mother brought a note into these galleries that was dangerous. She knew she was a good painter; what she didn't understand was that everyone else had forgotten it. Her ambition here was an imposition; it forced the other painters to see her as a woman who was disappointed. This note was their note, too. Many of them were also not doing as well as they might have liked. Anyone seeing them together with Mom would think they were all complaining. So their impulse, I saw, was to avoid Mom, or to talk with her in small doses.

I saw that in the art world reputation was everything. So, by talking with someone, you were *taking* something from them. Their seal. "If Neil Hollander spent that much time talking to Joan Freeley, she must really have something on the ball!" People guarded their social time like treasures, treasures of a weirdly elastic nature, for who they talked to determined the value. "I think this is character-building," my mother sighed to me, in the aftermath of openings, looking for the bright side. "But it's a little late to still have my character built."

We learned their particular styles of brush-off. Lara Kilmer would draw her foot back carefully over the floor, pointing it away from you, as if stepping out of a trap. Jack's silent nod meant what was between him and my mother was too complex for words at an opening. Of course, there *never* was the right space to talk about it, so they never spoke. Leonard Chichikov simply turned his back. When you did talk to him, he watched everyone else while you spoke, his eyes never quite looking at you but his mouth pointed right at your sockets, going, "Right, right, yeah, right."

We devised strategies. When I thought she was talking too long, I would say, "Let's go grab some Brie, Mom. I didn't have a chance to eat this afternoon at school." The Brie, our all-purpose excuse. Who knows how much Brie I ate, as a high school junior, a high school senior—that Brie was packed into my veins, my muscles, my brain. For three years, it seemed I *lived* on Brie, and even now, when I eat that cool, slimy food, something is triggered, and I look around for fear that I am being ungenerously judged. If, on the other hand, my mother wanted to keep talking—if she thought it was going well, and my anxious presence, like a manager watching his heavyweight from the corner, towel at the ready, was becoming too much—she would subtly unfold her arms and reach down and tap me on the back of my hand with her plastic glass. "Richard?" she'd say, widening her eyes. "Can you get me some more wine?" I'd go and hide myself and watch from across the room. When the person's head started twitching about—looking for someone else—I would bring Mom the wine and we would move on. Or I would duck down to the bathroom. I got to know where the bathrooms were in every gallery. I fixed my hair and checked my sweaters, and tested out my facial expressions. One lesson from high school did seem to apply here, not the specifics of science or math or the humanities. It was the basic: neatness counts. Everything counts, you are graded on everything. I would rejoin my mother and steer her through more rooms. She would talk to Hiroshi; he was a safe haven, a foreign port grateful for visitors. She would talk to Tom Dancer, who had a crush on her and enjoyed making her laugh.

I couldn't leave her alone, not even for a second. That dropped the value of her treasure, because then it seemed no one wanted any part of her. This meant that value was nil. The thought that soon—in two years, a year, six months—I would be at college, and she would have to face these situations without anyone by her side, would make me guiltily panic at openings. Wasn't it my job—I, who had helped plunge her into this mess—to stay by, stand with her, until the mess was cleared up?

She was more cheerful about it than I, I who only saw us being shunted away from where we wanted to go. No, she was less pissed off, as if these were the contours of a world she knew, the world she'd known she was joining. I think there was her love of painting—that held her. I didn't have that. I only saw the end result.

I found after-school jobs, to pay for my own clothes and school supplies, so that my mother could use the spare cash for grander and more intimidating outfits. She spent it on oil paint and canvas. "Magic *beans?*" I wanted to ask, Jack-and-the-Beanstalk style, as she came home with handled shopping bags of oils and brushes and turps. Her work wasn't going to give us the burst of growth we needed, for climbing back into the art world. Her work was great as it was; it was intelligent and pointed, with the something about it that was *her* that was heartbreaking. It wasn't going to get any better. But in an awful way it *did* get better. As far as I could see, her showing connected with socializing; I thought that once I had all their minds in order, everyone thinking well of Mom—each single person—then somehow this would flip the stalled switch in the art world and a dealer, receiving her slides in the mail one sunny morning, would think: "Joan Freeley. Painter. Hmm. Seen her around. Isn't treated like a pariah. Say—these are *good.*" I hoped to have her reestablished in the art world before I left for college; otherwise, who would take her to openings? What would happen if Hiroshi took English lessons, or Tom Dancer developed a crush on someone else?

Every few weeks, she put her slides and résumé and

optimistic letter into an envelope and I licked the stamps; the good luck of a family project. Then the dealers returned them, with courteous notes. The sadness of slides returned in the mail; as if they couldn't bear to be away from home, and had snuck away from summer camp or wherever and hitchhiked back, their faces dirty from the road but ready to be loved. That was the sight of slides returned in the mail. The horror of having raised something that could only find value at home, that could be treated with respect and consequence only in the environment in which it had been created.

I went to college and fell in love. Mom wasn't showing yet—I had to give up on my idea of having her settled before I left home. I'd postponed it; I hoped to have her showing again before I left college, when my own life would inevitably have to begin. She found a job teaching art at a small college in Connecticut the same year, so we went off to school together. In the fall, she took the day off, rented a car, and drove me to Bennington College. For four hours she seemed quiet and distracted. Though she didn't voice it, I knew her well enough to know what she was thinking. Our family sorrow was sucking me back to Vermont, to Dad's idea of paradise. We drove to our old property first; the river I'd swum in at Jon's instigation, the hill we'd bicycled down blindly. Our house had burned down. In its place was a one-story ranch house. A fat woman was sitting on the porch, and two Dobermans cantered over the lawn like small, snub-nosed horses. "Don't upset my dogs," the woman called to us. We got out of the car, chunked closed the doors. In the center of the lawn, Mom pointed out where the barn used to stand, where she had done her paintings—this nostalgia was new to me; I had thought, in her anxiousness to charge ahead, that she didn't look much behind—when all at once the dogs charged. We turned and ran and they raced after us. We made it back to the car, and the Dobermans kept hammering the windows with their paws. The woman ran over, red-faced and sweaty. "I told you not to upset my dogs!" she shouted, patting their necks. We drove away. My mom said, "God, if that isn't symbolism, I don't know what is. You can't *get* a clearer message from the past than that."

The episode, rather than depressing her, cheered her up. She seemed pleased that the world's sense of things and hers were the same; that her intuition had been proved correct. We drove to the college. Some students were sitting on the lawn of what was to be my house. They had moved a living room's worth of furniture onto the grass—a sofa, an easy chair, a lamp and stereo plugged in by an extension cord through a window. They smoked, and watched us unload the car with lizardy eyes. It was the dead hour of late afternoon, with the sun idling toward setting, when you realize all at once the day is about to end, but you haven't yet visited the bed where you're going to sleep. A boy called to my mother, as we walked back and forth with our armfuls, "We'll take good care of your son, ma'am," and his friends laughed.

I walked my mother back to the car—I could see, in her face, that she was trying to find the right note for farewell to our strange companionship for the four high school years. I didn't want to say goodbye to her in front of these students. "I'll drive with you to the gate." We skirted the little campus in silence. At the gate we stood out of the car. "Well," Mom said, looking at me, the brown-haired boy she'd produced. "This is goodbye, I guess. You're a very bright young man. If you try hard, things will always work out of you." We hugged, her hand firm on my back. She said, "Let's not drag this out." I released her. "I'll miss you. It's been nice raising you. One of the great moments of my life is the day you moved back." I remembered how close I had come on that day to saying nothing. She stepped into the car and drove off. I followed the taillights a little ways down the hill, feeling a nice, weird, unsettled emptiness in my chest. Then I turned around and walked back to campus.

The year in Bennington I learned my mother's pain firsthand. Bennington was not a good school. Or, rather, it wasn't "good" in the way we needed it to be. It didn't

impress anyone, at the gallery openings I attended by
her side. When I said "Bennington" to the ambitious
middle-class parents of my high school friends, they
looked at me with a little puzzled sadness. Here was a
topic they had to leap past quickly, or the ground would
plummet beneath their feet to reveal some spiky bottom
of pain. It was strange to see their eyes reorganize, to see
them realizing that your fate was not the best, that you
were hurtling for some second-class destiny, and their
job was not to tip you off that it *was* second class. I did
what Mom had told me. I tried very hard, mailed my
transcript, and got into a school in Providence, which
was Ivy League. There was a snag. They needed to see
Dad's tax records before they would give me financial
aid. Dad would not release them. He was still cham-
pioning Vermont, as if that part of his brain were
stalled. "What do you want to go to *Providence* for? It's
an ugly town." By August we still could not budge him.
This only intrigued Brown more; what hoards of gold
was my father secretly sitting on, that he didn't want to
show his tax returns to the school? We couldn't afford
tuition as it was. I said to Mom, "What the hell, I'll go
back to Bennington." Mom said, "The hell you will."
She got on the project herself, did some back-and-forth
with Brown. Her school started a week before Brown
did. She left classes to take calls, and followed up in the
evenings, from the motels she lived in three days a

week. The first day of September she called from Connecticut, voice triumphant and tired. "That's it," she said. "I did it. You're in."

So she drove me to Providence. The town looked so beautiful to me. Small, with its three shy skyscrapers towering over the low federal buildings, like embarrassed, gangly students in an elementary school who had come to puberty early. Students were strolling around the huge campus, bright and happy-looking. Mom and I had earned this together; I was about to join this stream, be restored to first class. "Well," she said, as my legs itched in the car to meet my classmates, "soak it up. This was what you wanted. Now you can bring your Charm Boy act to perfection." My "Charm Boy act" was what she called my good manners and sweaters, which she considered phony; always a double message. We parked and joined the line at University Hall for registration. Ceiling fans burbled over our heads as we moved from table to table, signing forms, getting receipts. When she saw my name on the class folder, she walked out of the hall. I found her on the grass, crying. "I can't believe we did it. We pulled it off," she said, meaning college. When she called me from home that night, she apologized. "I didn't mean to get emotional like that. I never told you this. But I hated leaving you up at Bennington, with those deadbeat kids. I thought they were all stoned. Not that I'm against drugs per se.

But I felt like a criminal. Halfway home I wanted to turn back around and say, Wait, there's been a terrible mistake, my son doesn't belong there. But I thought you were so happy. You didn't notice. In your New England locale, you know. I didn't want to spoil it." "I *did* notice," I said. "I didn't think you had. I was hoping you hadn't."

I thought it wonderful of her not to have said anything until the situation was resolved; that was how she was. Some years from now, perhaps, she would say, "Remember when I didn't have a gallery? When I didn't have a boyfriend? That was so *painful.* I *hated* those years." If we didn't play everything exactly right, she would never get to make this speech; it would go unconfessed, because the disappointment would never be abolished. I lay in my bed that night. I had cautious and conventional ambitions—but that was fine, because conventional ambitions were the ones most likely to be fulfilled. I had seen the pain of unconventional ambitions for five years. I thought everything was likely to go fine for me now. But Mom—who had allowed things to go fine—was not in a good spot yet. She was back in New York, alone. I would graduate in three years, and with this behind me presumably any nice thing could happen. She had allowed for that; I was leaving for life from a good gate. Now, I thought, I must make sure, in the three years I had left, that she departed from a good gate too. It would be wrong for me to progress from here, from where she had gotten me, if she wasn't progressing also.

That fall Freddy Beaumont opened his own gallery. He hadn't been lying to Gregor about his wife not having any money. But his wife's sister had married the heir to a first-aid fortune. Adhesive bandages and tape, and antiseptic cream, and fat pads of gauze had provided Freddy with the front money he needed. A nation of clumsy children, scabby-kneed boys from east to west, had all without knowing it given Freddy a gallery, and artists, and a staff. He had never forgiven Gregor for his flinty matrimonial advice. He rented a space in his old boss's own building. Right away, he went after Gregor's collector base, and there were rumors, too, of attempted raids on Gregor's artists—Jack, the sculptor Oliver Thrush, Neil. It filled us with enthusiasm. The only defection was in what he showed. Freddy filled his gallery with whatever was *in*. He showed: Neo-Geo, Neo-Expressionism, Conceptualism, even, for the few months it briefly and inexplicably flourished, a style called Storybook Art. This consisted of large, vivid canvases, with fanged wolves and tough-looking gnomes battling it out under moonlit skies. It surprised some people, this revelation of personal taste. But I understood the commercialism; Freddy was trying to make sure he could always tip the rug shampooer.

I asked Mom to hold off until I was home for

Christmas. She asked, "Why wait?" She paper-clipped her slides to her résumé inside an envelope, crossed the park, and strolled down Madison to Fifty-seventh Street. The large wire snowflake was already strung between the four lampposts, free-lance Santa Clauses rang bells (their costumes this early in the season still clean), and the air smelled of roasted chestnuts. From the street, she could see the two windows, with the gallery names lettered in gold. Gregor's, on the ninth floor. And then, five stories down, Freddy's—or rather "Frederic Beaumont"—and the sight filled Mom with fear and hope, for this was the purely professional side Freddy always tried to show the world, though perhaps, on the back of these letters, would be a picture of his huge behind. In the elevator, it felt strange for her to press 4. She walked into his gallery; Freddy already had the requisite Fifty-seventh Street touch, the money-hush, the whispering discretion of a bank vault. There was a woman behind the desk. She gave first a look of welcome—here was a visitor to the gallery—and then she saw the envelope under my mother's arm, and her face went narrow. Mom was an *artist*. Had I been there, I would have turned tail right then—a sickening feeling, my chest spinning around and trying to run through my back as my body continued forward—but Mom stood her ground before this woman and chummily called Beaumont by his nickname. "Is Freddy in? I'm an old friend of his. Joan Freeley. From the Krumlich era."

"I'll see," the woman said. So Freddy *was* in—in the inner office, behind closed doors. Mom inspected the gallery. On the desk was the current artist's résumé and a review, in a black ten-ringed binder. Everything was orderly and precise; Freddy hadn't wasted his training years at Krumlich. If *God* were having a show at one of those galleries, there would have been the black binder open on the desk with a résumé. 3000 B.C.: Creates heavens and earth. 2500 B.C.: Destroys cities of the plain. 2000 B.C.: Great flood.

The door opened. The woman emerged alone. "Mr. Beaumont is in a meeting," she explained.

"Oh—" my mother said. But if this woman thought my mother was going to be shaken off *that* easily, she was greatly mistaken. "Look, I'd like to leave these here, for Freddy to glance at when he has some more time. We've known each other for years, and I'm sure he'll be interested in what I'm up to now."

Something about Freddy's attitude to Mom's name—Mom saw from a certain impatience in the woman's face—had made it clear she had some leeway to be as direct as she wished. "Mr. Beaumont says that we aren't taking on any new artists at present. I'm sorry."

She walked outside. I had thought Freddy and my mother had so much in common: they both had such good reasons to be angry at Gregor. It had been one of my best hopes. On the way home Mom took the same envelope, wrote Freddy's address, and dropped it into a mailbox. She told me this story by phone a month later, reading the note Freddy had sent back. He hadn't taken her on, but he *had* added another paper clip, pinned to the corner of his gallery stationery. " 'Joan: Thanks very much for sharing these with me. We have a full plate at the gallery, but I'm <u>sure</u> good things will come your way. Best New Year wishes.' " She finished the holiday close, and laughed. A laugh I knew well—lowering her head to one side and blowing air through her lips and nose at once.

I took courses. Even if I'd had any talent in the arts, my mother would have been careful to shoo it away. She didn't want me in her field. She wanted me out of the art world, beyond the place where opinions so intensely mattered. She wanted to see me get a good solid footing in something like business. You were safer in the normal world, a world where other people made up the assignments for you. Then you could just be graded on those. In the arts, they had to first decide if the assignment you'd given yourself was worthwhile, before they could decide whether you deserved a grade. I tried management-behavior classes. These were vast halls filled with suffering athletes, all squeezed into their seats—for these desks were designed with students of very different builds in mind—who looked as if they would have been more comfortable hoisting the building from its foundations and carrying it on their shoulders than they were scribbling notes for two hours. I tried the sciences. But whatever gene it was that allowed for retention of minute information—the Brown applied-biology department had a pronounced pro-gene bias—I simply did not possess, for the information I tried to remember from these classes slipped away, my brain was like a pocket with a hole in the bottom. I tried English, and this stuck. It was in my English classes that I first saw Maggy Weatherly. What struck me first were her gloves. She had on fawn-colored fall gloves, like the gloves of Neil Hollander I'd once stolen. It was as though they had disappeared from my childhood to reappear here, on the elegant fingers of this pretty, black-haired young woman.

Mom loved her paintings. Even when they didn't sell, it made her happy to put them on the walls of our apartment. It was a private Joan Freeley Museum. When I was in high school, I'd come home and she'd nod. "I've been looking at this painting all day. It's *beautiful.*" When I was in college, she'd call and ask, "You know the green picture? That usually hangs in the dining area? That blue at the top has been bothering me. I'm thinking about changing it. What do you think?"

We had grown used to my giving Mom advice; like a husband, I was always there, in her home with her.

But unlike a husband I could provide tips on romance, from my double-agent, insider's position of being myself a man. So she called to ask my advice again. About the men she dated, the divorced businessmen her old friends fixed her up with, forty-five-year-olds who had found themselves suddenly ejected from comfortable marriages. They had lost the talent for speaking with women who were not connected to them by habit and law; their eyes went everywhere as they thought, *Is this how I used to do it? Is* this *the right way?* They stared helplessly at my mother like soldiers in lonely foxholes, watching the advance of an enemy they couldn't protect themselves from. She called and complained of cappuccino. Every first date ended up that way, in some Italian place for coffee. Initially, it had seemed stylish to her, and unexpected. But after the sixth or seventh time, she realized it came from the same playbook, all these divorced men were scouring the same magazines. "How's the steamed milk?" they would ask, watching her, wiping cinnamon from their lips. *You're supposed to mention the steamed milk.* "Richard," she told me on the phone, "I'm becoming a percolator. I am *peeing* espresso." I asked—testing out how much I was allowed in this new position—about sex. Mom's voice turned shyly hesitant. "I'm not sure I should talk about this with my son." "Go ahead," I said. "You have to understand, Richard, these are men whose marriages ended because of, oh, middle-aged sexual problems, or because their wives were unfaithful. So they're not the most confident." It thrilled me that we had become this close; how many of the other sons at school were, at that moment, talking to their mothers about sex? "On the other hand," she said, "they can be quite generous, physically speaking. And grateful."

I tried to be confident, generous, and grateful with Margaret. I tried to learn, from what my mother told me, what women wanted to see from men. They wanted to be considered, and called, and *let in*. They didn't want to feel that men were keeping things from them, that every conversation was shadowed with second thoughts. I knew I could use this knowledge in the reverse way, as a method of keeping Margaret off balance. But this would have been a betrayal not just of her but of my mother, who was trusting me with her own insider's information.

So I was generous, confidently. On an early date, I took Maggy to the Rhode Island School of Design museum, where one of my mother's pictures was hung. It was an early work, from the year she sold seventy-five paintings, a picture called *Jonathan*. I thought of my brother, at school in Berkeley, whom I had abandoned and who had become my father's son. "Wow. It must be an honor," Maggy said, "to walk into a museum and find a painting by your mom." I shrugged. We loved the wrong things about each other. She loved the art world

in me, which I longed to escape from. And I loved the
Westport in her, the businessman stepfather and drink-
mixing mother (when I took her for dinner and she
ordered a gin fizz it floored me; she sipped it and playfully furrowed her eyebrows, saying, "I get better ones
at home"), from which she must have wanted to escape
or she wouldn't have been dating me. We wanted out of
our own worlds and into each other's, which seemed to
mean there was nowhere for us to meet at all. In the
winter of my sophomore year, we met in New York and
I took her to see the picture my mother had in a group
show. My mom looked sorely outnumbered here, strain-
ing out from this chorus line of pictures. How were
collectors, dealers, or critics supposed to see how *good*
she was? It irritated me, for Maggy to be seeing this. In
the elevator of the gallery was a couple who were obviously collectors. Maggy grinned at me and said, loudly,
"What was that picture we saw on six, Richard? The
abstract, by Joan Freeley? That was some picture.
Wasn't that a beautiful picture? I wish we could afford
that picture." How dare she try to step into my world, to
become my mother's daughter, another helper? I sulked
all afternoon, and when I put her on the Connecticut
train in Grand Central she asked, "All right. What's the
problem? You've been in a bad mood all day." She knew
why. She was daring me to say it, and I did not.
"Westport's calling," I said. "Don't be mean. Did I say

something wrong? How can you act like you don't like what I say, if you don't tell me the things that are off limits?"

Mom listened to tapes and the radio while she painted. Jon and I—Jon, from his California perch—competed to make her tapes, and there was the great compliment if we won, because then she would play something we'd made for her all day. She liked: R.E.M. and Lou Reed and Leonard Cohen. She didn't like: Paul Simon and Edie Brickell and the Indigo Girls—"Too mousy."

She was forty-three. Age began to appear on her face. Age climbed out of her eyes and mouth, making lines there—as if it were something she'd been storing in her body all these years that was now crawling out. I got a summer job, and before I left for school I bought her a deluxe boom box, with two tape decks and auto-reverse. I felt I had trumped Jon forever, because whatever he sent would at least be played on something I had provided. I plugged it in and showed her the radio. Old folk songs, men with guitars who seemed to be singing inside boxcars. She shied at the expense. "You can't afford this elaborate a gift. Look at your luggage. It's a disgrace. You don't even have a toilet case—you carry all your shaving stuff in a plastic bag. A boy your age should have a leather kit. You can't go around giving me elaborate gifts like this." I tugged the cord from the wall, in irritation. She flung her hands out and said,

"Wait—that was 'Woody's Children.' " I saw then the contours of her life without me—that she spent enough time alone to know the names and programming on NPR.

I traveled with Maggy's parents. They didn't know what to make of me. They were hesitant talking about their own lives, for fear the expense would offend me. How could they know the taboos of the poor? My junior year, I took my disgraceful luggage with me to their home in Jamaica. It was a surreally beautiful place. Maggy and I got our own little guest villa, set into the hillside. I couldn't have asked for something more surely first-class, and I showed my gratitude by using my Charm Boy act for one week. Mr. Weatherly opened a letter from his Jamaica club, and tossed it to the table with a nick of a frown. "They've raised the golf fees again, Jill," he sighed to his wife. I asked Maggy what those fees were later. "I think something like thirty-five thousand dollars," she said. I felt the difference between us then. It was more than my mother made in an entire year, teaching art in Maggy's home state.

We made love all week. I have so far put sexuality to the side—this has been me chatting Margaret up to a choir of angels. (In the lower world, of course, it would have been a different explanation: "Gentlemen, she was hot.") Her body had surprisingly large breasts. Her skin was covered with a kind of sandy texture I loved, a kind of sweet-smelling dust, as if she had come to me freshly made from a draftsman's table. Holding her in my arms, with our lower bodies connected, I felt a kind of *sureness* I'd never known. This was an easy thing, a simple thing, which I could do well. It was as simple as Mom imagined the world of business to be, and the combination of rough, panting activity and this solid *person* I was holding was something I didn't want to lose. We tested our way over various sexual territories— Maggy surprised me here, too—and these held us together like shared secrets. When she came, she would fall asleep, for exactly ten minutes. When I did, she would smile and tell me, "I could feel that." In Jamaica we couldn't stop touching each other, the sight of Maggy in a bathing suit kept reminding me of that smile, the soft and dirty smile when she looked at me during sex. At dinner, I would find a blurred version of that smile across the table from me, and after a round of excellently mixed drinks we would wave our way past the tremendous Jamaican bugs to our villa, and clothe ourselves in each other. I had never been happier. At the end of the week, we walked on the dock at dusk. We watched the showy Jamaican sunset—the sun trying to throw out all its colors at once, before night came to blot away color entirely—and I felt my chest sink, and I thought of my mother. She was on the other side of the world. *What was I doing here, while she was at home listening to the radio?*

Maggy had the most beautiful manners. My mother and I made faces across the coffee bar the three of us visited in Providence when Mom came up for the weekend. When my mom and I went to dinner we plotted. We cursed like sailors. We were making believe this wasn't us around Margaret, who was like a walking videotape of perfect manners. My mom held my eyes from across the table. And, one old grifter to another, she agreed to play grande dame, to put on the East Hampton face I adored, for this girl I was trying to impress. She used the word *lovely* a lot. She shook her head at me ruefully afterward. "Couldn't you have come up with something better than a cappuccino bar?"

Mom was showing her work to critics. Ernest Steinman was the head critic of my mother's circle. He was seventy years old, the author of *Sensibility*—the book Gregor had been searching through in my mother's bedroom that night long before—and it had been Ernest who'd first written on Jackson Pollock and Mark Rothko. She did not start with him. Lara Kilmer and Ken Worthy were both critics. Ken would always stay, after looking at her pictures, and chat solicitously about Ernest's declining health. Lara was squinty and curt, but Mom thought she had the better eye. Mom found that when she wanted Lara to come, or Ken, all she had to do was say the other had just visited, and then they would show. They were both trying to line up factions of the art world behind them. Finally, when she had Ken and Lara coming regularly, she told this to Ernest. He agreed to come.

I returned from Providence for the great event. We tidied up the studio and went through the order of the pictures. The order had an extreme, nearly narrative importance; you could never show more than ten— "people can't *focus* after ten"—and you were trying to shape the viewer's response, create the mood in which to best view you, building to your strongest work. She held up her finger and announced, *"Scotch!"* It was well known that Ernest could not look at art without having three drinks first. She bought the most expensive scotch the liquor store carried—she was willing to skimp on herself, but never on her career. We sat in the living room and waited. Mom crossed one leg; then she switched and tried the other. She pinched her lower lip between her fingers, clicked it juicily back and forth— the same gesture, I saw, that I made when I was thinking. The doorbell rang. There, in our apartment, stood the famous man. A short man, all in gray, whose features were settling into age like a collapsed stack of pancakes. Mom took his coat, and we sat in the living room, where she had tried to add to the atmosphere of an opening by putting out a plate of crackers and Brie— Brie!—beside the bottle on the table.

They small-talked. Ernest was surprisingly considerate of us conversationally, asking my mom about shows they'd both seen and me about school—but then attention from a celebrity has that odd quality of seeming so much more generous than attention from just another person. I watched the customary first, second, and third glasses of scotch disappear down Ernest's throat into his complex, art-judging machinery. I watched as he allowed Mom—in an exquisite moment straight out of forties musicals—to lean across the table and light his cigarette. I sat slightly behind him, and he kept turning to make sure I was still involved in the discussion—and I saw that part of his strength as a critic had to do with keeping an eye on the details of a room, not forgetting where anything was. I had read *Sensibility*, of course—you couldn't grow up in my mother's world and *not* read it. Long sections had been about ethnicity, the need for painters to substitute for their own heritage the heritage of the arts. Ernest had a large round bald spot on the back of his head, and it was as if his ancestors, pooling their resources as ghosts, had not wanted this to happen, and had seen to it that he would wear a phantom yarmulke forever.

Finally, his internal motors sufficiently lubricated, Ernest placed his glass on the table. He narrowed one eye at the wall, measuring the distance. "All right, Joany. Let's take a look at some pictures."

I had hoped, as when a boy, to be released. I could have sat and read in the bedroom, or maybe called Margaret to brag that Ernest Steinman was in our home. I learned then how attentive Ernest was—for he felt the escape in my body and turned and asked, "You're going to look too, Richard, right?" My mom caught my eye and, with a clenched nod, told me I must stay. So I stayed. Ernest was famous for his studio visits, the speed with which he made decisions—Leonard and Jack, when you *did* talk to them, would broadly toss around this information. My mother walked to hang the first picture. She reached her arms wide, almost embracing it, and lofted the stretcher up to the waiting nails. As soon as she had stepped away, Ernest squinted both eyes and said, "Nah."

"Nah?" Mom asked.

"This picture isn't working." He opened his mouth, as he waited for his brain to give him, after his response, the reason. "Too stiff. It's the stiffness that does it in."

"OK—" my mom said. "Should I leave it up for a few seconds?" "Let's see another," Ernest said. To distract my mother—for I knew she had spent many months on this picture—I reached for Ernest's pack of Camels. "Would you mind if I . . . ?" I asked. I saw now that the attention Ernest had spread so wide before was concentrated; he didn't speak, but nudged the pack in my direction. His hand, which I saw for a moment framed by our table, had gone shapeless with the same age as his face. Someday my mother's hand would look like this. I had never smoked before, and Ernest's cigarettes had no filters. The first cigarette! It didn't hurt my throat, as I had expected, but it was like a fist had been slammed into the back of my head, leaving me dizzy.

My mother hung up a second picture, and then another, and each time Ernest quickly said "Nah" or "Nope." He reached his arm back to where he knew I was sitting and squeezed my shoulder. I was still, my forehead sweating, holding his pack. He lit one, exhaled with a kind of wood instrument *ffff!*, which I imitated on my next exhalation. He reached to his tongue and removed a fleck of tobacco.

After the fifth, he again searched himself for reservations. "It's the color here, Joany." He squinted again. "Yeah, it's *contrasty* as hell. Too *contrasty*. I've always *agreed* with your color sense before." So he knew her work; that was flattering. During a critique, you grab what you can.

My mother rubbed her hand over the middle of the sixth, as she used to demonstrate for me Cézanne's brushstrokes. "What I was trying to do in this canvas was mix the colors hot and cold together—"

"Joan, do you want me to look at the pictures, or do you want to explain the pictures for me?"

So she went about the rest of the hanging in silence, with lips primly pursed. I didn't know if it was just the cigarette making me dizzy, or whether it was watching Ernest dispose of a year's work so quickly. She put up the seventh painting. Ernest twisted out the neck of his Camel against the ashtray. "Ah—" he said. "*Here* is the first picture where I can see what you're driving at. Now I get you. There's a *facility*. You gotta take the colors *warmer*, keep the values closer . . ." My mother left this picture up slightly longer than the rest. "Next," Ernest said.

The eighth picture was the last. Mom's closer, a very big canvas. Mom looked at it against the wall, gauged it. "Richard," she said, and she revolved her hand in a get-on-with-it gesture. "Help." I stood and walked into the viewing area. The track lights, coming from separate directions, gave me three twisty shadows, making me feel like three different people, and this made me more dizzy. I came to Mom's side, she nodded, and together we lifted the stretcher. We lugged it to the wall, hefted it up, the nails took the weight from our hands. We turned around, our hands holding nothing. This was the first time Ernest didn't immediately respond. His eyelids fluttered. I had gotten so used to watching from the side that the sight of his full face was a surprise. The age didn't matter. His eyes were strong and alive in that old face. His arms were hanging softly by his sides. Everything in his body, and in his memory, was coming out through his eyes. I couldn't imagine how my mother had been able to stand in front of them.

He let us stand there a half minute. Squinting, tilting his head, taking a breath.

"Why don't you build from this one," he said.

He left soon after—we all came back to the table, and the force departed his face, and his arms, working again, reached out for crackers and cigarettes, and he was simply an older man, a man whose fame and intelligence were titillating. When he left my mother and I cleaned up. ("I didn't know you smoked." "At school," I lied. She thought it over. "Well, it's not so bad. You look good with a cigarette.") We stowed away the scotch and I finished the crackers. She brought the ashtray to the kitchen—and then, for a few days, neglected to clean it. She did this as if casually, but I wondered if she wanted a record of the event, some physical representation of Ernest's visit, in the same way that I had once saved pennies from the tracks of the Long Island train.

She did what he suggested to the paintings—how could she not have? And he visited every few months, and his visits kept Ken and Lara coming too, and sometimes he would ask what they'd said and then agree or disagree. "I *like* Ken personally," he said. "But I think he has a tin eye." He came to like the pictures, and my mother as well. When he was in a good mood, he would stay and talk about other painters, and sometimes about his childhood. The liquor store man grew to know Mom, so that whenever she came in the door he would take the bottle of Jameson right down from the shelf and smile. "Another dinner party, huh?" he'd ask. Ernest never quite solved the problem of how nice to be to her in public—where Neil and Oliver would cluster greedily around him—but we would run into him in odd places. Once, during Easter, when we were walking across the park to the Met: there was Ernest coming out of his building. He had a white plastic bag full of empty soda containers. "Just taking these back to the store," he explained, lifting the bag. It seemed so intimate. How could he *not* help us, this man who had shown us his bottles? He had lived with Celia Kapplestein during the fifties—people nicknamed them "the Steinsteins"—but had never written about her. Mom didn't want to repeat this mistake, and was careful not to let their friendship grade into something else. But when I was a senior, and Ernest hurt his hip, she was the one who picked him up at the hospital. They walked outside and Ernest was smiling. "The nurses asked if you were Mrs. Steinman," he confessed. "I told them *yes.*"

That year, he came to her studio and looked at ten paintings, each one for longer than a minute. "Yeah, you're hitting it. These are *good.*" Her work was strong—he felt she was ready—but this didn't do anything, and in a way was as frustrating as if he hadn't liked them.

Lara was close to Chuck O'Donnell, whose gallery was near the Guggenheim. She talked about Mom's work with him, and he visited, and Mom called me at school. "Don't get overexcited. He's taking two pictures." He wouldn't show them at first. He kept them in his office, to show to clients, and sometimes would display them in the informal group shows that filled gaps between official exhibitions. I was close—she was almost showing again, which meant, perhaps, I could go on my way when I graduated.

I had dreams, finally, where I was involved with her bodily. Our bodies tumbled over each other's. Mom was alone in a bedroom—a bedroom, it seemed, someone had recently left. I came in and started to undress. My mother and I were both grim about this. She was doing this for me, as a kind of stark favor. I was doing this for her. There we were, compelled into this silent, tangling chore. If I had one of these dreams while I was home, it was impossible to look at her in the morning. I wondered if she knew. I learned not to fight these dreams—that seemed to make them recur more quickly—but to accept them and put them from my mind.

At Thanksgiving, feeling I could avoid it no longer, I bit the bullet and invited Margaret to our apartment. She put on the gloves I loved, and a long cashmere coat, and I saw something I must have first loved in her: she looked like an apprentice collector. Mom met us at the door enthusiastically. We had drinks in the studio, Maggy turned her head around at the paintings on the walls. I was especially talkative, to distract her from the small size of the place. She went to the bathroom, and I knew that then she must see the apartment had only one bedroom. When she came back her fingers were cool and she whispered in my ear, "How long has your mother lived here?" It was the first time I lied to her— that I closed a door in her face, and showed there were truths about my life into which I would not permit her to enter. "Three years," I said. "She moved into this apartment after I went to school." *"Ohhh,"* Maggy said. "That makes sense. I was wondering." Then at dinner—this being the second time they'd met—Maggy said, "I wanted to say, Mrs. Freeley, that Richard has shown me some of your paintings before, and I've always been impressed, but I've never seen so many. They're lovely." My mother smiled. "Well," she said, "I had some problems at first. But we've lived in this apartment for seven years, and I think I'm finally learning how to paint here." I hoped Margaret hadn't noticed; the rest of the evening was a blur.

In February, Mom ran into Jacob Boyden at an opening. She called me at school—I could tell as she spoke, from the guardedness in her voice, that he had slept there. "What time did he leave?" "Late," she said.

"How late? He didn't leave, did he?" "No, he didn't. He just left a little while ago." "That's *great,*" I said, for I knew she had loved him back in Vermont. Her voice loosened. "Really? I was afraid you might have mixed feelings about him, because of the divorce." I remembered Jake, with his big beard and body—it seemed as if the men she'd dated during her success, the sculptor and the cameraman, had been different versions of Jacob, this one getting his beard, the other his artistic talent. They began to see each other, and this seemed a further chance for me to leave. Jacob could take my place—it would be Jake who would accompany her to openings. Jacob had a show in the spring; she invited me to come down and see it. We went to the gallery where he showed, and the dealer knew who Mom was and escorted us around, and spoke about the pieces. I saw this was another way to earn consequence in the art world—by who you dated. Jake had not wanted to see the show with us—"I can't stand to be around my work when someone is looking," he said. "It's bad enough to wait for reviews"—but was waiting outside.

She called to tell me about their dinners, their museums. Her voice on the phone sounded guilty. I asked why. "I just don't want you to feel I'm running out on you, or turning my back on you, before you graduate. I know it's a strange time." "Jesus, don't give me a second thought," I said. "Don't be in such a rush to marry me off, Richard," she said sharply. "I'm not in a rush," I said. "But Jacob seems like a nice man, and . . ." I trailed off. My mother was silent. "I could fall in love with Jacob," she finally said, as if this were a simple proposition, an offer her emotions were making to her (this man would be suitable to us) and she could decide whether to accept it or decline. "Do," I instructed. "You *are* in a rush to marry me off. It's not very flattering. Has it been that hard for you? Has it been that much of a burden, having a mother in the art world?"

She called and said, "I just saw Celia's retrospective at the MOMA. It was heartbreaking. It was so *beautiful.*" She sighed. "I could say it's nice for a friend, and all that Pollyanna bullshit. But it was heartbreaking."

Margaret's stepfather's brother—is there a name for such a tenuous connection?—owned a magazine of the Arts and Opinion in Washington. There was a job there if I wanted. Margaret would be at graduate school in the same city, and I had no other post-graduation plans. My body was thirsty for it. Or rather, my *ambition* was, the dry-voiced and reedy spirit that shared my spine with me and spun endless beautiful versions of my future. This little pickpocket wanted that job. It projected fantasy visions of my beautiful future in Washington onto my brain in order to bewitch me, and leaned one elbow over the projector, coolly smoking a cigarette. But I didn't feel right about taking it unless Maggy and I were to become closer still. That struck me as wrong. So that fantasy version of life wasn't possible unless Mom was ready for life herself.

She got a letter in April from Lara Kilmer—Lara was organizing a weekend at the Triangle Workshop in upstate New York with Oliver Thrush. There would be dinner and a party, and lots of other painters, at this art fair. Jacob asked to take her. This was perfect: she would not be alone, and Jacob could show off to everyone—not just his dealer—that Mom was his girlfriend, that they were together.

Maggy's birthday was in early May. Her other birthdays, we had met and gone to dinner. This was the plan our senior year too. I was to be at her house by seven. At six-thirty, the phone rang. "Richard," Mom said. "I have a dealer coming in ten minutes."

"A dealer?" I asked.

"Grace Bordenicht. I was sure she was going to cancel, because I hadn't heard from her in two weeks and didn't want to get my hopes up. But she just called me and said she's on her way over. At seven."

"Well," I said. "What's the order of the pictures?" She told me. "And what are you wearing?"

She described her clothes to me, and I made a few counter-suggestions. All the while, Maggy was ticking in my head—putting on *her* clothes, walking down the stairs of her house, sitting on the sofa with the look of quiet readiness that would perk up as she saw me through the window, as she heard me walking over the soggy dead leaves that had made it from last fall. I waited itchily on the line while Mom swung open the closet door to receive the opinion of the full-length mirror.

The phone faithfully continued to broadcast her movements. I heard her dress shoes click across the floor of my old bedroom, and then the receiver was swung through space to connect with her ear. "This phone conversation is going to make someone at AT&T very happy," she said. It was a quarter to. I would not be officially late for twenty minutes. I did not tell Mom where I had to go. She would have insisted we hang up—she *liked* Maggy—and it seemed more important for me to help her through this. Chuck O'Donnell had proven slow about showing her; I knew this was on my mother's mind.

She said, "Would you mind terribly, Richard, could you please just *chat* with me for a few minutes, just until she shows? I'm terribly nervous." So, to calm her, we talked. Our conversation hungrily gulped up minutes. I hoped that Margaret would assume I had been somehow delayed in transit; then I realized she was trying to call, and getting the busy signal. She knew I was here. At seven-fifteen, the intercom in my mother's apartment buzzed. "Whoops," Mom said. "That's her. Gotta go. I'll call and report in after she leaves." And before I could explain that I would not *be* there when she reported, my mother was gone. Then I decided to stay. The hell with it. I had known my mother twenty-one years—I'd only known Maggy three. This was Mom's *career*, after all, and if I was an hour late for Maggy's birthday, I could explain that. After all, if Mom was showing, she and I could dance together to Washington in perfect good conscience. I had told Mom I would stay, and I sat by the phone.

By eight, she still hadn't called. At eight-thirty, I called; no answer. At nine, there was a knock on my door. The rapping was at the level of Margaret's fingers—I knew her body so well, exactly the height to which she would reach on a door—and I seemed to smell her perfume seeping under the door. "Richard?" she asked. She called my name three times, each time in a higher key. Then I heard her breath—not a sigh, but a heavy breath, and her slow, light step as she walked away. It was the last time I heard her voice—my name, those three times. "Richard? Richard? Richard?" Each one expressing some different question to me. At nine-fifteen, I stretched in the chair.

At ten, my mom called. I had been prey to fantasies—Grace had taken her on, they were at a restaurant celebrating. Grace had hated the work, Mom was strolling in the park. These all proved more luridly colored than the reality. "She liked the pictures. They don't have any space in the gallery for two years. I wonder why these dealers come, when they haven't got space."

"Where did you *go*?" I asked.

"What are you upset about? I went for a soda. It wasn't particularly interesting news. I thought it wasn't urgent to report in. You didn't have anywhere else to go, did you?" I had made the sacrifice; to tell her its details, its stupid details, would be to *un*make it. A sacrifice isn't a sacrifice when the other person knows how much it cost. I had learned that, too, from her. "No," I said. I didn't talk to Margaret again; that solid feeling of her body was lost to me. Mom came to pick me up for graduation, and we danced together at the party afterward, she teaching me the box step, and Margaret—though I searched the dancing crowd for her—eluding my eye.

We had always been strangely synched up. I came home from school, and a week before the art fair in July my mother and Jacob broke up too. It was as if we were trying to stay free, always, for each other. She did not tell me the details of their fight, only that it had been in some way final. She did not want to go to the art fair alone. So I said, in my old ex-bedroom (mine again for the summer), that I wanted to nominate myself.

This is the story of the weekend my mother and I finally broke up. She came to pick me up in a rented car—a little compact Japanese thing, a Sentra, that was beautiful to me. As long as we were inside, we looked perfectly normal and well established to anyone *outside*. In the car, she was nervous and quiet and ready for business. Her makeup was firmly in place over her features—like an invisible system of clamps and nets, holding the skin in place, though the flesh under her chin was going a little soft. We scooted up the Henry Hudson Parkway. Then we turned onto the Saw Mill and followed its crazy green curves north. This was ironic—as we pointed out to each other—because it was the way we used to drive back and forth to Vermont when we lived there, and it was the route she'd taken when she first drove me to college, that sad afternoon on which she had been so silent and supportive and brave. I had by now perfected a trick of letting old spots suggest my old selves. I sat there, and I was myself at six and myself at seventeen and myself at twenty-one at once, comparing and sampling all those different impressions, adjudicating among all those competing ghosts.

I asked my mother who was going to be there. "Gregor, of course." Of course. Gregor was Oliver Thrush's dealer, and Thrush—an English sculptor—was the director of Triangle. "Celia will be there. And Ernest, too. He's the guest critic." "They're there together?" I asked. Presumably, Ernest's drinking had ended things between them, but Ernest had a soft terror of accomplished women, and I wondered also if her success, as it established itself, hadn't made him leave. When Celia had her MOMA retrospective, Ernest attended the first night but stood upstairs in the permanent collection, and even when she sent delegates he could not be cajoled down. Mom asked me to make a list; I wouldn't have complied—but since I was going there for her, it seemed stupid not to. Making lists was one of the superstitious ways she tried to exert control over her world. She made lists for everything: her telephone talks with dealers, her dialogue at openings. Now this list of people who would be at the art fair. It's a list I still have: forty names, the names of everyone we'd known in that world. It was Triangle's first summer, and my mother's whole aesthetic section had been invited. The paper felt like a bomb in my hand. After making the list, my mom shook her head—with the harsh energy she had, which is always so near the surface of both of us, and which was such a trial for her socially—and said, "Jesus, making this list, I'm wondering if we should even go. I mean, what's in it for us?" "See Richard and Joan Freeley act against their own interests as *The Lambs to Slaughter*," I said. My other trick was to convert our lives into the ad copy for movies. "It's funny to you," she said. "But this is my life."

It was my life too, of course. It wasn't necessary to add this. My mother—one of her strengths—was that she never failed to complete a project once she'd started it.

She said, "I did kind of a stupid thing."

"What?" I asked.

"I'm not sure I should tell you. I got kind of angry at Charles O'Donnell and wrote him a nasty letter."

"Did you mail it?"

"Don't get excited. I was just so fucking pissed *off*, you know. He wouldn't come to see the work. He wasn't acting like a real dealer. And he thought I wasn't *noticing* that he wasn't acting right. That was what got me. It was like he was giving me an IQ test."

"What," I asked nervously, "did you say in the letter?" And another question I'd thought closed had popped back open, for I had hoped she would eventually show with O'Donnell.

"I told him that I didn't want to deal with him anymore, that I didn't want to have my paintings there anymore. Et cetera." I knew what had happened—she had probably read something. When she read *Flaubert's Letters*, she came across Gustave's goodbye letter to his mistress. He had written, "Madam: When you stopped in last week, my footman announced that I was not in. As far as you are concerned, I *shall never be in.* Gus-

tave." Two weeks after reading this, it was still rever-
berating in her head, and she sent a version of this letter
herself to the man she was seeing, a tiny Scots chiro-
practor who was giving her a hard time. Mom played
me his bewildered answering machine message over the
telephone. "What are you talking about? I *didn't* stop in
last week. And you don't have a footman." "I think he
got the spirit of it, though," she said.

"What'd Chuck say?" I asked.

"He said OK."

"So he's sending the paintings back?"

"Look, you could say it's liberating, and nice to have
my position clarified, and all that stuff. But it's a fucking disaster. I get into this fugue state sometimes. I only
come out of it *after*. I'm forty-four. I've accepted that I'll
never *not* get into these fugue states. I think the real
progress will be, you know, when I come out of them
before, instead of *after*. After it's always like, OK: What
did I do this time?"

"Will he be there? You didn't put him on the
list."

"Yes. How am I supposed to talk to him? Should I
just apologize? Explain, 'Hey, Charles, sorry. I'm just
sort of crazy?' "

"Semi-crazy."

"Semi."

"I think you should avoid him."

"The standard Richard Freeley advice."

"Dick Freeley as *The Predictable Worrywart.* I say let's avoid him."

Triangle was in the town of Pine Plains—a tiny little town that had the feeling of a western outpost, a few buildings grouped together around the trickle of a street and signs everywhere saying TRIANGLE. We drove through towns that had grand names like Genoa and Biarritz and Lisbon. Whatever ambitions the town fathers had once had to make a mini-Europe here had long ago been disappointed. Pine Plains had been named after some wider experience. There were Pines. There were Plains. That was it. Mom stopped in town and we got sodas—I could see the sweat trickling down her forehead, lightly, and there were little feminine dots of wet in the rough cotton of her tennis shirt. Walking out of the store, to see her leaning against our car gulping down Canada Dry seltzer, I had thought: Yes; that's my mother. She looked like just what I wanted her to look like. I had turned her into what I wanted her to be.

I have wondered, ever since, why the afternoon was such a disaster. Why from that one nice moment everything else was such a trauma. I did all the things I had learned to do in the art world. Yet the afternoon was a calamity, the worst opening we ever went to. Worse, even, than the first one, where I had gone knowing none of the rules. It was the last time I would ever try to control her. There was the same danger of knowing too many of the rules as knowing none of them: if you knew none, you would blunder and capsize yourself. If you knew too many, your steps became brittle, you took on too much protective ballast, and you capsized yourself. This is what happened that afternoon.

The first person we saw was Hiroshi. We parked our car with a long line of others in front of a white cement barn. Many cars were parking as we arrived—this jazzed me up. The sight of other people arriving somewhere always excites me—at a school, at a concert, at a party. It seems I have at last come to the exciting, beating center of the world, and that's why all these other people are there too. They were mostly New Yorkers. You could tell, because as they stepped from their cars, their heads twitched automatically around, looking for signs with the parking regulations. The idea of a world where there were *no* parking regulations was an unthinkable paradise for New Yorkers. My mom and I had time for a last anxious once-over, standing by the car. Suddenly Hiroshi was in front of us. Dragging a woman behind him, a woman in her middle thirties. The woman had a strange look, of not quite being there; of seeing us, humorously, from behind a protective barrier of glass.

"Joan—*Rich*ard. Hi, hello." This was normal, and as it should have been: Hiroshi being warm to us at openings.

"How you doing?" I asked.

"Fine, nice, good." Hiroshi's English had ceased improving but his vocabulary had continued to expand, so that he often spoke as a kind of thesaurus, assuming some of the phrases would stick. He said, "I want you to *meet* someone. Say hi. Ah, polo player's *sister.*"

"Whose sister?" I asked.

"Hel*lo*," Mom said, and reached out her hand, very ladylike (I loved all her gestures of good manners; it was her Charm Girl act), and shook hands. "I've been hearing about you for years."

I wondered who the woman was. I wondered, in fact, who the polo player was; was there someone in the art world who played that sport? I tried to manufacture the memory of a polo-playing artist, and could not. But the woman had the look on her face—slightly ironic, slightly *outside* both the normal and the celebrated worlds—that is uniquely generated on the lips of those who live in proximity to the famous. Maybe it was Prince Charles that was her brother.

Everyone was looking at me. My mother tipped my arm, to remind my hand to go forward and shake. "Darryl Bayer's wife. Paula. This is her sister."

"*Oh,*" I said, and put out my hand. Hiroshi adored Darryl Bayer above all other painters. When Hiroshi arrived in America in the early seventies, Darryl had been at the height of his own power and influence. Hiroshi had looked at him—at Darryl Bayer, with his addiction to jazz and cool—and fastened upon Darryl as the model of the American artist he had flown so many miles to become.

"I drove her up. In my truck. Because Darryl asked me." Hiroshi went suddenly quiet, at the notion that this solemn duty had been entrusted to him. He was dressed for the occasion: small loafers, a dark corduroy blazer, black pants. But this was summer—he had gotten the fashions right, the season wrong—and he was sweating. "Have you, ah, *seen* Darryl yet? I want to bring him his *sister.*"

"Sister-in-law," Paula Bayer's sister corrected.

"Yes, right, of course. So have you?"

Mom said, "We just got here, Hiroshi. Maybe he's inside."

"Of *course.* Well, see you," Hiroshi said, and right away he turned around and walked. "I'll see you *later.* Inside. OK?" That was pure art-world civility. You were always telling people you'd talk to them later at parties—as if your departure might otherwise be so devastating that you had to sweeten it with reassurances. You had to give them a little verbal pawnshop ticket, which you would redeem by returning. Once a person was gone, of course, that pawn ticket got smaller and smaller until, at the end of an evening, you looked down and it was gone. It had evaporated in your hand.

We followed them, down the path around the parked cars. The cars had just arrived, many of them, and their fans were still going, cooling down the engines. Those cars were huffing and sighing like track stars in the locker room after a race. The path became a field, and at the end of the field was the barn. Hiroshi was in the middle distance, the polo player's sister behind him.

I'm a fanatic for omens. There were horses behind a fence; brown horses, trying to wipe flies from their backs with their whisk-brush tails. I said to my mother, "Let's stop for a second." I pulled some grass up and thought, If the horses walk over, this weekend will go well for us. I held it out and the biggest horse plodded forward, blinking some flies away from its soft, creamy eyes. I felt the strong tug on the grass, and then the horse was chewing. I pushed: I thought, If I can pet this horse, then the weekend will go well. I reached out my hand and the horse shook its head back and forth and thunked away. A half-omen. My mom asked if I was finished playing with the animals.

The barn was an opening. It was supposed to be a showing of work. Twelve young artists had come in mid-June to spend two weeks at Triangle, to soak up our branch of the art world's approaches and codes. Today, at the end of the two weeks, there was to be an exhibition and a party. But instead of an exhibition, it was an opening. You bring the art world somewhere, anywhere, and it remains the art world, no matter the setting. If we'd traveled to the North Pole for Triangle—and that wouldn't have been so bad; it was terribly hot outside—Leonard Chichikov would have staked out a pretty good iceberg as his, and Gregor would have sauntered back and forth over the snow deciding which polar bears had the most salable pelts, and you wouldn't have been allowed into Darryl's igloo unless you'd been invited.

I could never go to a big-time social event without hoping it would change my life. I'd go, and feel that *there* I would meet the people who would put me on the right track, onto the path I'd sensed twisting around me but had never managed to discover on my own. That's the lure of socializing, for me. I thought I would get my mother established here. I was hoping the *something* would happen, to make us dispensable to each other at last. I sketched out a plan for myself: I would pilot her through this afternoon without fuss. There would be no moments when she would speak too long, no rooms in which she would demand too much attention. The idea of these people hurting her—my mother, who had done so much for me, who was so *proud*—was more than I could bear. I would pilot her through the day, and maybe at dinner convince her to go to Chuck O'Donnell and apologize. This would hold, I hoped. This would be enough of a release. I could bundle the past this way into something safe and *limited*, something with a clear end to it, and then I could go on with my own life.

We walked down the center of the barn. Triangle artists stood beside their wares—paintings on the floor that cautiously imitated Jack Atski's style. My mother had had the same idea twenty years ago. Copy what was around and give it your personal spin. The only thing that had changed in the twenty years was that the personal spin was gone; the copying was now just copying. Here was Jack's style, of dark blues, with gels beneath to give the surface texture. There was Neil Hollander at the end of this room, with his wife. I haven't told you *his* brush-off strategy yet. As an old-line WASP, Neil had the idea that he was supposed to be polite to everyone, regardless of the enormous gaps he knew perfectly well loomed between them. He had made his mark in the early sixties. In the eighties, some loyal critics had done their best to get excited about a new series. But this had been abandoned, and he now gave the impression of staying alive solely as a courtesy to his biographer, so the inevitable book would have a plump second half. When he had time, Neil told you stories—carefully detailed anecdotes about his early shows, his art school years, his tastes. This seemed flattering. But one afternoon Ken Worthy and my mother compared notes and discovered he had told them, word for word, the exact same experiences. It was as if Neil had taken a treasure map that was his life and torn it into a number of careful pieces, and distributed them deliberately among his associates, for some future investigator to find. The only problem was his *wife*. Like many couples, they had delegated to each other different levels of message-giving. She guarded Neil's attention like an aide. You walked to Neil, and while he made lazy attempts to communicate, there was his wife, to scare you off with her intensity. Then Neil could seem blameless and sociable. We walked to them slowly. "Hey, Neil," my mother said. When what I wanted to do was run and hide.

"Joan, right? It's good to see you."

"Joan, we'd love to talk, but we have to go back to the car to make sure the phone isn't ringing. Neil's expecting a call." And they moved on. The car-phone defense.

We walked. There was a big fan in the barn over our heads, and the artists' materials were nostalgic to me: they made me think of Mom's studio back in East Hampton, the brushes and water pots and Tupperware bowls of color. There were artists everywhere—I saw Lars talking to a stocky woman, and Philip Cowls piloting himself wearily across the barn on his crutches—and they seemed very intent. Mom and I were silent, as we always were at openings. In our roles: She looking for an opportunity to make contact, and I longing to supervise that contact. We were not that different from the Hollanders.

Phoebe Eagleton padded up behind us. The years had not been kind to her. (The years, like a kind of swarm, sensing she was without defense, had moved in and done a little number.) She wore a purple sundress. Beneath this dress she bulged and wrinkled in unforeseen places, as if she had been crammed into it by a clumsy second party. The fact that she saw my mother as a friend, whose conversational attention she could not doubt, worried me. "Joan, Richard!" she said, and her voice made some heads lift. I didn't want us to be seen with her too long. I had internalized those ugly values; the longer we talked with Phoebe, the cheaper our company would seem. It could be had at any price. When we should have been allies.

Phoebe herself seemed to understand how she was looked at now. "I have *news,*" she said, as if the news would earn her some extra time. "Let me tell you," she said. "Jack? Neil? Leonard Chichikov?" "Yes?" we asked. "They're all out of Krumlich. Guess where they're going?" We tried to. "Frederic *Beaumont.* He's been trying to cut a deal with them for years. He stole away Gregor's artists, for the fall season. He finally took it to Gregor. Lord knows what's going to happen to Gregor now." So Beaumont had finally gotten what he wanted;

Gregor was in hot water. Phoebe asked us to wait; she was going back to get a drink. When she left, I looked around—I hated to admit it—to see who might have seen the three of us together. My mother was silent.

"What are you thinking about?"

"Gregor must have three holes in his schedule. Maybe I can show with him." It was the obvious thought; and I understood something about the artists in the room, why the energy level seemed so high. It was the dangerous atmosphere of artists smelling money. They were all well aware of those three holes.

"I don't want to wait for Phoebe. Do you?" I asked.

"Why not? She seemed nice."

"I don't want to spend the whole afternoon with Phoebe Eagleton, that's why. I wanted to spend the afternoon with you."

My mother considered my lie, and didn't fall for it. "This really hasn't been a good environment for you to grow up in, has it, Richard?" Nevertheless, she walked.

They were English, many of the Triangle artists. I made that out from the bits and pieces of their dialogue that I overheard. And then—because I rarely looked at paintings at a show—I saw on papers next to their spaces names like Brian Higgins (U.K.). They were approaching the trauma of an opening differently than Americans; staring out with a little shock in their faces, or sitting on chairs with their legs crossed watching as people strolled by. The Americans made believe they had something *else* to be doing—tidying their spaces, doing extra work, trying to suggest that *invulnerability*. The English just sat there; as long as they behaved correctly, they could remember the afternoon as an OK one. With the Americans, everything depended on how *others* behaved. The barn was full of us. Lots of New Yorkers, in their great clothes—Mom and I, with our safe tennis shirts and shorts, looked a little like a lost doubles team in here, or the people who scoop up mishit balls at Wimbledon. There were also some Pine Plains residents, who had come in families; moping kids, distrustful husbands, and eager mothers, who'd grasped the opportunity of a local art show as an enriching experience. They had the sense that art was something *good* in life, like church or healthy food, that was at the same time bewilderingly tedious and unappetizing. I watched one mother lead her family to Brian Higgins's space. Brian Higgins stood and politely answered their questions. He was getting it wrong, of course—the people who truly cared abut the arts were the ones who were treating this as an opening, as a place to score social points. I imagined planeloads of English artists soaring home and blithely misinforming their countrymen, "It's only among the rural classes that the spirit of art still thrives in America."

Oliver Thrush thundered into the room—he was flanked by collectors and friends like a kind of bodyguard coterie or press corps, and the room parted in front of him, reeled away in waves, and he laughed, his merry art fair in operation. Chuck O'Donnell was chatting with him—a small man in a light suit. "Now in *my* gallery," he was telling Oliver, "we'd call this trompe l'oeil." His eye caught my mother's, and I felt Mom stiffen—there was this *thing* between them—and right away I said, "Come here, Mom, I want to see what's behind *this.*" There was a kind of canvas tent against the wall—the three blank sides of the canvas out, making three new walls. We slipped in. There were paintings on the inside. Thick, sludgy surfaces, with Ping-Pong balls and bits of twine and carpet clogged in with the paint. It looked like a demonstration of what would happen if you put an American rec room into the microwave. "What's this?" I asked.

"Darryl Bayer's new work. Crap, huh?" she asked. There was a ladder built into the corner of the room. I almost suggested we climb up, to get to the second floor. But instead, I kept her in here, until I figured the coast was clear. I stalled her by asking about Darryl Bayer and Ernest, but she wasn't listening. She had her hurt expression on. Her hungry expression. The good things were happening *out there*, and somehow, by some mischance, we were *in here*, away from that good stuff. We peeped out. Everyone was gone. Oliver was gone. Brian Higgins was sitting in his chair again. We scurried toward the end of the barn, past rows of artists with their blue and gel paintings displayed, all hoping *some-*

how, in these two weeks, that they'd found the secret, and their work was going to loft them up into the realm of acclaim and respect they'd always known was their truest habitat. It wasn't so much their work on display as their ambition—their hopes for the future. They could do Jack Atski's work; now they wanted to *be* Jack Atski, and none of us were quite seeing their immense talent, their intense personal specialness. Lara Kilmer was suddenly hurrying toward us. With her squinty eyes, and long nose. There was the moment—her feet skipped a little beat, those expressive feet of hers—when she was deciding whether or not to be friendly. Then she said, "Joan," and passed.

At the end of the barn there was a display that was not of gels at all, but competent watercolors and oils of Pine Plains. The barn, the fields. "What's this?" I asked. "Is this from some other show?"

"Edith's work. She's Oliver's wife. I think some of them are actually not bad."

I squinted. Yeah, they were fine. I saw Mom was waiting for my opinion. "They're OK." I asked where Edith showed, and Mom said nowhere, and this pleased me, that this powerful man's wife was having the same troubles as we. At the end of the room were stairs, and we walked to the second floor. One floor done; one to go, and the afternoon would be over and we'd kill some soft time till dinner. She'd talk with O'Donnell. We would drive home. Already, I could feel the space of time between that happy Richard who would be chatting with his mother and the at-work Richard who still had to polish off these rooms. At the top of the stairs, Frosty Fuller was hanging around, one hand in his pocket, a drink in the other. His big square rump was toward us, and he was squinting above his thick mustache. There was always a moment of dissonance, looking at Frosty. He looked so much like Lars Stevensen—he looked like a man *playing* Lars Stevensen in a movie. But of course the producers had gotten their facts wrong, they made him too coarse, and given him a little too much physical power.

Actually, it was the reverse. Lars was playing Frosty. Frosty and Lars had gone to school together, at the Kansas City Art Institute. Frosty was the star there—sculpting and showing and *teaching* before he was twenty-two. Then Lars showed up. Frosty was tickled when Lars began picking up his sayings, his sculpting style—when he even grew his own Frosty-style mustache. When Frosty couldn't make it to class, he'd call in, "I'm going to send Lars. Same difference." And then they began letting Lars teach. And then Lars went to New York, and when Frosty showed up three years later he discovered that Lars had already made his personality a hit. And no one really needed Frosty. When he went to a gallery, the dealers would glance at his slides and say, "You've been looking closely at Lars Stevensen's sculptures. That's *smart.*" Frosty showed up at openings to haunt Lars—the man who'd taken his life—and I could see he was trying to find him now.

Up here, there was a mass grave of cigarettes in a big cracked plate, graying up one corner of the room with their ashy smell. There was a large pile of hay bales in the corner. There was a tub of Golden's acrylic, the sop stains on the side making a lovely zagging pattern that for some reason—my mother's old studio, our summer 18 years before in East Hampton—again spoke to some old haunt in me, and again broke my heart. That had been such a sweet time: when you could look at something like a stained pail, and because the rest of your life was all right, it held your attention. The difference between then and now.

There were artists up here; more artists than on the first floor. They had all come upstairs. When I saw how many, I thought about directing my mom back down. But she—proud woman—walked forward, and I struggled to keep up with her. There were the Tingleys again. Herbert, with his angular face that looked like a handful of chunky stones flung into a bag that was then twisted tight. Bea, with her crabbed posture. Herb looked at us with a little whiff of contrition, a little request for forgiveness. Years ago, Mom had explained to me, Herb had suggested that he and my mother should sleep together. My mother had wondered if it might not be better if they stayed just friends. In response, Herbert hadn't spoken to her for nine years. So that had probably been a "no." Bea turned away, fiercely guarding her treasure of Herbert. There was a furious woman painter—another U.K. person—who could not bear the tension, our slow walks by and pauses over her work. She was reversing the equation. Anyone who stared at her, she stared back, and sketched them. She drew all of us as grotesques. Hiroshi, Celia, Leonard; they were drawn naked, without consideration or regard for self-image. I could tell—a little trailer on her pages—who was in the rooms ahead of us by whom she'd drawn. She'd drawn the Tingleys as vultures.

In front of us, Jack Atski. "Joan! How you doing?"

"How are *you* doing?" How are you doing? had replaced hello as the form of address. Conversation was being sped up, chopped down to its unavoidable necessities, and eventually all conversations would begin and end with "Goodbye!" "Fine, fine," Jack said, waving his hand to dispel the conversation.

Perhaps someone a long time before had told Jack it was disreputable to speak about business—even a business as personal as the art world—in conversation. For all you knew from talking with him, he was a realtor, or a sport fisherman. He would talk about his houses, or his plane trips to and from the city, but his work never came up at all. Art had passed from a passion to a kind of expert pursuit and now was simply the basis for his living, the enterprise with which he was connected. He was removed in distance and in mind-set—quite far removed—from the young, art-mad boy he'd once been. The art-mad boy who had given a fake name and made believe he was an artist's agent, and had shown Gregor Krumlich slides of his own work claiming they'd been painted by someone else. When Gregor asked, "I would like to *meet* this Atski," Jack had dropped the pretense and said, "Atski—c'est moi." I wondered, if you could have introduced that art-mad boy to the older man he had become, whether the boy would have liked him.

Now his business was on everyone's lips. I had the impression, up here, not of ease on Jack's part, but that he was hiding. He was standing by the wall—I guessed he was looking for Gregor Krumlich, so that if he saw his old dealer coming he could scram.

"I see you've made a switch," Mom said.

Jack cocked his head. "I did, I did. I felt now was the time. Gregor is a very personable man, and I will always appreciate what he did for my career—but it's all a question of energy level, no? I have gone with the younger man." Then he did a strange thing. He took my mother's forearm and held it in his hand. He asked how she was doing again, but in a tense voice that suggested he didn't really want an answer. I had coached my mother about never telling the truth: when someone asked that question, all they ever wanted to hear was that you were fine. He kept glancing at me as he spoke to her, with a little odd question on his face. The question was, did I know they had slept together?

I did. Jack, we had no secrets from each other. I knew when and how many times she slept with you, for my mother's sexual résumé was no more mysterious to me than her professional one. I could have put it down on paper. It would have read:

JOAN FREELEY
Born, New York City, 1942

    m.   Paul Freeley 1962–1972
                 (Granted Divorce, NYS, 1974)

Crushes:

1942–61	Nathan Roseman (father)
1954–58	Marty Fox, Stephen Klein (now M.D.), Robert Gordon (LLD; joint crush with mother), Mike Brown (hood)

One-Person Relationships:

1987–?	Jacob Boyden
1984	Bill Crouch (cappuccino)
1978	Ray Willet (Canadian critic, remanded to chilly Banff)
1976	Perry Boyle
1975	Alby Thompson (mistrusted by her children)

1973–74   Ken Maple
               (mistrusted by her children)

1972   Jacob Boyden

Affairs: (casual, unless indicated,*)

1986	Mickey Silk* (casualty of Flaubert)
1985	John Bishop
1980	Jack Millay* (transferred by network to California; sad)
1979	Stephen Klein (finally)
	Ron Piddel
	David Shainberg (Canadian; missed Ray)
1977	Sidney Colton* (still fixated on first wife)
1975	Orrin Bannard (not understood at all by current wife)
1974	Jacques Atski
1973	Peter Ferri (New Year's Eve, wine)
	Dan Bellamy (friend of Ken's; one-time error)
1971	Jacob Boyden*

Therapists: (includes major themes)

Canter, Leonard, M.D.,
    "Your Marriage Is Unhealthy," 1969–72

Greenberg, Jay, Ph.D.,
"Why Didn't Your Marriage Succeed?",
1974–77
Weinberg, Alma, M.S.W.,
" " *(not very chatty)*, 1979
Freeley, Richard, B.A.,
"Marry Jacob Boyden," 1987–

Even with me mentally reviewing this, Jack showed no inclination to leave. Whatever he was getting from my mother—this affirmation of himself as a powerful man, as someone whose attention mattered, at a moment when he was exposed—was something he deeply needed. Jack asked if she had any shows coming up. My mother, bravely, did not fudge the point.

"It's not a great time," Jack said, nodding. "Don't get discouraged, keep painting."

Jack had given her an opening, and she took it. "You should come by and see the work sometime," Mom said. You could see he thought he'd made a mistake. He now got the worried look you find on people when they fear you're going to ask a favor.

"I'd like that," he said. He looked at his watch, as if checking to see if he had time right then, and this allowed him to slip ahead to the next part of the conversation. "I'm not sure now whether I'm going to stick around for this whole thing. If I don't see you tonight, will I see you tomorrow morning?"

"Where?" Mom asked.

"Oh," Jack said quickly. "Around. In Pine Plains. You're spending the night, aren't you?" And it was plain to me, right then, that though we had taken the trouble to come and display ourselves in every room, there was still some secret party going on, at the center of Triangle, from which we were going to be excluded.

"Yes. We're over at the Ramada Inn."

I brightened. "Really?" I asked. Mom laughed. "What can I do?" she told Jack. "My kid likes Ramada." I loved motel chains; they were so reassuring. Like our rented car, they suggested that we belonged smack in the dab of middle-class life. And since I believed that by pretending to be something you became it, this was a relief to me.

"Joan, don't despair. You're not responsible for the tastes of your children." This struck him as a good enough exit line. We walked on. I turned immediately to see if anyone had caught us talking to Jack for so long—if they'd seen this little triumph. There was the angry caricaturist. I made the mistake; I looked. She'd drawn Atski as a kind of panting satyr, with goat legs and bats around his head. With this representation I had no quarrel. But my mother and me she had drawn as a single two-headed being, sweating bullets. She smiled sweetly at me. We moved ahead.

"You slept with him, didn't you?" I asked. I knew it

kept my mother calm to talk, and made us look secure to anyone around.

"Richard! What kind of question is that to ask your mother."

"I know you did anyway. Why didn't it—you know—take?"

"It's complex. I think it was just a curiosity thing on both our parts. As it goes back more in the past, I'm glad I didn't. He's been married four times. He tends to pick very interesting women, and then once he marries them he proceeds to make them *not* interesting. They all become Jack's aides. I don't know anyone he's married who wasn't better off before than she was after."

In the next room I saw the top of the ladder I'd seen downstairs, in the Darryl Bayer show. There was a bald man here, talking to a group of people who were obviously collectors. *"Chichikov,"* my mother whispered in my ear. Leonard was a greedy man; a hog for attention and for stuff. Even here, he was standing in front of the window, so that his neck alone would be cooled by the breeze. Leonard was a year younger than my mother; I think, of all the artists, he had been happiest about my mother's fall, because it had preserved his status as prodigy in the group. Now he was old. But he was still fighting. His bald head had a kind of dent on top, as if he used it to cleave his way through the art world. With

him were the Worthys, Ken and Viola. Ken was once
again unsure how to greet us.

If Jack and Neil had been unnerved by their attention for the day, Chichikov was exhilarated. He spotted
my mother and waved us over. "Hey—Joan Freeley.
That's right. C'*mere.*"

My mother raised her watch face and patted it. "No
time," she said. And I thrilled at this. We were people
on a tight, demanding schedule, not just there to social-
ize. But gloating was like a warm bath you could comfortably sink into, and I needed to stay sharp. We
walked across the room. Leonard stepped a little from
the window, and I could see over his shoulder a plump
figure moving past the horses on the grass. To rev myself back up, I tried to imagine this was Jacob Boyden.
The horses nervously watched him pass, this hustling
bearded figure in jeans and a white work shirt. Then, as
the figure came closer, I saw it *was* Jacob Boyden! I
couldn't think of anything to do then but to get my
mother out of the building. I didn't think she was ready
to face him. I turned us around, but it was like one of
those scenes in a horror film where the zombies con-
verge. The Tingleys were walking into this room, and I
didn't want to have any little moment with them. At
the end of the hall, Phoebe Eagleton caught my eye.
"Joan!" she said. "I was looking for you downstairs.
That was naughty of you, not to wait." We couldn't stay

in this room. There was still the ladder. If nothing else had happened, and I had gotten my mother out of the building right then, the afternoon would have been a success. "Let's go," I said.

"You want me to climb down a ladder?" Mom asked.

"Why? Are you too old?"

"Fat chance," she said.

I went first. The rungs felt good in my hand. I stepped to the ground level, and watched my mother above me, her legs coming down inside her shorts. We were not alone in the room. "Richard!" Hiroshi's voice said. "No. I found Darryl! It's OK." Then I looked around and saw who was in the Darryl Bayer room with me, and understood that I had made a terrible mistake.

My mother came down to the ground, with a little leap. "Whew," she said. Then she saw who was in the room too. Hiroshi and Darryl and his sister-in-law were all having their picture taken. Gregor was holding the camera—a little self-focusing Nikon, which was making a sharp sound as the flash warmed up. Gregor was in here to enjoy his two remaining big male artists: Oliver was beside him, giving advice on the pose. And there was Ernest Steinman, too, watching from the corner.

"Joan, the reason we closed off the entrance is that this is a private affair."

Gregor looked at us. "Joan," he said. "How very *agile.*"

Oliver looked for a joke. His lips quivered for a moment as if shaping themselves around words his brain had not yet provided. He said, "Joan, you know, I'm not sure we're even insured for ladder-climbing!" and he laughed. Charles O'Donnell laughed with them. I had thought we were safe downstairs. But here Mom was, looking foolish and unpredictable, somehow, and I had done it to her. This wasn't the bad thing. What was going to be worse was how we would get out of the room. Because once we did, they would all realize they hadn't wanted her there, she had barged in on them, she had approached without invitation. They would talk about it when she was gone. This was my doing. The canvas entry parted, and Jake Boyden came in, too. This was all too much. My mother was deciding what to say. I couldn't stand to hear it. Without looking back, I walked out of the room, leaving Mom there, alone, hoping she would follow.

W e moped around all afternoon. Oddly, I could tell I loved Margaret—I mean, that she had entered the chamber in my head where I kept my loved ones, where I brought them my gifts of days and impressions, and where I ran to them to be soothed for disappointments and trials—because right after I left the barn, I wanted to call her up. I walked into the field. My mother caught up with me and put her arm on my shoulder and kind of patted me. She began, "That wasn't *great*—" and when she saw my face she stopped and flapped her hand to shoo the thought away: "Well, forget about it. We can't change it." As if she were *my* coach, and we would get them the next time. We stood by the horses (they'd been right after all, those demonically intelligent horses) and she put both hands on my shoulders for a moment and stood behind me and then we walked on. And I knew I loved Margaret right then because I wanted to call and hear in her voice that she loved me, too. That no matter my screwups here was a person who had trusted me with her love.

We walked to the other side of Triangle, where the sculptors worked. This perked us up. The sculptors were young men, a few years older than me. They were wearing gloves and seemed happy, drinking Rolling Rocks and chuckling with each other. Sculptors have it easier than painters. At least they're working with materials. They can see they have the power to melt stuff, weld stuff, bend big pieces of steel together. With painters, it's all so *attenuated.* You are trying to put the right colors in the right pattern so someone else will like it— you're safe-cracking their artistic tastes—and if you fail, what you've failed at is solving a *problem.* For sculptors, there is the reassurance of actual and solid objects. I left Mom outside in the exhibition garden—big bronzes with a dust of rust on the edges, like burn marks on toast—and walked through the sculptors' group studio. My thirst for a phone was very great. Inside, the sculptors were sitting around with more beers, many of them wearing goggles. They seemed like a battalion of the Army Corps of Engineers on break—the happy atmosphere of men who have finished some satisfying physical work. A torch was sizzling away somewhere, and there was also the cool smell any cement place will collect on a warm day. There *was* a phone. I dialed O and then Margaret's number. The operator asked my name. I hadn't spoken to Maggy in six weeks. I thought better of it; it would be shameful to call collect. Then I dialed again. By chance, I got the same operator. This time I said, "Richard." The operator laughed and said, "So you're feeling lucky now, huh?" The call clicked through, and Margaret's phone started ringing. I knew its particular purr—it stuck to the side of my heart like a burr. The machine came on. I said, "Hang up," because operators—maybe trying to help all of us thwart AT&T now—sometimes leave messages of collect calls. I didn't want Margaret to think of me lost somewhere, in the woods, without any money to call her. It wasn't a romantic image. So we hung up and I walked back outside, where my mom was laughing with some young sculpting kid.

We went indoors, to the sculpture galleries. Oliver had given himself one whole room. He was experimenting, for fun, with representational sculptures, big nudes that looked like Henry Moores. We walked out of the sculpture garden and down a little farm path. This was God's exhibition, but it wouldn't make His résumé. 1987: Another Lovely and Bakingly Hot Summer Day. It was humid enough so the trees in the distance were indistinct, the heat getting in there and fogging all our lenses. The landscape opened up around us. We didn't talk, which felt nice. It was just the two of us walking together. I was feeling horrible for her—for the real danger in my mistake had to do with the art world itself. It's all about associations, and when someone thinks about you, you want it to bring up a string of flattering memories. "Oh yes, Joan Freeley was that confident woman in the great shorts." "Oh yes, Joan Freeley is the woman I saw talking with Lars Stevensen." Instead, Charles and Oliver and Gregor would think, "Joan—yes, I just saw Joan Freeley barging in on us with her son down a ladder. What a strange person!"

I reached up into a flowering tree and put a blossom in her hair. Mom said, "Thank you," and fixed the blossom so it would stick. She was trying to cheer *me* up. I wondered then—as I had never wondered before—how much of her letting me steer her through openings and the art world had been a sort of favor to me. She had known I was a mess when I came back from Los Angeles: lonely and awkward. She had submitted to my instructions, and I had become confident in my role as social guide. She didn't want to discredit me, more or less. This seemed so much less important to me than her life, than her life in the art world! She asked, "Whatever happened to that girl you were seeing? To Margaret?" "I don't want to talk about that right now," I said. "OK," she said. "We'll drop it. You couldn't give me a clearer answer than that. I just wanted you to know I liked her. That I thought she was

a very nice girl for you. Adorable, pretty." "Actually," I
said, "I just tried to call her." My mother nodded. "I saw
you on the phone. I *thought* that was who you were
calling." "She wasn't home." "Well, you don't have to
let it go at that. Try later. Call again." Always encouraging me not to be passive—passivity my mother's great
sin, with TV-watching and not trying to propel yourself
forward and everything else. Dad must have frightened
her with some deep strain of passivity when they were
married; obviously, she thought Jon and I might have
inherited it. We walked past a long field, where the
claw hand of a sprinkler was sending a liquid version of
its fingers back and forth. There were blocky wooden
goals at either end. "What's this?" she asked. "Polo," I
answered, and laughed, thinking of Paula Bayer's sister.
"That *was* funny, wasn't it?" Mom said. We both had
that limited telepathy, which seemed to extend only to
each other. Like most family talents, it unfortunately
had no real play *outside* the family, and so was without
value. Certainly, had I been telepathic, I would never
have brought her down a ladder like that, down into the
lion's den.

It started to rain. Fine; the day was punishing me, I
didn't *deserve* any better weather than this. I stood with
the drops hitting my shoulders and said, "Oh, *fuck.*" And
Mom found a tree with some leafy cover and drew me
next to her body to wait. I asked about Jacob then. They

had had a fight, Mom told me. What fight? Mom was afraid I wouldn't understand. But I pressed and she told me it was a fight about children. They had been driving to New Jersey when Jake brought up his daughters. One daughter was living with a man who hit her. Not often—only when things got out of hand. It didn't seem to trouble Jake. Mom insisted he call her immediately and tell the daughter to leave the man and come home. It was as simple as that; Jake thought it wasn't her place. Mom kept at him, and they ceased talking, and when they reached his foundry Mom said she wanted a cab. She sighed. "So that's where you find me," she said. It made me sad—because I didn't understand. What I *did* understand was that what Mom had been defending, fighting for, was me, my own sadness in California, which she had been so insistent I leave. She had been defending her own choices with regard to me—you are supposed to do everything you can for your children— just as I had defended her life with Margaret. And yet we had both made sacrifices that neither of us wanted. And this seemed to me to be the doom of families: to keep on bringing one another gifts that nobody de- sired.

The sun shone, we walked. We stopped just at the point where the bands connecting us to the afternoon snapped. It was nice; there was something elemental about the walk. Me and my mother and the planet was what it felt like. And whatever was going on back there—in the noise and bustle of the art world, in the crash of ego and money and success that was that world—the important things were me and my mother and the sky. We walked back, past the field where the sprinklers were still flexing their wrists, past the farm buildings, back to the sculpture and the art world.

Oliver Thrush was waiting for us. Or rather, he was standing by the sculptures, with two tall women by his side. He was thinking something over. My impulse was to keep walking—as I told my mother—but she said no and strolled right over. I thought the memory of us was still too fresh in his mind. But he said, "Joan! This is a terrific stroke of luck."

"Why?" she asked.

"Well, I will get to that. You *did* come up by car, didn't you?"

"Yes."

"Well, there's a late guest who couldn't drive himself. He took the train, but he's stranded in town, and we needed someone to go perform the rescue."

"So you want us to drive into town?"

"No no, that would be too much of an imposition. But we'd like to *borrow* your car if we could for a quarter of an hour. We'll leave it back at the lodge. You *are* staying to dinner, aren't you?" And Mom gave him her keys, and the two women walked off, and Mom chatted with Oliver for a few moments about the show and the exhibition, and then she returned to me.

At the lodge, which was a quarter-mile from the farm, we found our car in the lot. We got our bags out of the trunk. There was no way to learn who they had driven. The car seemed shy around us now—we had whored it out, and it no longer greeted us with its perfect machine trust. I said, "Look. Maybe we've hit on the secret. Maybe carpooling is the real warp and glue of the art world."

We changed in the bathroom. The other guests had gone to their hotels, for naps and showers. The Ramada Inn, Mom told me, was too far away. So I went first, and acted fast. I put on jeans and a white Brooks Brothers oxford, and exchanged my sneakers for loafers. I tied my sweater around my shoulders, which was that year the fashion. You were supposed to wear your sweater around your neck, as though it was the pelt of a lion you'd wrestled and then skinned. I would never have dressed this much like a College Student around my friends; they would have known I was trying too hard at the role. But around these people it was fine. They would see me only as the perfect version of that student. I came out. My mother said, still trying to reassure me, "Jesus, *that* was a switch. All right, I can see my work's cut out for me." She came out a few minutes later in her dark olive Banana Republic skirt, which had been a gift from me and which made her look like Meryl Streep. She came out smelling of perfume, and looking lovely. She must have known she looked lovely, because she didn't ask for an inspection, just stuffed her ex-clothes into my bag and walked on.

Dinner was held under a big tent on the lawn of the lodge. The lodge owners had set a tent outside on the lawn, beside a little round pond. Twenty wooden tables were arranged on the grass. My mom and I went to the outdoor bar and got drinks, and watched the kids working at the lodge set up. They came out shouting happily to each other, carrying big silver dishes and samovars and placing them on a long Formica table. One girl lit a match and then lit the end of a long brown stick. She blew out the match, making an "O" face; then she went like a fairy, carrying this little stick, lighting the small jarred candles on every table. When she was finished she blew the flame out. One of the boys called something to her, and she spun her head around and laughed and cracked the stick in two.

Mom and I drank our drinks—gin-and-tonics; this was the one social lesson I'd carried away from Maggy's parents, that between the great gates of Memorial and Labor days gin was what you sipped—and again it felt wonderful and it also felt like a lie. Here was something splendid. Standing beside your well-dressed mother, sipping a cold drink, and watching a party being organized for your benefit. It *felt* first-class. But in reality there were few such moments in our lives, and our lives depended on mastering a professional problem. The professional was how we would someday have a shot at these nice things. We were pretending to be able to enjoy such moments without tension, and the pretense made me hungry for the time when it would be true. "This is a not-bad drink," she said. "Every time I drink, I wonder why I don't drink more. But I guess that kind of thinking is what turns you into an alcoholic, right?"

"You could never become an alcoholic."

"I know. Too tense." We were the only guests there, and we stood as the light died and the kids finished up. The animal world came hopping and sauntering to the party first. Squirrels rummaged slowly beneath the tables, looking for morsels. One tasted the half-stick the girl had dropped, and tossed it away with a disturbingly human gesture of disappointment. Then gnats, figuring it was no longer too hot for them—that the coast was clear as far as the sun was concerned—began to fumble up from the grass. Moths jerked down through the air, on their paper-airplane wings, come to feed on the candles. When they landed, their wings would go slowly back and forth, as though they were purring with their whole bodies.

Then people came, scattering the animals. They

looked refreshed, wet-haired, calm. After the delicate arrival of the animals, they seemed brutish and unrhythmical and dangerously noisy. They banged through the screen door. Headlights whirled in the parking lot, and emergency brakes made their cranking sound, and then footsteps and voices crunched over the gravel. They came socially, talking to friends, but with their eyes firmly on dinner and their mouths falling a little open. The squirrels scrabbled up on tree trunks and watched carefully, quivering their tails. Mom and I joined the dinner line. She produced two tickets and gave them to a boy who gave us, in return, two sets of napkin-wrapped silverware. We loaded our plates with corkscrew pasta and cold rice salad and barbecued chicken and corn on the cob. I gave my mother a paper cup with two handles, and reminded her to get herself some tea. "Thank you," Mom said. And I could see how it pleased her that I knew her this well—that she had been so lovingly cataloged—that I knew what she drank with meals.

Was I wrong to sense a little less *resistance* to us as we paused there with our trays, looking for a place to sit? After all, we *had* shown ourselves at the barn. We had proven we were social and not an imposition. We had only made fools of ourselves to five people—the fact that three of them were the most important people here had not been *our* idea, and you couldn't hold it against us. We stood. Many of the tables were occupied.

I whispered, about our chair-search, "R. and J. Freeley in *Exodus.*" My mother spotted an empty table and led us there.

With no one else there, I had a terrible thought that we'd be alone all night. But then strangers came to our table. They plopped down their trays, spilled the silverware from their napkins, made the non-verbal sound *"Ouf!"* as they relieved their bodies of their own heavy, daily weight. Mom began to eat, and I made a decision. The decision was simple. I wasn't going to tell her what to do ever again.

Who came to our table? Not Celia and Gregor. But they were fine people just the same. A bearded couple over from Woodstock for the day—or only the husband, a sculptor, was bearded. But they seemed to have worked out between them that facial hair gave one the power of human speech, because whenever the wife talked, she leaned so close to the husband's face you could have sworn she was bearded too. "This is so *great* for us," the husband said, meaning Triangle. "There's no art scene in Woodstock to speak of. This gives you a little *lift*, some encouragement to get back into the studio, you know? A thing like this." There was a lady sculptor, from Montreal. She kept bragging about how she'd made the drive herself. When she learned Mom was a painter, she began a harsh argument about formalism—my mother's branch of the art world. Mom waded in as formalism's defender—an ironic moment, for she was defending a world that had more or less forgotten her. She was so much fairer than I—for I had only contempt and hostility for worlds in which I was rejected.

Every so often, I felt cold fingers investigating my neck and would deal that spot a tremendous whack, obliterating a mosquito. The mosquitoes, the least welcome, had been the last arrivals to our party.

I kept an eye on Chuck O'Donnell as he moved from table to table, trying to make alliances—first sitting with Oliver, then with Gregor, then with the artists who had fallen into Frederic's circle. I tried to keep track of where he was, for the moment when Mom might seek him out and apologize. Then I lost him in the crowd. I know what I said before about not telling Mom what to do—this would be the final instruction. The last-gasp plea of crazy people everywhere: this is the last time. I swear!

A collecting couple arrived—they were superbly, comically well dressed, as though their life's audition were for a part in a *New Yorker* cartoon. They changed the dimension at our table. We responded to their presence, all of us, like the moths trying to get at our candles. We all wanted to feed from them, while they—our unsuspecting nourishment—sat with that clouded look collectors have, of staring out at a world made foggy and soft-edged by the presence of money. My mother was the only artist at the table they'd heard of. So they talked to us. The Canadian sculptress lit a cigarette and settled with it by her ear, as though the cigarette were a white radio that was broadcasting a very interesting program. The collector husband wore a phases-of-the-moon watch. A starry cosmos was contained in the center—it seemed wonderful, to own the heavens like that. "Torneau," the man replied. The woman talked to Mom. She had that midwife's response to conversation, saying "mm-hm?" and "yes? yes? yes?" very brightly and noddingly, until finally she'd helped my mother deliver herself of whatever she wanted to say. She took Mom's card—it said, JOAN FREELEY, PAINTER. Simplicity itself.

"Joan?" Tom Dancer was standing by our table. I was happy to see him. I knew Jake Boyden was in the area—I was looking for someone I could really twist the knife with. And here was Tom, and the whole time he was with us I was auditioning him for the role. Could he flirt with my mother? Would he make Jake jealous?

"This seat taken?" Tom asked. "Or, you know, are you saving it for Elijah?" He sat down; he had brought a dog with him, a tremendous social mistake. Tom had the features of a worried gargoyle—a gargoyle wondering if some check it had written would clear—and the dog was no handsomer. Tom was an art lawyer.

He noticed my staring. "What?" he asked. "Is my *dog* going to upset Elijah?"

It was such a small dog it couldn't upset anyone; this was Tom's mistake. Pets seemed to confess people's hidden self-images, and poor Tom without thinking had bought a Chihuahua. It was all ears and pushed-in features and high, nipping bark; it was like a bat that had lost its wings. It wasn't that different from Tom in the art world.

Tom pointed at the puddle of leavings on my mother's plate; for the good of her waistline, Mom had relieved the chicken of skin. "You're not going to eat that, Joan? Lot of nourishment there."

Mom said, "No. Why?" and Tom said, "I thought I might . . ."—and in swift demonstration he scooped the skin up, flapped it over his fingers, and held it out for his dog. The dog showed tiny wet fangs. Then it darted forward to suck from Tom's fingers. While he nursed the dog, Tom asked Mom what she was up to. I tried to listen without tension; Tom was Gregor's lawyer, and Charles O'Donnell's for that matter. He was the sort of exhausting conversational partner who *leaned* over every question, sorting through it for the occasion of a joke. He wasn't listening to what you *said;* he was listening for what he could make further use of. When Mom had finished, it was clear he'd only been waiting for her to ask the reverse question, for he had a prepared answer.

"I've been on a restaurant search in New York.

Nothing fancy. I discovered a great new place on the Bowery. Bo's Buffet. All you can eat. Only a dollar, but hardy fare." And the image of Tom, with his nice suits and his prissy face, at a shabby restaurant in the Bowery, made both of us laugh.

He disentangled his own chicken skin, held it out for his dog. The dog suckled. "You see Mal Volli?" he asked. Malcolm Volli was a sour young critic. "I hear he's having his personality revoked. No, it's true. New York State passed a law: you can't go around with a personality like that anymore. OK—all right. I can see you only love me for my gossip. That's fine—no, don't apologize, I'm always happier to have the expectations right out there in the open where I can see them. Celia did her entire crit, of the Triangle kids, without once removing her sunglasses. 'It's all too *yellow,*' she kept saying. And Ernest. He was scheduled to go onstage at ten. Someone was doing some wishful thinking there big-time. The Pine Plains liquor store doesn't even *open* before eleven, so everybody had to stand on their hands till Oliver could race to town and pick up some Cutty Sark." Tom's eyes widened, gauging the charge of this. He could tell Mom liked Ernest, and didn't want to hear anything negative about him.

The collector wife skimmed the cream cheese frosting from her carrot cake. Tom watched. "You don't . . . ?" he asked, frowning. Tom picked up the frosting and held it by his ankles for the dog. "Come on, Touchstone. Come on out. We want you to participate in a cholesterol experiment." We laughed again.

Tom looked back at us with satisfaction. This man—my Jacob-weapon—would have liked to be a critic. All of his jokes, all his real wit, for all these years had been dashed off on the pages of nights like this one, in disappearing ink. The culture had made a decision that one kind of talent, the kind you could preserve on paper, was valuable, and that others were not. So no one beyond his friends would ever know what a clever keen mind Tom had, which seemed a shame.

He ran through a routine that felt prepared in advance. He was divorced—he seemed interested that Mom know this. He'd married an Italian woman, who had proved argumentative and jealous, just as everyone had anticipated. So he'd been thinking about other stereotypes in his life. His child had a disturbingly Buddhist nanny ("Your child is *missing?* Oh, don't be so *attached*, Mr. Dancer. We both saw your son yesterday. How do we know we won't see him tomorrow?"). His building had a WASP landlord. (" 'Your water is out? How *dreadful*. Here, come stay at our place—we insist.' And then, you know, when you're in one of those homes, you can never tell which *towels* to use. Do you ask for real towels, or use the show-towels in the guest bath?") He told us about the new gallery he'd discovered in Chicago. The ideal: seven Jewish former real estate salesladies. "Those superwomen could move anything. You looked at a painting five minutes? Nope, you bought it. It's perfect for you. Do not attempt to resist us. How soon can we ship it out?"

We laughed, and I kept watching him. After all, Mom had used Karl Olken to get into Gregor's gallery; maybe she could use Tom Dancer to get back with Jacob. Still, there seemed something *off* about Tom. Not so much gay, but that he seemed too *wispy*, as a person, to stand up under the full weight of a woman—her life, her experiences, her sexuality and jokes. That was the something shifty you saw in his face, the central fact his jokes were designed to conceal. But Mom could flirt with him, and it wasn't necessarily clear that Jacob would see in Tom what we did. Mom asked about Gregor and Freddy.

"It was a good move," Tom said, suddenly serious. "I shouldn't talk about it, because I handle a lot of Freddy's work, too. But he's just a very aggressive dealer, and we're coming up on the nineties, and a lot of galleries are going to have to close. The ones that don't are going to need *very* aggressive dealers, which is what Freddy is."

"Do you think I should give Gregor my slides?"

Tom flinched a little. "Maybe—though the résumés just came pouring in on Friday, after the thing with Jack and Leonard came out."

"Late again," Mom said.

"Not at all. Give it a whirl."

Two artists arrived, English artists, Patrick Jones and Frank Bolling. Friends of Mom's—she was more social in my absence than I'd assumed. Their arrival displaced Tom, as if the table were now a hot tub and their jumping in made too big a splash. Tom said, "I'll see you inside for the dancing, Joan. Remember, I have dibs on the first two. Don't let your card get too full." He took the dog's leash and left. I whispered into Mom's ear the plan I'd devised. "That's very moral," she said. Some of Tom's humor had slipped into her speech. "No, it's very nice, and up-front, and shows real consideration for other people's feelings." I laughed. I was pretty sure she would try it. Patrick and Frank started talking, and it was hard to watch them. It had been painful enough watching Tom talk. What did they know about her—what would Mom say?

We had that limited telepathy. I felt something; she was nudging me on the back of my hand with her glass. When I looked up, Mom was holding out four dollars. "Richard?" she asked. "Can you get me another drink?" It was our old go-away-Richard sign from openings. I stood up. We'd been to so many events together, we had these signals down pat.

I walked into the damp night, the glimmering night. It was so thrilling to be away from the table that for a moment I could forget all my tensions and just concentrate on sensation. The warm breezes that coiled round my arms and legs, the crickets and the night insects making their racket—screaming and competing; what's surprising, given what we know of the lives of our fellow animals on the planet, is not that human life is hard; what's surprising is that it's not *much* harder— the candles flickering in their jars like twenty captured, blinking eyes. Under my shoes I kept crunching plastic glasses. I could try Margaret again. And I had this terrible thought, that even four years before I had reached some ultimate point with Mom, and since then my own anxiety had been making her life harder.

She was always encouraging me to be more social. But I had nothing to say to these men. Without Mom there, they didn't mean a thing to me. It was wonderful; without Mom by my side, the guns they waved all were empty, or shot only those flags that uncurl to say BANG. Leonard was standing with Lara Kilmer. He was trashing Neil. Leonard talked solely about dead artists; the effect was gloomy. If you mentioned a live artist, he would blink as if he didn't quite know who you were talking about. Then he would mention something personal about them, like, "We had a real shit time at their place last summer," or, "Yeah, Herb's a fucking character, and he's a hound too, but don't tell Bea." So that when you left Leonard—everything about the living having been faintly negative—you realized the only people he'd spoken well of were himself and the illustrious dead. I saw how wrong it was for me to hate these artists for playing this game. After all, we were playing it too. What I hated them for, I saw, was for playing the game *better*. This seemed outside the rules, unallowed, poor sportsmanship.

Jack Atski was talking with the beautiful and angry woman from the barn's second floor. There was something about Jack's posture—he was trying to lean into her, lessen the distance between them; he was trying to seduce her. As he must have seduced my mom, so many years ago. For all her drawing him as a drooling ogre, this woman seemed thrilled by Atski's attention. More than thrilled. She mirrored the movements of his head. When he put out a cigarette with his shoe she watched with real interest, as if she hadn't known a shoe could *do* that. As if the shoe still had properties she was unaware of. I walked to them; I still smarted from the way she had drawn Mom and me. "Hey, Jack," I said. He turned. "You should ask to see her portraits sometime." Jack asked, "You do portraits?" The woman lost her composure. Whatever was between them had snapped. "No; um, on *occasion.* They're more like, oh—caricatures." "Not at all," I said, touching her arm. "Give yourself some credit. She's wonderfully talented. You should sit for her, Jack. I bet she could really get the true you."

As I walked, I sucked a little chicken from between my teeth.

It made me happy my mother wanted another drink; that was so *normal,* so much what I wanted from her. That she have ordinary desires, and I have the ordinary role of fulfilling them. It made me happy to pay for it, and not worry about whether the drink was overpriced. And it made me happy to hold the bills by my nose, and smell their dirty and sweated smell (my mother's smell, above the smells of a hundred others) while the bartender plopped together her drink.

I know what my mother did later; because I asked. But I had determined I wouldn't watch her, and I didn't. I know eventually Frank and Patrick got up. She was alone, and the Canadian lady sculptor—as if they had both been waiting for the same thing—tried to immediately resume their argument about formalism. I know my mother left. I know she ran into Darryl Bayer. They talked, and she mentioned that winter night when he had picked her up in the carriage. That had been a night which had haunted both of us. It had been like the whole art world picking her up. We had both had the impression, for years, that on hundreds of occasions Darryl had shown up with carriages and summoned quite other artists to his side, and taken them for wintry rides, while she and I had sat at home. "No," Darryl told her. "That was the one time, Freeley. I don't know why we never did it again. It was nice. I remember it, too.

Your boys came down, didn't they? And then stood there for a long time after we were gone?" I know that at some point she went to the car, and took out a slide sheet, and transferred it to her purse. She had two slide sheets; she was incapable of traveling without them. If she'd gone on safari to Africa she would have brought slide sheets, for any giraffes and hippos who might be interested in how things were shaping up on the New York City scene. If she were being kidnapped by terrorists, her request would not have been for water or kinder treatment but for someone to run by the apartment and pick up her materials, in case any of her captors proved to be an untapped market for the arts. I know she ran into Jake Boyden at the bar. When he tried to apologize, she sat down with Tom Dancer, and began talking with him, so that was where my little plan went into effect. And I know that later in the evening—since Oliver owed her a favor—she sought him out by the edge of the pond, and gave him her slide sheet, because that was where I found her.

After a certain point I had to admit that rather than bringing my mother her drink, I was drinking it myself. There was a strange, breathing shadow on the front steps of the lodge. The shadow stood and resolved itself into black cat. I blew kisses to it—"Mpuh mpuh mpuh"—and twiddled my fingers. The cat stretched. It smelled something on my hand—the gin—and licked. The grainy feel of its tongue tickled my brain. Then the cat and I played a little game of stroking, the cat deeply engaged in getting my fingers to the spots where it particularly itched for them to go. But our collaboration was not a success. The cat rolled over to offer me its belly. I petted, it nipped at me and stood up. Then the cat walked back to the porch, wiped its face on the doorframe, and left a little glistening smear of saliva, dotted with fur. Another half-omen.

Alcohol still went through me very quickly—just like when I was eight. I returned to the bathroom and peed again. The bathroom now smelled like gin-and-tonic. I left the glass on the back of the toilet tank; the mirror issued a cold report on the state of my features. Someone rattled the door. I opened it and apologized. There was a woman there. An older woman, with the short boyish haircut older women give themselves, as if they have abandoned the precincts of femininity to the young and are moving on to the frankly unisex region of age where gender matters less. I didn't recognize her. I said, "I'm Richard Freeley. Hello." It wasn't the best time for an introduction. She said, "Edith Thrush," and gave me her dry hand to hold, and then took it back. She really wanted to get into the bathroom. But I wanted to make some impression. "Um—this is a terrific party you guys have thrown for us. Really fine." "Well," Edith said. "I thank you, Richard, for your kind words." She peeked over my shoulder. "I bet you went to a lot of trouble," I continued, trying to make some point to her about my savoir faire, which I hoped would reflect well on Mom. "Yes, well, I hope it will be worth all your kind words." She put her hand on the doorknob, and left it there, and I stepped away. Maybe after she was finished peeing she would think what a nice young man she'd met.

I walked back outside. I overheard people saying Jacob's name, which made it clear he had recently passed. I was back on duty. I thought about Margaret and felt sorry for myself. It was a beautiful scene, and the way I am constructed, this made me wish there was a woman for me to share it with. This would have made it more real—for there would have been a person seeing *me* in that scene. I had vague thoughts of flirting with the girl who'd lit the candles, and I was looking for her. I started to play my secret game. Which older men looked the way *I* would look in my forties? I saw a blond man who seemed to be Jon—and so I played my second game, which involved trying to make myself believe these older people were really visitors from the future, where time travel was possible. They were my friends and acquaintances from the future, racing back with urgent messages for me. The future-Jon was going to turn in a second and say, *"Don't* let Mom marry

Jacob. The marriage sucks. They end up moving to Montana and running a chicken farm." Or something like that. I saw a woman who looked a little like Mom—but she was another collector, and even in a best case scenario Mom would never have that kind of calm. Then there was a dressed-up version of Margaret Weatherly—the way Margaret might look at age thirty, in a linen jacket and a tan skirt. A professional Margaret. A Margaret I would have come to know well, had I stayed with her. The Margaret I was never going to know.

"Richard!" this woman said. And God, maybe she *was* from the future. The woman walked over quickly. She had been looking in a compact, and she stowed the compact into her purse, a lovely Coach bag.

"Hi," I said. Were we married in the future? No—I saw, as she approached, that the woman was simply Margaret, my Margaret. She had never dressed up at Brown, never put makeup on her face. That was why she looked so much older. But there were no wrinkles in her eyes, her skin was as smooth as when I had last seen it. She had dressed up because she knew this was a workday for us, a business setting, and she wanted to be my ally. "What are you *doing* here?"

"What do you *think* I'm doing here?" She stopped and stood with her little shoes in the grass, pointing in two different directions, a few feet away. "I think it was absurd of us to just stop *talking* like that. I think there's much more than that between us. I think it was crazy of you to just hide yourself away all summer."

You know what my thought was—beyond the shock at seeing her here. It was odd; my thought was how sad, how unfair it was that she *hadn't* been in Connecticut to get my call. She would have liked hearing my contrition, and then I would have been the one to extend myself. As it was, she had had to do it. She had probably been driving when I called. Coming to find me. And she had used up her one prepared line, it seemed, so now we were beyond the point in the conversation she'd fantasized about.

I wanted to hug her and hoist her in the air. I wanted to spirit her away in a flash so she wouldn't upset the intricate negotiations we were making with the art world. I was embarrassed she had caught me in my Superman-sweater, my College Student role. I wanted to explain and confess and apologize. I wanted to say nothing because my pride told me I shouldn't *have* to apologize. I wanted to make love to her, and I wanted to wound her with my *not* wanting to make love. I wanted to say how fabulous it was that she was here, I wanted *her* to say it, I wanted to say nothing and listen, I wanted to scream.

Maggy looked around now. "Are these the people you told me about?"

"Most of them."

She was choosing to be matter-of-fact, boldly witty,

like a thirties movie heroine. It was so hard to make the transition between being Mom's son and being Margaret's lover that what I finally settled on wanting most was to tell her to go to the bathroom and blot her lipstick. I held off. "Who's who?" she asked.

"You tell me."

"OK." She took a breath. "Over there, that's Jack Atski, isn't it? I don't see anyone who looks like Ernest Steinman—though you know I'd love to meet him. I read his book, which I thought was very good. OK. That's Gregor—*ooo*, he looks like he could freeze you just by looking at you. Scary. Which one of these is Celia? No one. That's Lars. That's Hiroshi; but that's easy. Um, I don't know who else. That's Darryl Bayer—I've seen his photograph, so that shouldn't count."

"Do you want to know how you did?"

"You're going to *grade* me?"

"Sure. Right on Atski; Steinman *is* here, but not at this party. That's not Lars; that's Frosty, but people who are more clued in than you have been making that mistake for twenty years. Now I have a question for you. What are you doing here?"

She wouldn't answer. She had told me already, by coming. She had come, and it was up to me to respond with a statement that was as eloquent. We were standing there, with our brains in control, and there was all that difficult strategy establishing itself through our faces and mouths. But in fact our *bodies* recognized each other. Hey—my body cried—that's that Margaret I held for three years. Wait a second—Maggy's arms wowed—that's that Richard body. Gosh, we slept with *him* a lot. So why aren't we touching each other now? Our bodies were like two dogs, eager to sniff each other, and there our brains were tugging on the leashes. "The thing is, is that there was just nothing happening in New York. It was looking to be a very dull weekend. So I thought I would just mosey up here and see what the art world was doing."

It was a chore for Maggy to be witty; she was doing it for me. She had never been witty—she took things hard and seriously, absorbing them. She was just smart and loving, and wit was part of the social stuff she had wanted to slice away, to get to the affection that was for her the point of socializing. She was doing it for me. She said, "This was the only place I knew you'd be this summer where I wouldn't have to call you. We were never great on the phone. I *knew* you'd be here."

"I almost wasn't. I wouldn't have been, except my mother had a kind of setback a few weeks ago."

"So I was in luck. May I ask what the setback was?"

"It was nothing. Just personal."

"Oh boy. You hate it when I talk about this kind of thing, don't you? Your mother's career."

"No."

"I don't see your mother. How's she doing up here, by the way? Making connections. Oh—wait, I forgot. I'm never supposed to mention I know your mother has a career. I'm sorry. Can you find it in your heart to forgive me?"

"You can mention it."

"No I can't. Look at your face right now. Remember that day in New York? You think I don't know this, but you *hate* it when I mention your mom's work. Hate it."

"No."

My hands went out. I took *her* hands; it was too much not to touch her. There was a little fumbling resistance, and then she let me hold them. Warm and small. Her hands didn't know how much to commit to me; they got twisted up with mine as I stroked her fingers. They were just doing an improv number, those ad-libbing hands of hers.

"Hate it," she repeated, just to say something, though all either of us was thinking about was how electric our hands felt together.

"No. No."

Her hands gave in. They stopped trying to pretend they had better things to do, and went loose and stroked back at my fingers.

"What are you doing, Richard?"

"I'm just saying hello."

Her face was growing warmly red; a sexual sign I'd forgotten. "I think the rule is, if we're broken up, you're not supposed to touch me. I think that's a pretty well established custom in this time and place."

She asked, "Are you drunk, Richard?"

"I've only been drinking a little."

"Oh, this is great. I drive three hours by myself at night and my reward is to find you drunk."

"Just a little," I said again.

"There's something I want to tell you," Maggy said. "If you want to talk. If you think this is worth it."

There was a fluffy wet popping sound over our heads. And then there was a little doodle in the air, a little mark of yellow. The fireworks. This was to be Oliver's send-off to Triangle. Everyone was standing up, leaving their tables, and walking down the slope of the lawn toward the pond. The party belonged to the animals again. The squirrels came down from the trees and went prospecting through the damp grass, and moths regained their full access to the candles. Holding Margaret's hand, I led her into the traffic. There'd been a canoe I'd seen before. It was out in the pond; a couple had taken it, and their paddles made a delicate slurping sound, of water being poured into a glass, and stirred the reflections into a number of colors, purples and golds and blues. I stopped for a moment and went on tiptoe. I could see everyone sitting down, but I couldn't see Mom. "You're looking for your mother, aren't you? I mean, I'd love to say hi to *her*, too. I like her. I think one of the tragedies of us not speaking is that I can't talk to her, either. Why should that be the rule, that you can't talk to someone's parents if you're no longer their son's lover?"

"I'm not looking for her."

"Oh, that's right. I'm sorry. I'll stop noticing. I will."

I saw Mom talking with Tom Dancer, and Tom Dancer's dog, with his high ears. There were real bats in the air, and I wondered if the dog was trying to remember, deep in the species brain bank, what it had been like to fly. I saw Jake by the bar, watching them; it suddenly frightened me—my mother away, outside of my control, trying to do this. Margaret and I kept walking. Of course, there was no way of explaining to her my reasons for leaving, which would have spooked her anyway. And she was here, and in a lazy way I hoped I wouldn't have to explain anything. I knew, before a courtroom of angels, that my reasons for pushing Maggy out of my life would have seemed commendable. Only, when I considered making the exact speech to her right here in Pine Plains, I saw it would sound obsessive and crazy and weird. Maybe the angels just have a higher tolerance for craziness, having seen so much of it down here on earth. I took off my sweater— I hated to think of Margaret's linen clothes getting stained—and spread it on the ground. "Here," I said. "Let's sit on this."

I could hardly see her, but her voice came from

where I knew she should be: "Thank you." I sat down beside her and stroked her arm.

"Richard—remember what I said before about that custom? Don't confuse me. If you want to talk about these things with me, then that's wonderful. But don't just confuse me if it feels right to touch me now, but then, with whatever's bothering you, in the morning it won't feel smart anymore."

"That's sensible," I said. But I couldn't stop touching her. I grasped her ankle—which I figured counted less on the erotic scale of things. I could feel the meat under there, the smooth skin with that rubbery feel of having been recently shaved. "Ankles count too," Maggy said. But then she put her hands on my forearm, those small hands with their light grip, and we watched the fireworks.

There was another sound like the popping of a champagne cork, and a yellow streak rose up from the end of the pond, nosing its way to the sky. The fireworks went off over the water, and this doubled them— they would arc down toward the pond as if the reflection and the model were lonely for each other. Sometimes only one went off, sometimes two or three at a time. Each one left behind a little shadow of smoke that the next one, bursting, illuminated. Some bloomed like flowers. Others were simply mid-air explosions, flashes. A few burst and then zoomed forward, like the effect in

Star Wars when the ship goes into hyperspace. Some were designed to fool us. One popped open very high in the air, sending out a circle of streamers like the frame of an umbrella. The crowd began to *"Ooh."* Then one of these falling streamers popped open itself, sending out a second series, and the rest of the crowd went *"Ahh."* Finally, one of these popped open right over the pond, giving off a final shower of color, the streamers plopping and hissing into the water around the canoe, and all of us whistled and applauded.

I sat there and let my mind go; I tried to turn that telepathy we had in the family outward. I tried to relax. I had Margaret's hands lightly squeezing my arm, kneading it. This was right. And I tried to let myself go and think about the other artists, why they treated Mom and me the way they did.

I watched Gregor Krumlich moving across the lawn. He saw Mom sitting there, and he must have thought how *right* he'd been. There had been a lot of money to make off Joan, and now there wasn't so much to make anymore. Her career, after leaving him, must have been reassuring to Gregor; it must have looked like a train wreck he avoided. A man like Gregor probably no longer saw people as individuals anymore; just as zones of emotion, of personal force, that either attracted or repelled him, opening into problems or ease. So that was why he avoided us.

I looked at Lars; he wasn't thinking about Mom or

me. He was hardly watching the fireworks. He was probably thinking about Gregor. And then he was probably and more immediately thinking about how soon the fireworks might be over, how soon he could get himself a drink. If he ran into Mom and me at all, it was just—we slowed down where he was trying to get to. Who knew where Lars's money came from, after all? It was hard enough, probably, being Lars Stevensen, without having to worry about any other people.

It wasn't hatred of us—it was just too hard, in this world, to have any feelings like sympathy. All these art people were fighting against money and time—the two great opponents down here on earth. There was Jack Atski; there was Neil; they had climbed up as far as you could in this world, they had scaled up to the heights. But they must have felt the great distance there was to fall beneath them, and they were like the cartoon animals in all the shows Jon and I had watched all those mornings, who could not look down because then they really *would* fall. And perhaps they were even waiting for Mom to be powerful again—if she was going to be—so they could indulge her society guiltlessly.

And I extended myself. Lying there, under the real stars, and under the man-made stars that kept sizzling up over our heads, I imagined Dad in California, in his workroom, pausing under his mountain of papers. It must have been seven o'clock there, the light just beginning to leak out from the long Los Angeles summer day.

I wondered if he could feel my mind exploring. I was looking at a firework over my head, so I imagined Dad standing up and walking to the window and watching an airplane glide slowly down over the Southland horizon.

I've never said what happened to him. His fourth year in Los Angeles he left advertising entirely. I don't know what prompted Dad. But I knew his jobs had become progressively less good in California. He had squandered his profession to get back at Mom. In New York, he had been a first vice-president; now, he was just a copywriter.

He started another book; it was as if the arts were a dangerous infection, and once touched you could not rest until you had made your mark in that world. He hadn't succeeded at fiction; this was nonfiction. He devoted himself to an endless examination of the economy, while Jane supported him. By the time I was sixteen, he worked at this book all day—worked, but never finished. It was frightening. On our drives home from the airport, once he had bundled me into the car, he would grow jolly with plans. His book would revive trade unionism. His book would pitch the Republicans from office. I tried to believe Dad. But I was old enough to see that the world didn't change much, and that if it *were* going to change, the change wouldn't come from an ex-advertiser in Westwood, California. He would

chuckle, to the other drivers, "Capitalist lackeys—are
you quaking in your boots? I'm after your asses!" Had
he stayed in New York, he would have been successful
and happy. Now, he had only his days, clipping newspapers and going over notes. Endless notes. Each year he
spent enlarged the debt of time he needed to recoup.
After three years, the book had to be giant; after six
years, huge. I almost felt sorry for Dad, when I imagined him facing that note pile every morning. That
burden of years was beyond what a human being could
support.

Dad had gotten what he wanted—and was it any
surprise, as I lay there beside Margaret, that I also
feared getting what I wanted? My mother had gotten
what she wanted, and somehow that had been the end
of our family. My father had gotten what he wanted,
and it led to his living isolated in California, with a
book he could never finish. I had gotten what I wanted,
too—I had gotten out of SoHo when I was a boy, and
that had played into my father's hands, and had brought
him and my mother low. Getting what you wanted was
dangerous. When you knew someone, you knew them
as a person who was thwarted: they are living in your
world half the time, and the other half of the time they
are living in the inaccessible reaches of their future life.
On those rare occasions when people *do* get what they
want, they become strangers—the versions of them-

selves they had waited to become all along. When they got what they wanted, they became someone you had never quite known.

So I imagined my father getting up from his desk, and walking to the window, and thinking about Mom and me. I wondered if he was happy; I wondered if he was frightened. For his present life was so much the result of his past choices, and I wondered if, standing there, watching the red airplane lights I'd given him to watch, he would have undone it all, gone back in time, not taken Jon and me away from Mom, not lobbied to move all of us to Vermont. I wondered if he would have liked to go back to the moment when everything started, to the front seat of our old Thunderbird, to have said to Mom: "No. We've already paid to go to Connecticut. I say, we're going." I wondered if he imagined the man he would have become, and if he regarded that lost Paul with some kind of longing.

A wet breeze came over the lawn and across the water and smelled like grass and pond. Margaret shivered. The women near us wrapped their arms more tightly round themselves and their men carefully changed position. Three or four men put their arms around the women by their sides, giving the women the benefit of their body heat. I did, too. "Don't get the idea I'm trying to break any rules," I said. "I thought you might be cold." "They're your rules, Richard," Maggy said—which was as close as she came to declaring the scary fact, which was that it was up to me. I smelled her hair, and her skin. I kissed the top of her head. What a thing, for another person to confide themselves into your care like that!

I tried Jon's mind, but I couldn't jimmy that lock. He was living in Berkeley, had taken six years to get through school, as if he didn't want to enter the world either, as if our family situation had yet to be resolved for him, too. I tried, but I couldn't get that lock open. I had left him there, and he was closed to me.

The display got more and more elaborate—until, for the last few minutes, there were ten or twenty rockets in the air at once, bursting and unfolding simultaneously. Everyone started cheering—the shouts came from all our throats—and the noises kept booming over us, making us duck our heads. The air smelled like sulfur.

In the jostle of leaving the fireworks, I saw Tom's dog; it was yapping at my feet, its wet teeth very white. A second later, Tom appeared, in the humorous role of man looking for pet. *"There's* Touchstone. Thank you, Richard, for finding him. Your mother tells me you're very considerate." "He found *me,*" I said. Tom ruffled the dog's neck. "Yes, well, he has a nose for the quality, doesn't he?" I could feel, in the tension, Margaret waiting to be introduced. I introduced her. "You work fast," Tom said—meaning that I had found a girl. "No, I'm Richard's *ex*-girlfriend," Margaret said. "Until further notice, no doubt," Tom said. He smiled at me, "Ah—you Freeleys lead such complicated romantic lives. I thought I had a lock on your mother, but she seems to have disappeared entirely. Watch out for them, Margaret. Just when you think you have a handle on them, they slip away."

"She is here, isn't she?" Margaret asked, after Tom had gone. "I mean, you didn't just come here on your own, did you?" There was music coming from one of the big rooms inside; modern music, the music we played in college.

"I should find her," I said.

"She can get along without you. She got along just fine for twenty-three years before you were born." I had the sense this was another prepared statement, because Margaret looked down before she said it. Then she looked carefully at my eyes, as if this was a thing she had long imagined saying and was curious to see my reaction to it.

"I did a pretty shitty job for her today, actually, as it was."

"You don't have to do *any* job for her except to be her son."

But I knew that she had done an extraordinary job for me, in this extraordinary world, as a mother, and this required an extraordinary effort on my part just to keep things nice and even. I didn't want to think of her as a star player surrounded by an incompetent minor cast. "I should find her," I said. "If we get separated, you have a place to stay, don't you? I think there are a lot of hotels around here—but they're probably booked, I mean with all the artists."

"Richard. You're doing it again. It's not your job to take care of everyone. That's not why we want you around. We want you around because we love you."

I was so plugged in, and this was such a compliment, that I looked hoping someone could have overheard it. I was loved! A Freeley was loved, by this rich and pretty woman! But this wasn't only about point totals; this was personal, and I had to stop responding in this impersonal way, of wanting to share my triumphs, of wanting everything as *proof* in some larger scheme. "I'll be right back," I said.

I found Mom by the water, where big puffy cattails were swarming in their own little agricultural cocktail party. When another breeze came up, these rattled crazily back and forth. Mom was talking to Oliver and Edith. She was speaking in her confident way, in the way she had once the initial tension of whether a person was going to accept her was gone. She was so *good* with people, if they would just allow her to get past that difficult initial part. Then the personal force that screwed up the light social stuff could come out, and prove masterful. It seemed a shame to come by and squelch it; but I was unnerved by the idea of her being so long without me. Edith saw me coming first, then Oliver. Then my mother, who looked in my direction last. "Hey, Rich!" she said. Her face was dazzled with social success; as if she were throwing her own fireworks display here.

Mom introduced me to them. Oliver's palm felt papery in mine. Sculptors' hands tended to be meaty and strong, from their steel work, but Oliver's was dainty. "Good lord, so this is your *son?* When I saw you together earlier, I thought: Hmm. Here's a woman of a certain age who has managed to come up with a very young and handsome escort. Bravo, Joan. I thought he was a student of yours."

Mom looked at me fondly. I shook Edith's hand. "Sorry about before," I told her.

"Sorry for what, exactly?" she asked. I shrugged. And in that way, our bathroom moment disappeared from human memory.

I said to Mom, "Margaret Weatherly is here." And then I felt I had to inform on her, and my voice got fast: "I didn't invite her, but she knew we'd be here, and she drove up."

"I know. I saw you together. I was happy for you. You looked *happy* with her."

"Did I?"

"We're talking about Richard's ex-girlfriend, a very nice and intelligent young woman. I'm always astonished, actually, by how young people date now. At that age, I would never have felt the freedom to follow a man somewhere if we'd broken up."

I couldn't tell if she meant this to be a good thing or a bad thing. "I was glad she came," I said. And then I didn't know if this was a betrayal or not, or who I was betraying.

"I could tell that. They do so many things differently than we did."

"You broke up and she came here to find you?" Oliver asked. "That's quite brave. She's quite a heroine." And I saw that we were using Margaret after all, that we'd found a way to incorporate her into our little scams. What a treat, a strange treat, to be talking about my romantic troubles with Oliver Thrush. That's the strange power of celebrities, that they make you so dizzy, that just by doing the normal things they take you up with them on a Ferris wheel and everything in your real life looks tumbly and more brightly colored. I looked at Oliver and tried to remember, Yes, I left her to help my mother get around creeps like you.

"Now, Richard, Edith is a painter. You saw her pictures today in the barn. Edith, you show—don't you—where?"

"That remains to be decided," Edith said, and looked at her husband. He nodded. And it made me happy again that even with her powerful husband this woman had the same troubles we did in the art world.

"Yes, well, Joan of all people knows how hard it can be to find the proper dealer," Oliver said. He looked over my shoulder, at the lodge, where the music was playing. "Well. I should return to my hostly duties, Joan. I've loved chatting. Thank you again for the loan of your car. And thank you for your slides, which I *am* excited to get a look at. We'll be seeing you in the ante meridian. The three of you, I trust—Richard, do bring that heroine of yours, to our place." The couple departed. Because they had not asked us to go back with them, Mom and I lingered by the pond for a moment. We watched the couple walk, their two small heads, and their feet squeaking on the grass. I waited until they were out of earshot.

Then I asked, "You brought your *slide sheet?*"

"Oh, Richard, don't be a coward. I came up here for business, and that's business. The idea isn't just to skulk around so nobody notices you. I don't think there's any terrific gain in that."

Training wheels. I was her training wheels. "No. Well, I'm proud of you. You swung a private audience with Oliver and Edith Thrush. That was brave."

"You always think I'm braver than I am. And that's not the only thing I swung. We now have an invite to the mystery party tomorrow morning. At Oliver's."

"How?" I was surprised at feeling my chest swing

open into gloominess. On some level, I realized, I had
been looking forward to our chastened drive home tomorrow. I was the only person who understood Mom's
talent and value; it was her and me against everyone.
Now that drive wasn't going to take place, and I might
not be the only person. I wondered if I could find some
flaw in her performance, some space that would justify
my constant presence to her. "You didn't just, ah, come
right out and *ask* him, did you?"

"Richard. You must think I'm very stupid. I think
you have this idea in your head of me as this consis-
tently brave and very stupid person. Oliver told me he'd
assumed we'd show up anyway. It's an all-artist brunch.
A reunion."

The music stopped. Then someone turned it up
much louder: a techno-pop song I had danced to at
Brown, with Margaret. I said, because here I truly *could*
help, "You're planning to dance?"

"Yes of course I am planning to dance. I didn't drive
up here just to go back to the Ramada Inn and fall
asleep while you soak up cable television."

"That's great. I want you to. But here, let me just
show you something first. Don't talk. Just listen for a
second. We'll hear the music better if we don't talk."
For I had an image of the last time I saw her dance.
Three years ago. I'd found an old David Bowie album
while I was cleaning up my room. I'd thrown it onto the

turntable, as a reasonable sweetener to this boring task. A moment later, Mom had come through the door— dancing. "Whoa!" she said, "this stuff is great. This stuff really *moves*." She danced, in her grubby painting clothes. The music probably meant something special to her, for these mid-seventies songs had been the sound-track of her success. But the dancing style was all wrong for now. She simply hadn't danced that much. Like her clothes—which I had tried to be helpful with—it told things about her that made her look bad.

"Dance with me, please," I said.

"The arms about you. The charms about you," she joked.

"Just for a second. You showed me how to dance at school. Let me dance with you."

"Richard," Mom said. "I'm touched." We stood there for a second. "Let me just get the beat."

When she started, it was all wrong. She had the music wrong, and she had the style wrong. For some reason, it intensely irritated me "No, no, no. Stop. Don't use so much energy in your *hips*." I put my hands there to steady them. "Just a little swing, back and forth. This way looks like somebody is shooting bullets at your feet."

"You don't have to overreact so much. It's not life or death."

"It's wrong," I said. "Just do like this." I showed her

how. After a minute, she began copying me. Her eyes
closed a little, and she smiled. She got it quickly, and
then we were on our way dancing out there, so that
anyone seeing us would never have guessed we were a
mother and son, just two people dancing. It was embarrassing to be in rhythm with her; it really *was* like sex,
dancing, I saw. My hips went out, hers went out. Mine
went in, hers did. I hoped she wasn't noticing, as I was.
It seemed intimate to see her eyes closed that way—the
face she might have worn during sex. She wasn't dancing with me as if I were her son, but as if I were any
man. It felt spooky, but it felt nice, also, to see how she
was picking this up so fast. This was the kind of thing I
could teach her. She had raised me to be her dance
coach. Mothers and sons had to stick together now; we
were the scouts for our parents, as they were the base
for us.

We danced by the pond. We swayed back and forth,
our hands sometimes brushing against each other. Need
I add she looked beautiful, in her skirt and her blouse,
with the cattails crowding by the shore to watch us. I
worked up a little light sweat, and she did too, from the
two of us being out there. The lights from the lodge
made a fire in the pond water, a long yellow reflection
separated into boxes, that had thrown itself over the
surface of the water like a glowing rug. We danced
there. I took her hand.

"OK, Richard. Do I pass? Am I set?" Her eyes were still closed.

I answered, "You're perfect."

As we walked to the lodge, I said, "Don't dance too much with Tom. And if you see Jake, don't dance with him at all."

"Jealous, Richard?" she laughed. She liked my behavior best when she was able to convert it into Freudian terms. I was tried and convicted along the lines of basic psychology.

"No, Mom. For strategy. Richard and Joan Freeley as *The Brazen Manipulators.*"

"Well, Richard, you try to have some fun too. This isn't just my thing, I hope."

I left her at the entrance to the lodge. Then I tried to find Margaret. She had gone. I wondered if she had seen my mother and me together—and if this had spooked her. Maybe she'd seen us and had ducked into her car and driven home, and I admired her for this choice, because there was so much more in that bond than there was likely to be with anyone else, with someone outside. I looked around the lawn, where I had last seen her. My sweater was gone from the ground. There was no one at the tables—just the crew cleaning up, and the cat I'd petted working over a barbecued thigh, chewing in the choking way cats have.

208

I looked inside. Herb Tingley was in one of the rooms, looking dead beat, like a Popeye who had unwisely taken the pledge against spinach. The Triangle students were sitting together in the living room, with their legs crossed, comparing impressions on how the day had gone, looking relieved and lightly drunk now that the weekend was over. Lars was by the bar. He slapped me on the shoulder and once again invited me to have our pinecone fight. Drunk, with problems of his own. It was sickening, though, how hungrily I reacted to his attention; I wanted a stepfather that badly. Margaret was nowhere to be found inside. I walked back outside. I walked around to the porch, where the dancing was. Through the screen I could see my mother dancing, with a young man I didn't recognize. Her own seventies moves were coming out through the thin layer of what I had taught her, but she looked good on the dance floor. She herself looked young: fifteen or sixteen, a woman I'd never gotten the chance to meet. I stood outside and watched. When it seemed I'd caught her eye I left. I didn't want her to be self-conscious.

I walked into Tom, sitting with his dog outside. "We're both out of luck," he said. "She's gone wild! crazy! mad! She's just dancing with everyone now." I was tired. I went onto the porch. There was Margaret, dancing with Jacob. The perfect combination: people rejected by the Freeleys. I tried to imagine their conversation, and could not; it seemed perfect and normal and horrible at once, as if we were all on a TV show, and they were shaking their heads while the laugh track knowingly sounded. Hiroshi was standing to one side, drinking a beer. I walked up to my mom.

"Richard," she said. "Are you cutting in?"

"You should dance," the guy said. "That's right. A mother and son dance."

"Why not?" my mother asked.

"I'm embarrassed," I said. "I'm tired and I'm ready to leave."

"Why? You danced perfectly well before, out by the pond. He taught me how to do this just now. He was very worried about my style, apparently."

People were crowded around. "You dance with your mother," Hiroshi said.

"That's right," Mal said. "The Freeleys are going to dance."

And they were all waiting, and Margaret was looking too. So we danced for another second, a pleasant curiosity. But the song was halfway finished, and when it was done I said, "I'm ready to go."

"I raised a stick-in-the-mud."

We talked with Margaret; we'd meet her in the morning. I couldn't imagine that I was supposed to sleep with her, that night. But Margaret seemed disappointed, leaving, and my mother seemed oddly quiet as we crunched out to our car, as if I had let her down, too. That I was too careful; she wanted everyone to be having a good time. She seemed disappointed by my lack of initiative. We got into the car. Jacob had spoken with her. He had seen her dancing with Tom, she said, and had come over, and she had stopped for a second and had a drink with him. He wanted to apologize, she thought. We drove. We drove past nighttime pines. The drive reminded me of all the drives we'd made, all the summer places we'd driven to. The calm nice feeling of nothing much at stake, except the mystery of a new route. The big fronds of the heavy pines. The road looking gray under our headlights. We reached a small empty highway, and paid a toll to cross a bridge.

Then we were at the Inn. My mother produced a Visa card, and gave it to the woman behind the counter. For all she knew, we were the sort of people who stayed in motels every day. Normal, nice people. The room was thrillingly and apologetically nice. We try to make these rooms as comfortable as your own home, the room said. Actually, it was *more* comfortable than our own home. In bed, I had a strange moment. We had two double beds. And though I felt weird dropping down to my T-shirt and underpants with my mother in the bathroom, I did it and slipped quickly under the covers. My mother was washing off her makeup. "I didn't know you were wearing any," I said. "That's the point," she said. "When you do it right, you can't tell." Then what was the point of wearing it? I wondered to myself. We were back in the locker room; our locker room lives.

I lay there and thought about Jacob; what a strange ending that would be to our saga, too. Jacob. If she married him, I would be free, and I could go off with Margaret to Washington, and she could go off to New Jersey to Jacob. I imagined her as his wife. The *settled-ness* of it. It was such a routine and mundane end to the ongoing open story of our lives. And I wanted to ruthlessly advise her to cut it out. Say, "Stay away from Jacob. The whole thing's not good enough for us." But we were both blissing on a good night, and my mother came out scrubbing her face with a towel and said, "I think it went well," and I said, "Yes," and then I watched her, vaguely, drop down to her underpants and T-shirt, and I thought I wouldn't try to end this after all. Because whatever my second thoughts, we were almost there.

In the morning, my mother wore the dress I'd hoped for. It was a tan cotton dress, with a Greek cut. This was the dress in which she delivered me to and picked me up from college. I told her once, after freshman year, how much I liked the dress, and then every time afterward when we were driving she made a point of wearing it. I don't think she knew why I liked the dress so much. She'd bought it the summer after I graduated from high school. We'd both been sitting restlessly in our tiny apartment, drugged by the New-York-in-August heat. My mother stood up abruptly and announced, "We have *got* to get out of here." We walked out onto a street that was like a twisted dream of summer. We took the subway to Penn Station, and walked down tunnels that smelled like dust and urine, urine with a lot of sour alcohol mixed in. We dropped deeper into this smell, as if we were searching down into a cave where the city itself lived, the great slothful disheveled animal that *was* the city. At the LIRR counter, Mom bought two tickets to Southampton. We

took an old train east, a train with red leather seats that
had cane backs. I got up and sat between the cars—the
conductors left the doors open, so a breeze would come
in, and I watched the yellow landscape turn beachier
and scrubbier, the trees and bushes flattening out under
the constant pressure of sunlight and salt. As we approached the water, the telephone poles beside the
tracks began to be covered by vines, by great beards of
vines, as if they had been left out here so long they had
turned into unshaven hermits. This was my father's
train, the train he'd taken all those weekends to meet
us. I looked into the car, and tried to imagine an army
of young fathers in dark suits, the anticipation, the eager boyish loneliness of young men being factored back
into families. But the train was empty: the conductor
sitting at the back counting tickets, and my mother with
her legs crossed, in the blue jeans she used for painting.

When we stepped off in Southampton, the air had a
sharp smell of salt water, like a great clean sheet that
had been left to hang dry over the same clothesline for
months. And though I'd had the eerie feeling someone
might be there to meet us, there was no one. Some
crickets were humming; seeing nobody was around they
were tuning up, turning this empty platform into a
daytime rehearsal of night. This was one of the August
afternoons when the moon shows up for work early. We
walked into town. My mom said, "I am *baking* in these

jeans." At a small boutique—the kind of place where I
licked my lips with anxiety, where the idea was not
bulk but price—my mother bought that tan cotton
dress. She paid for it in cash without protest. We walked
outside with her wearing it. "Richard," she said, "can
you—there's a tag in the collar." I bit it off. We threw
her jeans into a wastebasket by a big square piled with
cannonballs. The confidence of this gesture thrilled me;
it seemed a promise that she, like me, felt our situation
would surely improve. That it could be shaken off as
simply as that.

We walked beside the houses of the rich, shielded
from the road with dense shrubs. We walked under cool
shady tunnels of trees, which smelled of honeysuckle
and cut grass. Where bees did motiveless figure eights
in the air, as if to say, I may only be a bee, but I live in
Southampton. Then we walked down Dune Road, the
beach road. This was the road we had lived on, many
summers before. The bay was on one side, the ocean on
the other, and depending on which way the wind came
from, there was a rich, mucky fertile smell or the clean
salt and blue of the Atlantic. We walked onto the ocean
beach. My mother removed her shoes. Here were families that consisted solely of mothers—mothers who sat
reading thrillers and fashion magazines, their children
in the water. My mother led me up a sand dune, helping me with her hand, and we walked along a path I

recognized. We walked along red wooden fence posts tied with wire. A bird twitted. My mother reached down, plucked, then sucked on a beach plum. We stood above an old stone house, the house we'd rented one summer with Lars and Hiroshi, the house where Lars and I had had our famous pinecone fight. The house was empty. My mother tossed away the beach plum.

"Lars owns it now," she said.

I knew this. We watched for Lars's fat figure to emerge from one of the porch doors. We waited for him to see us standing on the dunes above our old property and wave us down for a drink. That was the last element missing from our trip; the element of someone *welcoming* us. For no one had spoken to us since we stepped onto the platform, and we had been moving as ghosts, drifting invisibly over the landscape. Since we were ghosts, there suddenly seemed to me no reason why we couldn't simply walk into the house; we had entered a place where time was porous, where it could open smoothly back into the past, where you could beat your way down the curtain of the present to find the rent in the curtain through which one could walk backward. Why couldn't we walk down the rest of the path and go back through our old door, and my mother would be thirty-two again, and I would be eight, and Jon would be there too, ten years old, smiling, his hair extra blond from a summer of sun? It seemed that time

was offering us to take this risk, to dream ourselves
backward. Mom watched the house with a look of hunger and energetic ambition, as if the whole of the art
world were going on inside its walls. She stared—and
then she turned around and walked back toward the
ocean. My mother walked into the water and let the
surf cool her toes.

We walked back to town. She bought me a bag of
Doritos and a smoked-turkey sandwich, and I sat on the
platform crunching while she sipped a diet cola. In her
new dress, she looked beautiful and mysterious and
poised and elegant. The dress seemed an emblem that
she would never give up, that she would find that rent
in the curtain and we would enter it together—and
then she wouldn't need me, and I would lose her again,
into the circles and circles of the art world. That would
be my reward; it chilled my heart. But that dress was an
emblem that we would walk back into our old life as
surely as we had stepped onto trains and beaches, and
onto sandy paths that had carried us in one afternoon
from our tiny, hot apartment to this cool dark station
that was singing with crickets.

A s we walked to the parking lot, the sun pressed
through the fabric of this dress and I could see that
underneath she wore a red one-piece swimsuit. It was

touching, that at the start of what promised to be a difficult morning, her main desire was that she get a chance to swim in the water of the Mashomack pond.

She opened the door of our Nissan and turned to me. "Do you want to take a shot at driving?"

"Really?" I asked.

"What the hell. I know you've been practicing the last few years. When I was your age, I could drive. When *he* was your age, your father was on his second car." My father's upbringing—its suburban cushiness— was the way she justified any small extravagance toward me. My mother was trying, on her small salary of one, to give me the sweet entrance to the world my father's parents had provided him, so that I might believe it was as welcoming as he had believed. She said, "Why not? I trust you."

I took the keys from her, and she sat down confidently in the passenger seat. I did a run-through on the car—pedals, the stick thing that shifted the gears, the mirrors that had to be adjusted for my height—all the time trying to ignore my erection. I would have made a good witness at a congressional investigation on the connections between violence and sex. The first few times I drove, I always had to fight down this pokey little awakening, at the thought that a heavy and dangerous machine had been entrusted to me. All that power; I suppose my brain—the unpredictable part of it that was responsible for sexual response—associated power with romance.

I made some jerky stops and starts as we pulled out of the lot. My mother ignored my mistakes; she was that kind of mother. We turned out of the lot and onto the highway, and then the wheels rolled smoothly over gray road. It made me feel suave and exhilarated; like drinking, and talking to accredited adults, it made me feel that the motions of being a grown-up were not complex, and that their mastery would come with a simple introduction to them. To show off my cool, I turned on the radio and fiddled the dial for a decent station. My erection, at this scent of danger—maybe it was the sense of risk that set off that little part of my brain—made a fleeting comeback. As I was fiddling, we crept up right behind a slow-moving van, and I braked quickly, and our heads rattled back and forth. This was too much for even my mother to ignore.

"Maybe you should just concentrate more on the road," she said.

At the lodge we parked and my mother held out her hands for the keys. "That was a very nice job, Richard," she said. "I knew you were a good driver."

"I can hold the keys. Maybe I can drive again later."

She waggled her fingers. "We can see," she said.

There was no way of knowing that this would be our last morning together. There was only the

Mashomack, empty and recuperating from the evening's party. There were glasses everywhere, and ashtrays full of the corpses of cigarettes, and cushions and
pillows spread out all over the floor, where people had
sat on them. The house itself was sprawling. The house
itself had gone a little too far, as if it had gotten a little
drunk and now had a hangover. We went outside. We
passed by a mirror, and our reflections astonished me—
my mother looked entirely glamorous and I looked, in
my white oxford and tan shorts, cloddish and unsophis-
ticated, as if I were a cousin of hers who had just taken
the train up from Nebraska to be her escort for the day.
Under the tent, the crew was folding away the evening's
tables. They had set out some iron lawn furniture by the
pond, and Margaret was there, waiting for us as we
arranged. My love for her made my heart trill; it was
like a bell tolling very softly and delicately within my
chest. She stood up quickly. She had overdressed, and
had again worn makeup. The effect was not so successful as it had been the night before.

My mother's moods were unpredictable. Nine hours
ago, she had seemed disappointed that I had not taken
Margaret home, that I had not shown that much inde-
pendence of spirit, as though it reflected ill on *her* spirit.
Now, she seemed disappointed that Margaret was going
to be with us, and whispered to me from the side of her
mouth.

"There's your friend," she said. And then she waved

expansively in the voice of hers I knew to be fake. *"Hey, Margaret."*

"Just remember," she said, side-of-mouth again. "It's not my responsibility to entertain this woman. She's a friend of yours, and I'm happy to have her along . . ." Margaret was walking toward us, and my apprehension that she would soon hear Mom's words was mounting. I nodded, adding neutral "uh-huhs" to what my mother said. I faked a smile, as if Mom were giving me pleasant information about the weather. ". . . but this is a business morning for me and I don't want to have anyone cramping my style. It's too important. You can social-climb with the Connecticut gentry on your own time."

Was I social-climbing—it was hard not to look in my mother's utterances for truth, since she knew me better than anyone, and was as alive to momentary alternations in my behavior (the steps away from my "true self" with which the world is so temptingly full) as I was to those in her.

"Good morning, Mrs. Freeley," Margaret said.

"Good morning, Margaret," Mom said. If she had been feeling especially warm, she would have added, "Call me Joan," which she didn't.

Margaret looked at us. "I've overdressed," she said, and she took a tissue out of her purse—the beautiful black leather handbag, much nicer than any my mother owned—and began wiping off her lipstick. Her parents had trained her to try to match each occasion—and how different, after all, was the training required for a suburban daughter than the training I'd picked up in the art world? I was still carrying on a mental argument with myself over Mom's remark about the Connecticut gentry. "There," Maggy said. "Do I have it? Does this look all right, Richard?"

My assumption of such husbandly duties in front of my mother was unnerving. Her posture stiffened, and she looked lightly away, to let me do what was necessary in private. I told Margaret that she looked fine. "You sure?" She had heard a strange note in my voice. "I'm not a veteran of these sorts of things like you two. You're just old soldiers up here!"

She was trying to catch the family tone—but it was mixed in with WASP bonhomie, the strange tendency of these ancient pioneers to our shores to try to sell one on the excitement and achievements of one's own life. Still advertising America: You immigrants are doing a great, a bang-up job here! Our hats are off to you! We stood there together, the three of us, and I didn't know who to stand closer to, or who to play to. Should I play to Margaret or to my mother? I said, "Should we get going, Mom?"

"Do we know that woman?" my mother asked. She nodded her chin at a woman sitting at the far table—I knew Mom so well I knew the vocabulary of her chin—

a tall woman reading the Sunday *Times*. We walked toward her and she turned out to be Paula Bayer's sister.

She looked at us with plain relief—a relief I didn't immediately understand. *"Hi,"* she said. "I'm sorry, I'm bad with names, but didn't we *meet* yesterday—"

"Joan Freeley," Mom said.

"That's right. Joan. You're a painter, Hiroshi said. Well, Joan—I've been waiting here for three quarters of an *hour*. Hiroshi was supposed to come pick me up, but I think he's abandoned me. Are you . . . ?"

"Yes, we're going to Oliver's. But we don't have the directions—"

"I know Oliver's place," Paula Bayer's sister said. So the deal was struck, and the three of us ended up driving the polo player's sister to Thrush Manor. She and Margaret climbed into the back of our little Nissan, and I gloried in the fact that we now had a full house. She asked if we minded if she smoked, and though Margaret hated the smell of cigarettes—when I was with her, I smoked only outdoors, and had become a devotee of Certs and other breath-killing candies—she joined Mom and me in saying "Not at all." She was learning to subvert her own personal wishes to social goals, which meant she was joining the art world too. I had a sudden panic, that instead of helping me leap out of my mother's life, Margaret was going to join it, and Mom would have two helpers instead of one, a horrible irony.

Paula Bayer's sister cracked her window and then conscientiously exhaled only through the tiny slit. So as not to make any extreme demands on our conversational skills this early in the morning, she acted as though this little bit of business (smoking, exhaling) consumed the bulk of her attention. She didn't notice my mother's fast, reckless driving. I loved that Mom was always, as a young person is, in a rush to get on with it, to barrel ahead to the next thing.

We drove into the morning, which was chilly and had a kind of all-over light. Trees were having their tree conventions all along the side of the road, and birds were having their bird conventions in the trees, and we were off to our artists' convention. My mother spoke, and Paula Bayer's sister issued polite directions of where to turn, and how long to expect to enjoy a straightaway before the *next* turn.

I felt Margaret playing with my hair with her hand, reaching her tiny fingers into the scruff at the tip of my neck and kind of rubbing back and forth. I leaned my head against the seat rest, to get more of her fingers and so that my mother would be less likely to see. We still hadn't had our conversation, Maggy and me. Paula Bayer's sister asked a question or two about my mother's exhibition record, about her teaching, and I froze up, hoping she wouldn't answer negatively. We seemed to strike such a positive and upbeat note—the two of us, and then Margaret in her expensive clothes—that the report Paula Bayer's sister was likely to carry to anyone she talked to would also be positive. There was no reason to disabuse her of her notions about us. Mom answered carefully and properly, but this meant their conversation didn't exactly take off. It faltered, fell to earth, died, though Paula Bayer's sister and my mother both made attempts to rouse it. We drove. And then Margaret started talking with Paula Bayer's sister about her own life—and Margaret's social skills came into play. She knew how to talk to anyone, how to keep it light, and how—with the names of various restaurants and towns thrown in like footnotes to verify the high glossy truth—to suggest that she was a part of the same world. Margaret kept up this blather with Paula Bayer's sister in the backseat, and Mom turned to me and frowned her lower lip and raised her eyebrows playfully. Hm! I had to laugh back. Margaret was turning out to be a powerful ally, another plus for us, and when she asked, "Mrs. Freeley, it *is* OK for me to come to this brunch, isn't it? I don't want to horn in if I wasn't invited," Mom answered fully and charmingly.

"No, Margaret, in fact Oliver specifically asked Richard to bring you. You wouldn't want to miss this anyway: Oliver is famous for his parties. And please, don't call me Mrs. Freeley. Call me Joan."

"OK," Margaret said, and she squeezed those hairs on the back of my head, knowing she'd received a little bonus. Which meant she hadn't missed it before.

"One more right turn here, Joan," Paula Bayer's sister said. And then we were in sight of Thrush Manor.

Oliver's house rested on top of a hill. We could make out the red triangle of barn roof, freshly painted, standing out against the blue of the sky. We climbed a serpentine roadway. On top of his mailbox, there was a big wooden letter *T* with the letters for "Thrush" inside. This suggested a kind of self-promoting egotism that I would have thought was outside the cravings of an artist as successful as Oliver, since those needs were met—for free and without effort—by magazines and newspapers. But perhaps the hunger had to be very great, to come to the position where other people would fulfill it for you. We glided up the road. On our sides were concrete pedestals with old Oliver Thrush sculptures. They were bronze, and had been cured rust-red by the seasons. It was like a safari park of art. As we came around the first turn, Mom exclaimed excitedly, tapping my hand to get my attention, "These are all Oliver's sculptures from the early sixties, Richard, when he was still coming to terms with David Smith. Wow, he's just laid everything out! What a pleasure this must be for him." And it made me sad, that once again power and money were allowing people to do things my mother might have liked to do. It was so much more official than Mom's Joan Freeley Museum, from which she would call to ask my opinion of her work, as various pictures matured and ripened under her gaze.

We made another turn, and here were Oliver's sculptures from the seventies, a little more personal, the early influences shaken off. Then we were into the eighties work, the work Oliver is best known for, huge bronzes that looked as if they had been crumpled by a giant's hand, a hand far meatier than Oliver's own. Each sculpture had the year of its completion set down underneath it in the concrete. Where the most recent works should have been there was nothing. There were just empty concrete pedestals. This suggested the future was still waiting to be created in Oliver's workshop. Paula Bayer's sister, at the cessation of conversation, had lit another cigarette, and was leaning back in her chair, contentedly puffing: she had been here before, and didn't have to see.

We parked; I gave Margaret a hand out of the backseat. We stood there. "Thank you for driving me," Paula Bayer's sister said, squaring her shoulders and fixing her hair, in anticipation of brunch.

"It was our pleasure," I said. "Thank you for the directions." I wasn't going to let her get away so quickly, without anyone else having *seen* us drive her. Whatever social benefit Hiroshi had gained from driving her, I wanted us to derive too. "Let's go," I said.

Then I saw an odd thing, the first of many odd sights that morning. Frosty and Lars were standing together. There was no anger in either man, in the space between them. They looked simply like what they were:

two older men who had once shared student days together, and now were comparing their individual passages through the world. They looked also like twins,
with their jeans going faded in the same places, and
T-shirts, though Lars's was gray and Frosty's was green.
It was as though for the first time Frosty was appreciat-
ing the joke Lars had played on him, and Lars was
permitting himself gratitude for the favor of style the
older man had bestowed. For after all, if Frosty had
been the force behind Lars's early work, Lars had himself converted that force into something all his own.
Frosty pounded Lars happily on the back, and Lars
slipped his hands cheerfully into his jeans pockets.

We walked away from the cars and toward the
brunch; we could hear talking, that peculiar thrum of
many people socializing without discord, the sound of
the river of warm words we were hoping to jump into.
There were three picnic tables in front of Oliver's barn,
and the artists occupied them. There were no collectors
left; the weekend had been a kind of shaking out, a
winnowing down. Everyone had been at Triangle, then
only artists and collectors had been at the lodge, and
now it was only artists here, and we were among them.
God, *everyone* was here—if I had been dreaming the art
world, if I'd been dreaming my life in the art world, this
would have been the dream. And we were here too; if
we'd made it, we were among the survivors; there were
immense points to be collected for showing up. Leonard

Chichikov spotted us, and waved. The other artists looked up expectantly. There was no hint of resistance toward us that I could sense, no worry that we didn't belong here. People *wanted* to talk to us, for having made it here meant, in a sense, that you had weathered the art world. I stopped. The polo player's sister really did want to get to brunch. She said, "Thanks again," and I could tell everyone could see us from here. We had what we wanted; we let her go. Mom turned to me.

"Pardon us for a second," Mom said to Margaret. "We have to strategize."

"Huh. Go right ahead," Margaret said. "I know you guys like to do planning sessions before openings."

"You do, huh?" Mom asked, and looked at me. "Well, this is something Richard grew up with, and I'm sure it's had its advantages as well as its disadvantages."

"I didn't describe them as strategy sessions," I said. I still didn't know who to play to. And Margaret stepped a little back and Mom turned to me. "OK," she said. "How do I look?" I told her she looked fine. "Who do I talk to first? Should I talk to O'Donnell if he's here? Should I talk to Gregor?" I said, "Be yourself. Talk to whoever you want." "Really?" "Yeah, sure. Talk to anybody you like. Anyone you talk to, it will be an honor for them." My mother frowned. "You're just saying that because you want to spend the morning with your girlfriend, which is, by the way, perfectly understandable." "No—she's my ex-girlfriend, and I do want to spend the morning with her, but I say go with your instincts. You've done great so far. And I didn't do so great yesterday." "Yes, that wasn't the high point of my life in the art world. But you're sure I'm ready for this?" I laughed. "You're great," I said. "Just talk to whomever."

And Lara Kilmer had gotten up from the table and was walking toward us with a little smile. She was allowing her eyes to see us, and even her shoes seemed to be smiling. This was her decision to be friendly in public. "Joan, we didn't get a chance to talk yesterday, but I was really curious to get your impressions of the show. Sorry, I just had my head screwed on backwards, there was so much to *do,* so many people to talk to. I mean, I just went *Ga!*" And she flung her hands wide around her temples to suggest sensory overload. She and my mom started to talk. And then Celia Kapplestein appeared.

Her glasses hung by a beaded chain around her neck, and she was wearing tan slacks and boots and a man's blouse with an ascot—as if the only imaginable model for mature female success was Katharine Hepburn. I wondered how she felt, seeing Mom. For Mom had once been a great competitor of hers, a loathed competitor, and here Mom was a decade and a half later with no gallery and no shows, and two young guests, and Celia had quite clearly won. Celia had won just by seeing—what she couldn't have missed—how pleased Mom was to have her attention. Celia spoke with a military, geometric precision. Each statement led directly and without fumble toward the next—this was quite different from the achieved, moody ephemeralness of her paintings. There was no way to slip away from where Celia wanted to take you. "Joan! Why, what a long time it's been since I saw you in the flesh. You look *good*. I was afraid I wouldn't get a chance to visit with you this weekend at all."

It was strange seeing her outdoors; her power existed in artificially lit rooms, in small spaces with track lights and money changing hands above the hush of a church. The sunlight didn't show her any deference. "I wouldn't have let that happen, Celia," Mom said.

I interposed myself, and tried to put on my best manners, and shook her hand. I could feel the force behind Celia—or rather, it was a force I brought myself, from knowing who Celia was. You knew she was famous, and registered what a pleasure it was to make her acquaintance. This was how celebrities took the measure of their own power, by seeing what it wrought in you. "Hello Celia," I said. "It's been a long time."

"Yes it has. I can never remember which of you I saw last—whether it's you or your brother. I used to think how charming it was, that Joan brought you to all the openings." Talking of this let Celia think of my mother as less of a painter—for Celia's paintings had clearly been the great maternal passion of her life. It made Mom seem less serious; but on the other hand, children were something Celia would never have now. There were some things Mom knew that she could never know. "You know, Richard," Celia began. "You have a very good, and brave, mother."

Such a cutting and blameless insult. This was all she could tell me. I nodded. And Margaret—violating one of her principles, which was that you didn't speak until you were introduced, as if the world were one great polite variety stage and you didn't exist until the host had waved his hand in your direction—Margaret spoke up. "She's a very good *painter*, too."

"Yes she is," Celia said. And then Margaret and I excused ourselves to get to the food, leaving the three of them chatting—Lara, my mother, and Celia.

"You didn't have to say that," I told Margaret. That had been one of my mother's early mistakes, wanting to clarify too much.

"I didn't know if she knew who your mother was. I wanted to tell her."

"That was Celia Kapplestein. She knows who my mother is." I realized there was some pride in what I said, which confused me.

"I don't think of your mom only as a mother. But I've violated your rule again." This was spillover from the discussion we were going to have. We walked toward the tables—Gregor was coming up from the parking lot, and I saw him, in his calm way, taking the measure of the morning, seeing who was where and plotting his course. His eyes fell on the little group of women at the edge of the tables and stopped. This seemed to interest him. My mom—about whom he had mixed feelings—and Celia Kapplestein and Lara Kilmer, about whom his feelings were unmixed. We walked past the tables. I felt a hand on my arm. Leonard Chichikov had reached out to stop me.

"Richard," he said. "What's going on over there?"

"With my mother?"

"Some kind of girls' night out? A hen party?" He seemed wounded; he hated any group he had been left out of. He was addressing me here with a man-to-man loyalty, thinking that this would be more powerful than my loyalty to my mother. Leonard—despite his star position—must have felt his place as so tenuous that he imagined any group was speaking negatively about him. The danger of being aggressive is that you can finally only assume that the rest of the world plays by your rules.

"I think they're just catching up. Celia and my mom are friends."

Leonard still hadn't released me. "Look at them," he said. We looked. "They're plotting."

We went into the barn. Brunch was a much better menu than dinner—it made me feel like a rube, for having liked the dinner so much. That had seemed

exciting to me; now I saw it was just a meat-and-pota-
toes kind of thing, the kind of stuff you would serve to a
big group. This was better. There were halved Cren-
shaw melons, of a pink color disturbingly like human
skin. There was prosciutto. There were a number of
quiches, and slips of bacon slept in the yellow dough
like eels in groves of seaweed. In the corner of the barn
was a staircase, going upstairs to Oliver's workroom.
Edith came through the door looking a trifle nervous,
saw me, chose not to talk, and walked downstairs and
outside. Who cared? Margaret poured herself a cup of
coffee, then loaded her plate with muffins and croissant.
There was a plate of tiny-sized pastries, with blueberry
and cherry and raspberry tops, and I popped a cherry
one into my mouth, and greedily chewed. I filled my
plate as well. There were bagels and lox and champagne
and a kind of Boursin spread. It was all so lavish—so
convincing—that it seemed beyond the needs of the
party outside.

There was no place to eat but the tables. Margaret
and I walked back and sat down together. I felt Margaret's hip pressing against mine—the little extra bit of
heft her vegetarianism made necessary—and on my
other side I felt a promiscuous procession of hips. First
Neil Hollander, who had come, no doubt, hoping to be
photographed for that future biography: "In the late
eighties, Neil attended parties. Here, in a picture taken
in 1987, we see him at a table at Oliver Thrush's vaca-

tion home. (The young man at right is unidentified.)"
Then Herb Tingley, who absently took a bagel from my
plate. Finally, at one point, my mother—hips I knew.
She patted my back in hello, and she was talking in a
loud, confident way to someone else at the table. Then
Gregor took a seat beside her, and she spoke to him, and
I tried to ignore what Mom was saying. I made myself
ignore it. Her voice had dropped down to a rumbly,
confidential register. But she said, and this I did hear,
"You took a chance on me twenty years ago. Why not
now?" And I waited a few seconds, so it wouldn't seem
that the remark had driven me away, and then I got up
with my plate and left. Margaret followed me.

We ditched our plates in the barn and took champagne glasses and walked outside, down the hill, toward
Oliver's sculpture. First the empty pedestals, the ones
that would hold the future, which felt odd to me. Then
the ones from the early part of the decade. We were
waiting to have our argument, but neither of us wanted
to start it, so we looked at these beaten red objects and
felt the sun on our heads. I reached out and patted the
top of Margaret's black hair; I was surprised. It was
actually *hot*, from the sun, and there was her brain in
there too. I wanted this over with; I was so full of
feeling for her I wanted to put whatever was in the
conversation behind us so we could see where we'd go
next. I said, "You haven't really told me why you came
up," to launch our conversation.

"You know why."

"I'd like you to tell me."

"We couldn't just *stop* things in the middle like that. We've been together for a very long time. I kept worrying for months if it was some fight of ours that had made you do this, but I couldn't think of anything. There was my birthday, of course—"

"—that was horrible," I said.

"—which was horrible. But it seemed, and you can correct me if I'm wrong, that it was my part to be angry about that, and not yours. Wasn't it? So it couldn't be that. And I thought about it for a long time and would you like to hear what I came up with?"

"Yes."

"What I came up with is that I decided it couldn't be *anything* that had to do with either of us two."

It made her seem brave and misguided at once, to think you could mount an argument about emotions. Certainly things looked accurate listed that way—but feelings could change on a dime, without explanation, and to try to reason around them seemed wrong-headed, as if a very strong argument could convince the heart to produce feelings of love. The heart wasn't as easily per-suaded as that—it required wild proofs, sudden displays of insight, not solid and steady calculation. The fact that I still loved her had nothing to do with this. And in the part of my heart that wasn't feeling *that* for her, there was this sympathy that she understood love so little. But this sympathy graded into a kind of love, too. "No," I said.

"So then I tried to think of what *else*. Could be driving you. I didn't think it was another woman—not in the sense of what you normally mean by another woman. That's right, isn't it?" I nodded. "So I tried to think of what else was in your life, and I *did* think of another woman. Would you like to know who it was? I thought it had to do with your mother."

I didn't say anything. I had the stupid and desperate urge to change the subject—in the most laughably obvious way, to point out a sculpture, or the beauty of the day, or to ask if she was hot. I put my hand back on her hair. "God," I said. "You must be *baking*. Black really *does* retain heat. For all the times my mother has talked about color, I never really listened. But she did say that." Then I realized how stupid and taunting a change that was, since it brought us right back to where we'd been.

"I thought it had to do with your mother," she said again. "Don't interrupt, because this made a lot of sense when I've been thinking about it, and I had a very long thing I wanted to say. I can almost picture the way it was supposed to come out. But now that I'm saying it, it sounds like it's all over the place."

"No."

"And I know it sounds dumb, because I know you can't talk someone into loving you if they don't love you anymore. So I'm saying all this with the assumption that you still have certain feelings for me." She stopped and looked at me. "You do, don't you?"

I waited a moment, then said, "Yes."

"And you know I have certain feelings for you, or I wouldn't be here. Don't interrupt, because this is very difficult to just come right out and *say*—"

"Look," I said. "Can't the conversation stop here? I mean, I've said I loved you, and you love me, and I know I've been a little stingy about showing you that, but we have this established again, and so this doesn't have to go on anymore."

"Pardon me, I think it *does* have to go on, a little longer. There are some things I think you should hear, from *some*body, because I don't think anyone is saying them to you. I know you lied to me about how long you lived in your apartment; all those things. You think I don't *notice*. Your mother is a very capable and accomplished woman. I *like* her, and I've always hoped she liked me. So I don't think it's anything she said to you about me. But I think you feel *responsible* for her, in a very strange way. I think you think she needs you, and she doesn't. She doesn't need you."

We were alone beside the sculptures, and crickets were once again using the empty stage to practice up for their evening recital. You couldn't see them, just hear them. They were camera-shy. "I love how much you love her. I think it's admirable. But I think you don't have to be responsible for her. She's the parent, and you're the child. Not the reverse. I don't think she wants it to be the reverse either. I don't think any person would like that."

"You've been talking to her about this a lot, I take it."

"No. But I'm a woman. I've been someone's child. I hope someday to be somebody's mother. And I can tell you that this isn't what she wants you to feel. I think you have the idea that you can *rescue* her somehow, and you're very intelligent and capable and I can see how you could have that misconception. I remember that this is what I wanted to say. But she doesn't need you to rescue her. She needs you to take care of yourself. I'm worried about you." But I *could* rescue her.

"You're worried about *me?*"

"Yes. What's going to happen to you in the fall? I know you haven't thought about it. There's a job you could take, a job I know you would love. You haven't taken it. You haven't made *any* plans at all. You can't keep just helping out your mom, going to openings with her and parties with her and looking at her paintings. That's not a job description. I'm worried about what's going to happen to *you,* and I'm sure your mother is also."

There was the pleasure that another person had seen me so well—it shouldn't be as exciting as it invariably is that someone has watched you closely. It was flattering, in a way, that she had understood me so clearly. And then there was something else—these were things she *shouldn't* have seen. These were embarrassing things, the things I thought I'd hidden from her for the years we'd been together. The notion that she had seen them all was bewildering. She'd been in that room with me the whole time. I had tried to close off and lock the doors I didn't want her to open, and just show her the beautiful parts of the house; the parts with flowers in them and curtains. But she had snuck into those other rooms, where sheets were thrown over the furniture and the wallpaper was peeling. I could have just laughed with Maggy, and said she was right. But that would have meant stepping away from the whole project, the eight years I'd put in trying to steer my mother. Oh yes, I was wrong, and my mom was wrong, we were on the wrong track.

"This isn't my business. It wouldn't be—except that, as I said before, I think it's having an effect on my life, not just on yours. And it's affecting your life, and I care about you. But she doesn't *need* you. If there really isn't any room in your life for another person, then that's fine. But you should *tell* another person that. In fact, you shouldn't become *involved* with another person, let them develop feelings and ideas and attachments about you, if deep down you know there isn't any room for them. That's unfair. Let me finish, because I want to make sure I say everything I wanted to say. I

think that I would feel very bad, if nothing else happened between us—and you know, I would feel awful
about that—if I didn't get out everything I meant to
say. But I think you've latched on to this idea that you
have to save your mother, and you *don't* have to, and
you can't."

It felt horrible to listen to. I wanted to end the
conversation. The way you can tell if you are betraying
someone is simple. If you're in a conversation with
someone about somebody else, a person who's absent,
and you imagine them listening in, and you can tell
they wouldn't like what you are saying, then you can be
sure you are selling them out. I wanted to leave the
conversation, and it hurt me that I could think of no
better exit than the old mediocre trick of turning Margaret's words against her. To teach her that to speak
fully is to make the mistake of crafting weapons that
can furnish and outfit another. But she'd hurt me. What
did she know about my life, and who I was, this late
arrival to the scene, this gentrifier? She'd said, "What a
nice neighborhood this Richard Freeley is; I think I'll
live here, spruce up the place, put some nice shutters in
the windows." What did she know about my past, or
anything about me, the history of me? I said, "I think
you're right, that it's probably none of your business."
And I walked off, with the taste of that mediocre comeback in my mouth. She had taken us too far, and
pushed, and the same thing had happened. History re-

peats itself because the same figures always add up to
the same result. My mother and I could grow old and
odd together.

I walked up the slope of the hill, past the sculptures.
Maggy stayed there. We'd have to drive her back to her
own car, at the lodge—but she was independent-
minded, and maybe she would call a cab. I was dizzy; I'd
had her, I'd lost her again. In front of the barn, Oliver
Thrush was talking to Gregor—his hand pressing
Gregor's lower back, in a fond way. Gregor at least had
this man, and Celia, and Darryl Bayer. That kind of
casual warmth between men surprised me, as did
Gregor's nods. He didn't look shaky. But he was clearly
in some kind of jeopardy, his head a little less high. I
decided not to walk past them. I walked around to the
back of the barn—the party's backstage. The same kids
from the Mashomack last night were working here.
Hosing down dishes, chopping open melons, chunking
champagne bottles and soda cans in a big empty beer
keg filled with ice. Because I had been rude, it was
somehow necessary to me—for earthly compensation—
to be perfectly sociable to someone else. The girl who
had lit the candles yesterday. She glided over, and told
me, "I'm sorry, this area is for employees only."

"Oh—I'm sorry. I was just taking a look around. It's
a lovely property." My voice sounded froggy to me,
from the awful leadenness of having said goodbye to
Margaret again.

"Isn't it? It's a joy to be out of New York. Are you from there?" She had dropped the officiousness; now we were just two young people. I nodded. "I work as a caterer summers, in the city. Oliver hired me for the weekend. He's a friend of my folks. Most of this stuff is from New York. You know Zabar's?" I nodded—and the brunch seemed another ruse, because this was food Mom and I could have bought ourselves, ten blocks from our home. "You go in there and always buy a little *something*, and look around and think about all the other great food? Well, Oliver gave us this *huge* list. It was fantasy shopping. He said, Just buy the most expensive of everything. I had to ride in the back of the van to make sure none of the food spilled. That Saw Mill Parkway is really twisty."

"I know," I said. It brought up something. "Do you have any idea why Oliver's gone to all this trouble?"

"I think that somebody is coming up. That's who the brunch is for. A dealer arrived from New York yesterday. We were supposed to pick him up, but I was off with the van in Poughkeepsie, buying champagne. Frederic something."

It was Freddy Beaumont, obviously. I thanked her and walked around to the front of the barn. So Oliver Thrush was going to leave Gregor too. I thought of Oliver, standing happily next to Gregor—with his hand so fondly on his back—and all the time secretly plotting to be rid of him. It was as I had once told my mother:

You could not be too careful among people who lived and died, who earned their livings, socially. They were dangerous. What other people did haphazardly, without premeditation, for them was very icy and precise. This was the sort of thing my mother needed me for. Margaret was wrong about that. I walked back to the front of the barn. Oliver and Gregor were gone; I walked inside. The door at the top of the stairs was still closed. But I was curious to see what Oliver's studio looked like, before a showing to a dealer. Maybe I could pick up some pointers for Mom. And I didn't want to see Margaret again, because there was the risk that I would run to embrace her, and chuck away the folly of the life that had been before she arrived; I could hide in Oliver's workroom. And there wasn't exactly any *sign* saying the upstairs was off limits.

It was the same mistake I'd made yesterday. Surmounting a little flutter in my stomach, I walked quickly up the stairs and put my hand on the doorknob. It felt cool to my touch. The door itself was light, like the one Hiroshi had made for my mother's bedroom, in our old loft. I swung it open—would Gregor be inside, with another drink and Ernest Steinman's book? Frederic? my mother, as I had once seen her, sleeping in Jake Boyden's arms—and there was no one in the room at all.

I had seen the sculptors' studios yesterday, and I have been around sculptors all my life. Jacob was a

sculptor. So I knew what a sculptor's studio was supposed to look like. It was supposed to look butch, like
the engine room of a ship. But there were no acetylene
torches here, no goggles, no gloves, no apron, and no
metal—there was no evidence that it was a sculptor's
studio at all. Sculptors' studios have that *citrusy* smell,
of metal waiting in its unformed state. Not there either.
Instead, there was a clean floor, and a wheeled table
with some oil paints on it against the wall, and lots of
brushes. It wasn't Oliver's studio at all; it was *Edith*'s.

At this point, if Oliver had asked me, "What did
you go upstairs for?" it would have been possible to
answer. I looked behind me, downstairs, at the food.
There was far too much. I closed the door behind me—
and it was only now that I entered the territory of the
wrong, that I had passed on into realms that couldn't be
lightly explained. My beastly penis, at this fresh scent of
risk, began stretching and rousing itself. There were two
dimmer switches on the wall. I pushed up the first. The
ceiling fan, to the left of the skylight, began to slowly
revolve. I slid up the other, and the track lights dawned,
going from pale to very bright, like the stars rising for
the evening.

The studio was so *neat* it was hard to imagine work
being done here. It seemed merely to await visitors.
There was a table in the center, with three wineglasses
on it and a bottle of champagne, and a wheel of Brie,
and some of those awful round crackers. A private open-

ing. Footsteps scuffed on the floor beneath me. Someone paused by the croissants, shuffled to the coffee, and then went back outside. Maybe it was Margaret, looking for me. I froze. After a few minutes, I moved again. My being up here was becoming harder to explain. Oliver could now say, "You closed the door, and no one could hear you upstairs. Why, Richard?"

There were no paintings on the walls. But there was a rack against one corner, and all the paintings were there. I tiptoed over and slid out one of the canvases. A serene oil of the Triangle barn. It wasn't good, and it wasn't bad. It wouldn't have been *embarrassing* to have in your house, but it wasn't exactly going to get your blood racing either. On the back of the canvas, there was a Post-it note with the number 3. I pulled out another canvas. This had no number on the back at all. I pulled out a third; it said, "7." There were twenty paintings in all in the rack, and I went through at random. Nine pictures had the Post-its. Of course, you couldn't have more than ten if you were going to give a visit.

Then I understood. The weekend was for *her.* It was *Edith's* work Freddy Beaumont had traveled to Pine Plains to see. It was him, of course, Oliver had picked up with our car—but none of this would have been necessary if Oliver alone was going to Freddy's gallery. Freddy knew Oliver's work; he knew his collectors; so joining was all up to Oliver. But he couldn't know

Edith's work; this brunch had been arranged to impress him, and to get Oliver—this was clear to me after a second—Freddy would have to take Edith too.

It was wildly unfair. A day ago, I had thought Edith and my mother were in the same boat. But it wasn't the same boat at all. Her husband was famous, and had power, so Edith was going to get a show. Frederic hadn't even been willing to *look* at my mother's pictures. And her paintings—as Ernest had said—were exciting, and interesting, and innovative. And there was nothing she could do. The numbers on the backs of Edith's paintings signified the showing order. I knew the importance of this; you wanted to have a script in advance, you didn't want to have to pause and fumble. Awkwardness of any kind was not allowed in this world. Edith had planned her showing in advance.

I had taken few risks in the art world. I had always played the same game as everyone else, hoping things would work out. Now I would play a new game; not theirs.

Edith wasn't going to have that easy a ride in her life. I took all the Post-its off the paintings. That was the first thing I did. I removed each one and crumpled them into a starry ball together and stowed the yellow ball in my pocket. After the first, I had second thoughts—but once I had three of them off, I knew I could never have found the right paintings again. I took the paints off her painting table and strewed them on the floor. I heard footsteps beneath me a second time. I froze again. At this point, there could be no explanation for my being up here at all; nothing would fit the bill. So I stayed in position until these steps, too, had gone— and for that minute, I was the only sculpture in what I had assumed was a sculptor's studio. All the work I had done for my mother, trying to make sure she looked right, acted right, my leaving Margaret to concentrate on Mom more—it was all meaningless. It didn't matter *how* you acted. This was how the art world ran; on power. I determined that it would not work with Edith; maybe I was still angry from Margaret. But it seemed awful, too, to have had that argument with her, and to have lost it in this resounding way. Not to find that my mother didn't need me—this was what I wanted to believe all along—but that there was nothing I could do in this world anyway. That the boy I had been loyal to had been playing at nothing.

If presentation mattered—well, there wouldn't be any kind of presentation here. I scattered paintbrushes on the floor. For so many years I had longed to say something to these people, to *confront* them; I had held back because their impression of us mattered, and now I found it didn't matter at all. Brie. I took my revenge on the Brie. The Brie we'd eaten at all those openings— half my body was composed of Brie. I went to the window at the back of the studio. It overlooked the sculpture garden. Margaret had gone. There was no one out

there, and certainly no one to see. I opened the window.
The wheel structure of the Brie had always interested
me. Would it make a good Frisbee? No one had ever
done any preliminary research for me in this area, so it
was up to me to make the initial inquires myself. I
picked up the cheese. I leaned back, wound up, and
flung the Brie out the window. It wobbled and didn't
really spin, and landed with a fat whomping noise near
some crows, who flew away. Not a good Frisbee. It sat
there in the grass. I went back and crushed the crackers
in the plate, and that was that. I couldn't imagine it
would be an impressive visit for Frederic; they couldn't
even *show* the paintings now. Then I was finished.

It had been one of my mom's fugue states. The
studio was a mess. Even when I saw what a mistake I'd
made, there was no way to go back on it. Now I had to
make sure no one saw me leaving. A few people came
into the barn beneath me. I heard them laugh. I stood
there in terror for fear they would come up the stairs. As
long as I could get away from the room without anyone
seeing me, I wasn't responsible for it. The farther I was
from the room when it was discovered, the less chance
there was of me being linked. The people beneath me
were chatting. There was more laughter. Someone
reached into the ice bowl—I heard this distinctly—and
tossed some ice at someone else. Still more laughter.
"Jesus Christ," I said out loud. "Please don't be so *frolic-
some.*" I had never used that word before. Under duress,

you learn interesting things about yourself, and about your vocabulary. Those irritating people left the barn. I waited for another few minutes. I could keep waiting—because no time would *ever* seem like the absolute and safe time—but every minute I waited increased the chance of someone having the same idea I'd had and coming upstairs. I walked to the door. I turned the handle and opened it. The barn downstairs was empty. I closed the door and waited. Then I opened it again, still empty. I closed the door behind me, and walked quickly downstairs. I had to get out of the barn inconspicuously. And then Jacob Boyden walked in.

He had been looking to talk to my mother or to me. Social events bring out deep training—he was dressed all in white, a white shirt and white denim pants, as if he was off to play cricket at a club, or to officiate. He flagged me down. "Richard—hey, I didn't know you were *in* here," and his lips opened and closed soundlessly past his words. He had more to say. My impulse was to get out of the barn, to get away from Thrush's house, as quickly as possible.

"Hello, Jake," I said. "I was just trying to get outside—"

He put his hand on my arm. "Hold tight. I was just in here a few minutes ago and I didn't see you. Christ, every single person in your family is always running away from me. Stay here." His grip was strong, like most sculptors' grips. I remembered Mom telling me he had a bad temper, and I could see why it was frightening. "Speak with me for a moment. This is private in here."

"OK," I said.

"Were you upstairs?" he asked.

"No," I said.

"Funny. I could have *sworn* you weren't in here a minute ago. I don't think I saw anyone come into the barn. I was looking for you, you see." He squeezed my arm harder. "What were you doing? Were you spying on Oliver's studio?" He nodded his head up. "I'd be curious to see it too. I wonder what he's up to now. We could talk up there."

"It's not his studio. But I haven't seen it." These statements couldn't make sense together.

Jacob looked at me. "All right, Richard. I'll make a deal with you. You talk with me for two minutes and I won't tell anyone you were sneaking around where you weren't supposed to go." His breath was rich with fermented food—not a bad smell, but a rich and strong one, suggesting a kind of power, and there was his bodily strength, and I couldn't see what Mom loved in him. After all, I had trained my mother to be the kind of woman I could love: I had trained her into a well-mannered woman in first class. Mom had trained me to be what I was—but her training had obviously been more selfless, for this was the type of her desire, a rougher sort of man than I was. There was that strange

male richness to Jake. But trying to guess what moti-
vated her romantic tastes was as wrong as peering into
her bedroom; it was *more* intimate. "That will be our
deal," he said.

"OK," I said.

"What has your mother told you about she and
myself?"

"You had an argument."

"I've been trying to talk to your mother for ten
days! I called to apologize last week. I know I was supposed to drive her up here. I called her on *Thursday* and
told her I was still planning to go through with it. She
said no. You know how she can get. Maybe you don't.
Maybe with you it's always peaches and cream. You see,
I don't really know."

"You called and said you'd take her up here?" So I
hadn't been necessary at all. Or rather, not in the precise
way I had thought; I'd been *preferred.* On a deeper
level, this was flattering.

Jacob asked, "Is she trying to make me pay? Well,
she *has* made me pay. But your ma has to understand,
there's a limit to the price I am willing to keep putting
forward, in emotional terms. I tried to talk to her yesterday—nothing. I tried to dance with her—she would
only dance with that smarmy Tom Dancer."

"I don't know if she was avoiding you. She and I
don't speak that much about those things."

Jake looked at me in a steely way. I could see also

why he'd beaten my father, in their old beard competition. In America, there was always a little presumption that you weren't being *quite* earnest. That you weren't quite competing for a woman; that you were only doing this until the next activity came along. You were fiddling with it, and that you could just as easily have been playing a hundred other roles. This news of personal ambivalence had apparently never reached South Africa. Jake wanted what he wanted. "Oh come now, Richard. Don't you think your mother and I are close? I know she tells you everything. Tell me what she's thinking. Otherwise, I'm just wasting my time, and I'll drive home right now."

"I think she *likes* that smarmy Tom Dancer."

"Oh, Richard. Your mother has never thought about Tom Dancer for a single or solitary instant."

He didn't want to be told that she was his for the asking—and now I was no longer sure she was. But I thought about it. I thought that men didn't know what they wanted. That men, in the calculus of affection, knew women had value but were never precisely sure how *much*, and it was up to women to set that number. That was their part. My answer had to contain this, for if I said too much perhaps Jacob would be gone.

"Look at me, Richard. This is maddening. I'm a man who made a mistake, and I'm trying to apologize. I'll tell my daughter to leave; I'll set up a hotline number if your ma wants me to. That's what men do when they're in the wrong. They apologize. I have known your mother for twenty years. You can't find that with another person. And here I am a grown man having to talk to Joan's *son* about this."

"I'm a grown man too," I said.

He looked at me with more interest. "Yes."

I decided to do something nice; something non-manipulative. Here was a man—a man I sort of liked—who was speaking to me as a fellow person. I said, "I really don't know what she has in mind. I didn't even know you called her. But if I cared about someone"—I was thinking about Margaret—"I would talk to them. But not now. I think she's having fun. Look."

I pointed outside, to where Mom was talking at the picnic tables. It was as though I had invited Jake to peer into the sun. He turned his head away with a kind of *hish!* and I left the barn.

It was after one. People were getting up to leave. One man was walking in from the parking lot—a thick older man. The man wore a suit, and there was something in the jaunty angle of his head that I remembered, and my body got a little nervous. It was Freddy Beaumont. He had widened out. His behind had gotten to largeness ahead of him, and the rest of his body finally caught up. This was a walk Freddy had imagined taking for decades. The walk past Gregor's artists, when they were now his own.

A kind of ripple went out ahead of Freddy to the

tables—business kicked in a little. First one head turned, while other mouths kept talking, and then all the heads turned, and finally everyone was watching Freddy, and no one was talking. Gregor was right in his path as Frederic made his graceful way onward. I saw my mom watching Gregor, to see what he would do. It was the first time any of us—maybe anyone—had seen Gregor in a position of vulnerability. Who knew how he would respond? I tried to imagine what Mom or I would have done. Gregor stood his ground. I found myself rooting for Gregor. What a sad irony it was, that this man, whose considerations had been solely monetary, should come to stand for everything that was *good* about the art world. But perhaps this was the way of all symbols—that information everyone longed to see embodied hovered around over human heads and finally found expression through people who did not quite deserve it. This moment was what Freddy had waited for.

Gregor stood, and as Frederic approached, his face went into a very light social look and he reached out with his hand. "Hel*lo*, Frederic," he said. There was silence at the tables. "We haven't *spoken* in so long, I just wanted to *congratulate* you on the success of your gallery. I haven't *visited*, but I've heard it is superb. So I offer my *congratulations*. Good to see you." And with a quick handshake, he was gone.

It had been perfect. Gregor was simply not ever going to be rattled. My mom turned back to me and lifted her eyebrows with a smile, meaning that had been a nice, impressive surprise. Gregor continued walking—he went past me without seeming to recognize me, and into the barn. Frederic continued his walk by the tables. Oliver and his wife approached him, Edith looking nervous, and Frederic asked something and Oliver looked at his watch and answered.

I looked away, and heard a voice behind me. "Rich—ard?" Gregor asked. I turned round. Had we ever spoken since the day I'd seen him in my mother's bedroom? Never privately. Seeing him made my bladder squinch up, as if I still had to pee from that night fourteen years before. "I *thought* I recognized you." He had gotten himself a cup of coffee, and was watching Freddy. In private, I could see him noting who Frederic was talking to, who was being warm, who was not. It was like my mother watching *him*—his expression was unreadable. There was no alarm, just careful observation. "Please tell your *mother* that I have looked at her transparencies, and they are *very* exciting. Tell her please, that I will be back in the city *Tuesday* afternoon, and will call about making an appointment. If it is all right, I am *keeping* the slides." It was what we'd wanted—I nodded at Gregor, and he looked at me and tried to make conversation for a moment, opening lines of communication between himself and our family. "How, ah, how is your *brother?* Still finger-painting?"

He had gotten us confused. I saw everything of my

mother's difficulty in talking to these men. He had already given us what we wanted, and now all I wanted to do was end the conversation before some silly comment of mine would undo his decision. "That was me, actually. I was the finger-painter."

"Ah," he said. "Forgive me. All that was such a *long* time ago. What about now? Have you abandoned your artistic ambitions?"

"I just graduated from college."

"Ah. What are you doing now?"

"I don't know," I said. He was giving me the space to say what I wanted, and I learned that there was nothing for me to say. His old brusqueness had been a kindness as well. He was a professional, and all I wanted from him was professional things. Beyond that, there was no room for conversation at all. Gregor had known this. He went back into the barn for more coffee. I waited a minute in the sunlight, before bringing the news to my mother.

The silhouette of her bathing suit was clearly visible through her sundress. All these people, I saw, had *aged*. It wasn't just Celia; the sun was doing a job on all of them. Mom was talking, and beside her was an ancient, bald man—so ancient the top of his head was beginning to wrinkle. The wrinkles, seeing they had done what they could to his face, had moved on to the rest of his skull. It was Karl Olken, still alive—the dealer my mother had used to get into Krumlich the first time. Mom told him, "I never apologized, Karl, for not going with you that way. That was pretty shitty."

"It was just business, Joan. In this field, one has to be careful to keep separate the personal from the commercial. It was just business. I understood."

I could see all of them as I walked to join her. Their futures were in their faces. Time was working whatever tricks it could on them, like ivy climbing up their bodies. They were just people, not horrifying ogres, just people trying to make money in a difficult field, four-limbed animals trying to get their hands on money, shelter, each other. I don't know—maybe acting horribly, in a way that required forgiveness, made me forgiving myself. Hiroshi was aging—his floppy black hair was going gray. Lars had given himself to drink; his vitality was seeping out of him, and even if he took big gulps of scotch to plug it up it would keep trickling away. Neil Hollander would die into his biography, as he intended. They were men I had known my whole life, and their lives were settled and moving slowly ahead, into age, while I was moving into my own life, and this huge edge—the only edge that mattered on the planet—made me hate them less.

The sun was boiling life out of these men like sweat. I didn't think I was going to be found out—who knew what they would think had happened—but I felt ashamed for doing what I had done to the Thrushes, for time was playing far worse tricks on this group than I ever could. The simple passage of time was paying them off in ways beyond what I could dream of. This thought seemed an absolution—a release from the afternoon, from the weekend. I could feel it tumbling away down my shoulders. It seemed a suitable permission for me to retrieve Mom and get home.

I walked to my mother's side. She appeared still young; her life was still uncertain before her. She hadn't relaxed onto a track. There were still efforts to be made, her body hadn't settled in to the end part of its life; it had the freedom to end up anywhere. This freedom was the edge she held over these men. Seeing me coming, she did a quick nod, and walked to my side.

"What? You're leaving Joan?" Leonard asked in his soft voice. "Too much pressure, huh? Didn't feel like staying around and seeing how the afternoon turned out?"

A confident smile went over my mom's face—it overjoyed me to see it. "Leonard. You've known me twenty years, and you still don't have a clue about who I am. It's still warm out, and I want to get back to the lodge so I can go swimming."

We drove back to the Mashomack—I drove. My mother sat comfortably in the seat beside me. Margaret had gone—she'd called a cab and left, and told my mother. With her unpredictability of response,

Mom said, "You should be nicer to that girl. She's really very charming." But there was something behind her voice as she said this, a rote quality, as if no one was quite good enough to penetrate into our circle. Or was this only what I thought, while assigning the opinion to her?

In the car, I told her about Jacob, and about Gregor, and Mom—sitting there in the passenger seat, her seat belt off as if buckling it would have been a brutal criticism of my amateur driving—closed her eyes and didn't say anything for a moment. Then she inflated her cheeks and released the air and opened her eyes at the same moment. "It's been a long time coming," she said. And then she didn't speak.

We'd gotten what I wanted—we'd lined everyone up in the art world together, and they had *seen* her. They had seen there was nothing wrong with her, they'd seen her work, and it had done the trick. And now, at this moment I had so longed for, she seemed to be receding from me. For what we were together—the way we talked to each other, and helped each other, and knew each other—came from misfortune. Nothing brings a family together like bad luck. Good luck spreads people out—they want to go running off and brag about it. Bad luck locks a family in to ruminate on solutions. When I was with my mother, I knew the taste of my own soul. Away from her, I didn't recognize its flavor so immediately, and nibbled here and there, trying to find the things that were properly me. In all the years I'd spent with Mom in the art world, it had never occurred to me that this would be the result of success— that she would need me no longer, and I would have to find a place for myself somewhere else.

I remembered the day after she got me into Brown. She took me clothes shopping at Brooks Brothers. Our idea was that this was how young men in college should dress. She came to my room and got me out of bed at nine—"Come on," she said. "We've got a lot to do to-day. No dawdling." At the store she followed me from counter to counter, selection to selection, with a bashful, willed blindness, as if to look at prices would awaken in her something she didn't wish awakened. When we got home I unpacked the big shopping bag in my room. She came in and watched me. She said, "Go ahead. Try those on," for she felt free to admire the purchases now that they were officially ours. She watched me put on shirts and shoes with real pleasure. My head appeared above the top of a charcoal sweater, and we both stared with surprise at the mirror, in which I was the kind of confident, successful boy we both knew I wasn't. She watched me model the clothes I would wear into an-other world, the clothes in which I would walk away from her, the clothes in which I would leave her be-hind. In her face there was only happiness for me. I found I could not be as generous now as she had been then. I wanted to urge that she tell Gregor to go to hell,

that he had no *right* to be on our side this late in the
game. I found myself constructing an argument—and
then that argument unraveled in my chest, the words
fell out of alignment and were sucked back to my brain,
and I sat with my hands on the wheel saying nothing at
all.

She laughed about Karl Olken having been at the
Thrushes'—and since this would be the last after-open-
ing discussion we would ever have, I decided to enjoy it
with her. I asked about Olken's wife, whom I still so
clearly remembered from East Hampton. She had died,
Mom said. She had turned eighty, and for the first time
in her married life had decided not to wait to see what
her husband's policy was on something but had gone
ahead and died first. Mom was a hardier specimen of
twenty years in the art world than she had been.

We parked at the lodge. Mom slipped from her
dress in the car—I stood guard before the window,
blocking sight lines with my body—and she got out of
the Sentra and walked happily to the water, her red
swimsuit under the brown and green arms of the pines.

I searched for Margaret's car. It wasn't there, in the
lot. I walked down the crunchy gravel road a ways and
there was her red Prelude, with its blue Connecticut
plate. It was as stunning as seeing someone I knew. I
ran back to the lodge and found her on the pay phone.
She had washed away all the makeup—as if this was a
new self she'd tried, which had failed. After all the

made-up people I had seen that morning, her uncos-
meticized face looked charmingly and thrillingly naked.
She hung up, and I took her hand and said, "I never
wished you a happy birthday," and she laughed in a
mournful way and I hugged her, and patted her black
hair with my own hand. I saw why birthdays were so
important. You give gifts back to the person because
you are saying, You gave me a gift, this day, by becoming born. Thank you. This is a private holiday, and I am
spending it with you. We kissed and my lips fell into
the rhythm of her lips very quickly, the familiar, cush-
iony, muscular rhythm of those lips. Conversation in
pantomime. The lips spend all day forming themselves
around words, but it must be foreign to them, and kisses
are the mouth speaking in patois, in its own native
language. We kissed and I murmured things into her
ear and we walked clumsily—Maggy leaning her head
against my chest—into the library and sat together on
the couch. We sat and then Maggy rested her head on
my legs and I smoothed back her hair.

"When are you and your mother leaving?" she
asked.

"Soon, I think." And then I was hovering between
roles again. "Can you get back OK by yourself? I'd like
to drive back with my mother. We came up here together."

"That's fine," Maggy said. Her eyes had a soft quality. All the anger had been a ruse; everything she'd done

had been a false start to get to this place. This was what she had wanted, and she'd communicated it to me in the strange way we as humans communicate everything. I *don't* want you, I *don't* need you—OK, I do. We held hands and then I kissed Maggy again and she drove home.

Outside, the ironwork tables were all occupied. I sat down on the porch steps. Mom, in her red suit, was lying on a raft in the center of the pond. The big pale man beside her was surely Jake. By now, Frederic would be inside Edith's studio, and half of me was there with them. I regretted what I had done, but there was nothing I could do to change it now. At least it made it harder for me to go back into the art world, because Edith would always be at galleries and parties, and I wouldn't be able to look at her without my face communicating all those things—regret, embarrassment, shame, guilt—that would have made a little speech to be read by *her* face. The couples at the tables closest to me were all my age, or a little older. Maybe five years. They were the Triangle participants. And though they had their own anxieties, and were trying to enter a world that was fiendishly difficult, their poses at their tables, with cigarettes and drinks, seemed terribly enticing to me. They would trust their talents and their luck. They were watching Jake and my mom on the raft, and seeing in them models of artistic success they might someday hope to grow into.

Mom had been in the right place at the right time—that scary combination of circumstances again, just like East Hampton. I *had* to mess up that way in the Triangle barn so we could take our sad, moping walk in the fields, so that Mom could run into Oliver. She *had* to lend him her car, and had to have the nerve later on to approach him, to collect on that debt. Otherwise we would never have been at the Thrushes' party, and she would never have spoken to Gregor. If she hadn't brought her slides, there could have been no capitalizing either. And then my standing there, by Oliver's barn—what if Gregor *hadn't* seen me, and spoken to me, and a day later had thought better of it? I felt a weird, grateful fear for the world, for so often opening up opportunities—but there was the awful thought of how chancy those opportunities were, and how random the world's generosities could be. Who knew how many times one wasn't in the right place, or called only a minute after opportunity had gone?

I heard a car squeak to a stop in the parking lot. A minute later, Tom Dancer walked onto the grass, looking eager, his absurd dog tottering behind him. He did not see me. I watched his gargoyle face as he recognized Mom (it got happy), and then as he recognized Jake (it got sad). I felt guilty for having used this man. He was a person, after all, and I had used his feelings to make another man want my mother more, but the corollary of that had been encouraging Tom to think optimistically about Mom. I felt bad about that. He stood watching for a second. Then he turned and walked slowly to the parking lot, the dog in front of him. I waited another minute. Soon, I heard his car starting. A catch, a few roaring breaths, and then a kind of steady sigh. Then I heard gravel popping under tires, and the whir of an engine being swallowed by the afternoon. I seemed to hear this whir for a long time, until I realized that what I was actually hearing was the steady rummaging of wind through the distant tops of trees.

I walked down to the bank of the pond. It was here that I finally saw Ernest Steinman again. He was sitting with Celia, and the atmosphere at the table was comfortable. Ernest was puffing on a Camel. He flagged me over and, surprisingly, held my hand for longer than a handshake.

"We're just watching your mother swim," Celia said. "It looks positively *ravishing* out there."

"My mother," I told Celia, "is a good, and brave, swimmer."

Ernest was wearing a cap, to protect his yarmulke bald-spot from sunburn. "That's your mother out there?" he asked, blowing away some smoke.

"Yes," I said.

Ernest nodded. His head rocked slowly up and down. He squinted. "She's a damn fine woman, your mother." He was looking at her like a picture.

He asked, "How old is she?"

"Forty-four," I said.

"She has damn fine legs for a woman of forty-four."

Celia nodded breezily, as if Ernest had just delivered another sound artistic insight. It was cool by the water. I walked to the shore. There was no beach, just the grass needing a trim and meeting the water with a wet, bright-black mud. The canoe was waiting in this mud. I stepped inside. It rocked under my weight, and I felt the canvas in my sneakers swell up and grow heavy with water. As in driving a car, or starting a career, it was the taking-off part that was difficult. I removed my sneakers and threw them into the canoe. My toes slipped over the yielding bottom of the pond. I pushed the canoe out, until with a kind of sudden rising *pop!* it received the water's full support, and then I hopped inside. I sat in back and steered myself with the paddle to the center of the pond. Mom watched my approach levelly. She raised her body on one elbow and shielded her eyes. She hardly wanted to be disturbed. She was a glutton for fun.

"Richard," she called. "What's up?"

I paddled closer. Sunlight bounced from the water, in little trapped ripples. "I've come to get you. I'm itchy for home."

She looked at Jacob. Their hands were touching, the way Margaret's and mine had been. I looked quickly away. It was embarrassing. Then I looked at them to see if they saw my embarrassment, and then I looked back at their hands to make sure what I'd seen was what I'd seen; my instincts were constantly disobedient to my desires. "But this is the vacation part of the weekend." She smiled.

I glided forward. The canoe ticked the edge of the raft. My mother reached out a hand and caught the ring at the end of the canoe, mooring it. The back edge, where I was sitting, swung outward, and little waves further distorted the sky's confident reflection. I pressed my paddle onto the raft and pulled the canoe in alongside my mother and Jacob. I decided to try for courtliness. "I'm here to ferry you back to shore, my lady."

My mother made a decision. She stood up. Jacob did too, in his out-of-date plaid trunks and his fleecy gray chest hair. It was gray at the tips, as if someone had taken a paintbrush and tinted the end of each individual hair. "I'll speak to you in the city, Jake?" Mom asked.

"I'll call right when I get back to the foundry," Jacob agreed, in pale glory. My mother walked across the raft and settled herself daintily into the canoe. She gripped the wet aluminum for support. I looked at Jacob. "Jacob," I said. A drop of water slipped from the paddle and dripped onto my thigh. I meant to acknowledge our talk.

"Richard," he returned, with a nod.

I pushed off with the paddle, swept us a few lengths backward, and then turned the canoe around. From this perspective, the details on shore were indistinct, a kind of impressionist painting. As I brought us forward, the landscape became larger and more vivid. It became a Romantic painting by Delacroix, then a vigorous Dutch realist work by someone like Vermeer—until, as the bank sloped upward, I could make out individual blades of grass and dandelions, and we'd gone back to the early Renaissance exactness of someone like Dürer. I had brought my mother back through art history, back across the water.

We left the canoe. We stood on the shore and looked at each other. We were both going to be less happy apart. I knew that. She would end up with Jacob; I would stay with Margaret. We would build our individual lives from there. But the something between us was not going to exist anymore. That was OK, too. That was fine, that was growth, that was the progress we'd both wanted: to make ourselves *dispensable* to each other. She said, "You were talking to Ernest."

I clipped away what I thought was extraneous. "He told me," I said, "that you were a damn fine woman." My mother smiled, her eyes glowing in the related praise.

We drove back to the city. I had never driven at nightfall before. My mother remained spookily confident about my abilities. I had been wrong about driving—it was not so easy after all. Especially night-driving. One slip on my part would spill us into a score of collisions. We were all of us, this panicked herd of cars, trusting that this would not happen. My fellow drivers had no idea how misplaced their trust was in me.

My mother sat beside me quietly. We were driving back to the city; her eyes were focused not on the cars, or on the road, or on me, but on the plans taking shape there. It had been another successful trip for her. On our sides, beside the road, were the mammoth steel sculptures that hold up electrical wires. They were fifty feet high, roughly human in shape. They towered above the green trees. There were hundreds of them, trotting in long lines down through the hills, into the underbrush, sharing the weight of electricity between them, a race of origami strongmen holding up the world. I tried to think of a joke to banish the silence from our car, this comfortable distance that was establishing itself between my mother and me. I began, in my mind, "Richard and Joan Freeley, as the——" and then I stopped. I could think of no end to the title. There were no roles left for us to play. The Saw Mill, with its curves and hills, was tilting us down toward the city. I was becoming accustomed to the rush of the turns, the sweep of our headlights. Soon, we would see the necklaced lights of the George Washington Bridge, and beyond that the restless, glowing lights of the city, the towers and the windows. We were both going to leave each other, but that was fine. Once we were in the city, we could talk about plans, and what was going to happen, and what *had* happened. And I would begin to make ready for my own departure. But this was some time off, many miles away. I consoled myself with the thought that there was an hour, half an hour at least, before we would be home. And so that postponed the moment when I would have to say goodbye.

DAVID LIPSKY's writing has appeared in *The New Yorker*, the *New York Times, Rolling Stone, Details,* and *Harper's* magazine, among others, and has been published in a number of anthologies, including *The Best American Short Stories* series. A graduate of Brown University, he is the author of *Three Thousand Dollars* and a nonfiction work, *Late Bloomers*. He lives in New York City, and is a contributing editor at *Rolling Stone*.